We're all a little GUARDED

you are enough

BOOK 2

A NOVEL BY

TIFFANY ANDREA

Paperback ISBN: 978-1-990724-09-1
Hardcover ISBN: 978-1-990724-10-7
eBook ISBN: 978-1-990724-11-4

Cover Design by: Burden of Proofreading Publishing featuring Graphics by JemStock via CanStockPhoto

Interior Graphics by Yupriamos

To my father, Roger
Thank you for teaching me the value of being a good person.
Because of you, I know it's okay not to be the smartest, funniest, or
most successful person in a room. What I can be, every minute of
every day, is hardworking, courageous, and kind.
Because of you, I know I can have high hopes and a humble heart.
Because of you, I'll keep trying to be the best human I can be.
I'll keep trying to make you proud.
I love you.

Contents

In writing this book, I did a lot of reading and research on life with PTSD. What I learned is that it has commonalities, but still affects each person differently.

My intention with this book, as with We're All a Little Broken, is to bring awareness to what life is like with mental illness, and hopefully have people not feel so alone. Beyond that, with Chelsea's story in particular, I noticed PTSD is a very "trendy" topic to write about in recent years. What I didn't want was to write this story as if I were just following the trends. I sincerely hope the point of this novel comes across well. I never want anyone who is dealing with an internal battle to feel as if their condition is being belittled or used strictly for entertainment. I hope this book entertains you, but I hope you take things away from it, too.

You'll notice with this book (in contrast to Zara) Chelsea's PTSD doesn't appear as a separate internal voice, but her trust issues do. PTSD operates as a constant battle between logic and panic, motivating everything she does. I didn't want to write sixty percent of the book in italics, so it was my intentional decision to write it this way. It's not a separate entity from Chelsea—it is in every fibre of her being.

Chelsea is going to frustrate you and you'll want to shake some sense into her—that's my goal. If you get annoyed with her, I've done my job right. Why? Because moving forward, when you get frustrated with people's actions in real life, I want you to take a moment and re-approach the situation from a place of compassion. Writing a story, you have some insight into Chelsea's thoughts and motivations that you don't have with others. So, before you judge, take a moment to show compassion.

While her choices might not make sense to you, she is doing what she feels to be the best option in hard circumstances, just as we all are. You don't have to agree with someone's choices to show them love.

I hope I've portrayed Chelsea's life with PTSD appropriately, and still added in some moments that make you laugh.

Don't read any further if you don't want any spoilers, but I do want to offer a trigger warning.

This book contains reference to substance abuse, child abuse, and emotional manipulation. As with all of my writing, even though the topics are difficult to cover, I try to keep it clean and light-hearted, but if these things might upset you, I urge you to stop reading.

The heavy rain beats down on the driveway beneath my window; water droplets telegraphing their intentions to ruin my day before I've gotten out of bed. Some people find the rain peaceful and calming—I am not one of those people. The trouble is, I don't find sunshine, snow, or fog to be peaceful or calming either. My open curtains allow me to view the moon hanging low, and I silently beg it not to sink in the sky. I'm not ready to face another day.

The moon denies my request, turning the sky dark, and making way for the dreary clouds of a new day. At least today they're physical clouds, and not only the ones hanging over my head.

I force myself to pull back my heavy white duvet and drop my feet to the floor. If I didn't need to pee, I wouldn't be getting up yet, but my bladder is inconsiderate. I walk into my ensuite bathroom, grateful for privacy without shutting the door—one of my many quirks.

Morning college classes are a test of willpower and endurance—a lesson I've learned over the past few years. How long can you manage late nights, early mornings, demanding class schedule, part-time job, and still produce assignments sufficient to pass? I'm not sure how people squeeze in any semblance of a social life. Liam Davis is my only friend, and even keeping up with him is exhausting.

I promised Liam I would arrive on campus early today so we can grab a coffee together. He insists on meeting to make sure I'll show up. Our majors are different, meaning we don't have any classes together, but we've been friends since high school, and I'm glad he's at least on the same campus. He is the one person other than my adopted family who knows my past and tries to be supportive, even when he doesn't understand.

Once I finish my shower, I blow-dry my hair and do my regular skin-care routine. I rarely wear makeup because my face is covered in freckles; it becomes tedious covering them. I am a genuine ginger—right down to the flaming orange hair.

My typical college-day clothing, dark-wash skinny jeans, black T-shirt, black hoodie, and slip-on sneakers serves as a uniform of sorts to help me blend in on campus. Speaking of, the clock is ticking. I walk out of my bedroom and head down to the kitchen, where I find Zara, my adoptive mom, and Isla, my twelve-year-old sister.

"Good morning, trouble," I say as I ruffle Isla's blonde hair, resulting in a glare from her dog, Bond. She did not name the tenacious German shepherd after the womanizing spy; she gave him the moniker Bond because the moment Isla and him locked eyes at the animal shelter, they shared an unmistakable connection.

"Good morning," Zara's voice rings out. "Did you sleep well?"

"As good as usual. I woke up early and I couldn't get back to sleep because of the rain." I shrug my shoulders as if it's no big deal because this is a frequent occurrence.

"Oh, Sweetheart, I'm sorry. Do you want to talk? If not with me, to someone? What can I do to help?"

"You don't always need to be in counsellor mode, Zara. I've told you; you've done more than enough. I doubt you dreamed of having a young adult with a book's worth of disorders crashing your house forever."

"Chels, we've been over this. We adopted you because we love you. You're not a consolation prize." Zara walks around the kitchen island and pulls me in for a mamma bear hug. "I love you more than anything. You inspire me every day."

I surprise myself by not recoiling at her touch, but instead of discussing this any further, I change the subject. "I need to get to campus. Liam is meeting me there before classes."

"Okay. I've got a few clients coming today, and then have some errands to run, but call me anytime if you need me, okay?"

"Thank you. I know the drill. Trust me, I'll be fine." I won't, but I can put on a brave face as I try to "adult" like other twenty-somethings.

"Be safe and let me know when you'll be home tonight."

"I work after my last class, so it will be at least ten before I get back." My job isn't profound—working in a bookstore—but I enjoy it, and I want to make Zach and Zara proud of me. I don't want them to regret their decision to adopt me five years ago, so I try to earn money for myself and pay for my needs, despite their protests. They bought me an SUV, which I reluctantly accepted under the stipulation I make regular payments toward it.

Zara kisses me on the forehead as she turns to walk toward the stairs. "Isla, come up and get dressed when you're done, please. And Chels, make sure you get something to eat before you leave."

"We will." I wink at Isla, earning a giggle.

Once Zara is out of earshot, Isla turns to me and says in a hushed voice, "Do you know I had coffee?" She giggles again, and the sound makes me smile.

"Coffee? Who gave you coffee?" I ask, but I'm sure I know the answer.

"Daddy. It was gross, though. I don't know why he drinks it. Mommy's tea is way better."

I can't help but laugh at her innocent perspective. She has no idea that coffee is a life-sustaining nectar for, I'd guess, fifty percent of the world's adult population.

"Maybe you can stick to hot chocolate then, hmm?"

"Hot chocolate is yummy." She hops off her stool and skips toward the stairs. "I have to go get dressed now or Mom will have a cow." She freezes in her tracks. "Why do people say that? Have a cow?"

I love her curious nature too. "I'm not sure. You'll have to research it and let me know."

"Okay. Bye Chels." She carries on her merry way with Bond close behind.

Before I set off for the day, I grab a hard-boiled egg, an apple, and a rice cake. It's random, but I prefer snacking over having enormous meals. Even though it's been a long time, my past forced me to ration food, so I don't eat a lot at once. Another one of my quirks.

By 8:15 I'm pulling onto campus, but my first class doesn't start until 9:30. I circle the parking lot four times before I find a spot that meets my criteria. A parking space must satisfy three important requirements: I can turn left into the space, it's near a light source, and I have a clear exit strategy in place. I will drive around far longer than necessary to make sure I find the right

spot. If an outing requires an underground parking garage, I am not going.

I park my red Honda CRV, grab my bookbag from the passenger seat, and step out under my umbrella. Despite the rain, I throw on my trusty sunglasses, more to help me avoid eye contact than protect my light blue eyes from the sun—considering there isn't any today. I lock the car doors using the fob and head for the steps of the library to meet Liam. After many years of friendship, I have accepted that Liam operates in a different time zone than I do, so I will end up waiting. For someone who is pursuing business management, he has zero time-management skills. Early into our final year before graduating, he has gotten no better in terms of punctuality.

A very wet twenty minutes later, I see Liam's curly hair and light-brown skin emerge in the crowd. His fade is sharp, framing his handsome, friendly face. As the son of a Nigerian mother and Irish father, Liam has a unique combination of features that broke more than a few hearts in the time I've known him. He doesn't date much, and when he has, it's been short-lived, but he puts in more effort than I do.

How are you supposed to trust another person with your heart? It seems irresponsible. People can't be trusted.

Liam strides up the stairs two at a time until he's standing beside me. Of course, laid-back Liam didn't bring an umbrella, so he seeks shelter under mine. I'd happily share, but he's over six inches taller than me, so it's awkward.

His casual outfit, consisting of relaxed olive-coloured jogger-style pants and a sporty black hoody, somehow makes him look stylish. One glance at his comforting smile and I don't feel so vulnerable standing on these steps in the rain. I never thought I would find someone I could feel safe with, but Liam has proven me wrong; one step in managing my PTSD journey.

L iam's presence lessens my irritation over standing in the icy rain for twenty minutes.

"Hey Chels. Sorry I'm late. I slept in."

"I'd be willing to bet you woke up on time, but you laid in bed too long watching dog videos."

"You know me well." He shrugs and adds a trademark Liam laugh. "You wanna grab a coffee?"

His question makes me think of Isla, so I chuckle. "How about a hot chocolate?" I could use a kick start.

"Whatever the lady wishes. I'm buying to make up for keeping you waiting." He performs a dramatic bow, pointing his arm in the coffee shop's direction.

The college was onto something by having the coffee shop attached to the library. Both are open around the clock, so the coffee shop is always busy—especially before exams. Most post-secondary students are walking around like sleep-deprived zombies, barely alert after all night study or drinking sessions. Many of them choose caffeine to heal, or mask, their afflictions.

We walk into *The Thinking Cup Bistro.* The door shuts behind us with a rush of air, and the sensation makes me jump. Liam places a hand on my arm, accompanied by a reassuring nod. I return his gesture, note the exits, and head to the right to find us a table while Liam gets in the queue to order.

I choose a table within suitable proximity to the door—close enough to get out, but far enough, I'm not contending with the draft from its opening and closing. When I remove my sunglasses, I immediately regret it. A tall, muscular young man is staring at me, and I feel suffocated under the weight of his gaze. I meet his eyes, but he turns away. That suits me since I avoid eye contact whenever possible, but it unnerves me at the same time.

The hairs on the back of my neck stand at attention, and the steady breath I had maintained all morning speeds up.

Liam arrives seconds later with our drinks, taking a seat across from me, distracting me from the stranger.

"How have you been sleeping?" There's no lead up to his hard-hitting questions.

"Fine. As much as any other college student." I fiddle with my paper takeout cup, doing my best to avoid looking at Liam's face. Not a challenge. I'm quite adept at avoiding social interactions.

"Chels, be honest with me."

"It seems you know me well, too." I release an audible exhale, glancing up at Liam, then back down to my cup. "Okay, I haven't been sleeping much, but it's no big deal. I'll get through it." I hope he's satisfied with that answer because I don't enjoy diving into amateur therapy hour in the middle of a crowded coffee shop.

"If you need to talk, I'm here." He smiles—the kind of smile that makes you think everything is right in the world.

I'm grateful Liam cares enough about me to notice when I'm not "quite right," but I don't want to discuss my mental state today. I don't even know what my mental state *is* at the moment. How do you discuss something you can't wrap your own head around? How do you name feelings you don't understand? Beats me.

I look back toward the stranger and again catch him looking in my direction. I scan the immediate area to see if someone else is catching his eye, but don't notice anyone. My world is closing in.

"I'm proud of you." Liam's words startle me, redirecting my thoughts.

"Proud of me? What on Earth could you be proud of me for?"

"A lot of things." He holds up his left hand, counting things off with his fingers. "I'm proud of you for getting out of your house and coming here today. For sitting in this coffee shop with me. And for continuing to try, because I know it's hard."

I'm not worthy of his pride. Getting out of bed this morning wasn't a choice. I'm sitting here because I didn't want to stand in the rain. I *try* because I don't want to be someone else's problem for the rest of my life. "Just surviving, Liam. Nothing to be proud of. Those are things everyone around the world does every day."

"A lot of people are doing it every day, sure, but they're not doing it while carrying monsters on their backs."

I pause for a few seconds, raising my eyes to scan the room. "Liam, speaking of monsters. I'm getting a weird vibe from that guy over there. Can we take our drinks to go?" I'm speaking to Liam but looking at the questionable patron standing near the hallway leading to the washrooms.

Liam follows my eyes. "I've never seen him before. He's probably checking out the pretty redhead, but if he makes you uncomfortable, let's go." Liam grabs his coffee and stands, his concerned eyes focus on me. "I'm going to put my arm around you so he thinks we're together, okay?"

I nod, willing to follow his lead. Being touched is not something I enjoy—another quirk—but in this case, it's the lesser of two uncomfortable situations. I stand, grab my drink, and Liam places his arm around my shoulders to walk toward the door. We exit into the courtyard and I'm thankful the rain has let up.

Once we've walked enough distance from the coffee shop, Liam removes his arm, dropping it to his side. He leans on the back of a bench, casual and cool, like he's capable of doing in any situation. I envy him for not being in a constant state of fight or flight.

"We'll stand here for a minute to see if he comes out. If not, there shouldn't be anything to worry about." Liam sips his drink, eyes darting across the grassy expanse, trying not to make his surveillance of the coffee shop obvious.

After a few moments, the stranger in question hasn't exited, so I chastise myself for being paranoid. He was probably another caffeine-addicted student looking for his fix.

Once we finish our drinks, we toss them into the nearby garbage can.

"Can I walk you to your class?"

I hesitate, but since his class starts after mine and is in the same direction, my reluctance to accept his offer dissipates. I'm relieved he is here and tolerates my lunacy.

By the time we arrive at the doors to my lecture hall, I'm shaking from a combination of wet clothes and fear. My heartbeat is rivaling that of a pigmy shrew. No, more of a Rhesus monkey; I don't want to be dramatic.

"Take a breath. You're okay. You're safe here," Liam reassures me.

I meet his gaze and thank him as best I can without a word. I'm embarrassed, shaken, and irritated all at the same time. "Sorry."

"You don't have to be sorry. I may not know how you're feeling, but I understand why."

In a fluid movement that surprises both of us, I lean in and give Liam a hug. For the entirety of our five years of friendship, this is the first time I have ever initiated any affection. He wraps his arms around me in return. Is it crazy if I stay here? I'm safe right now and that feeling is fleeting. Plus, he's warm.

"Thanks, Liam." I remove myself from our embrace, embarrassed by my moment of weakness. "You're the best friend a crazy girl could ask for."

His chin dips to his chest and his previously cheerful expression turns stone-faced. "I'll always keep you safe."

Drowning in self-consciousness, I worry I've somehow turned this conversation awkward. "I better get into my class so I can get a good seat. Thanks for the hot chocolate, and for getting me here without a meltdown."

"See you later, Big Red." Liam's voice is soft and lacking his usual enthusiasm.

I roll my eyes—I hate when he calls me that, but also love that I've had a friend long enough, we've come up with nicknames.

"Later, Arizona," I call after him as he strides away. I read a book about Pearl Harbor, where I learned two men with the last name Davis were aboard the USS Arizona when it was bombed, and they survived—so I thought perhaps that fortune would rub off on Liam. The ability to survive deadly circumstances seems like an excellent trait to possess.

I enter my lecture hall, which has theatre-style seating to accommodate over 100 students. A podium stands alone on a small stage at the front. The large classrooms can be intimidating, but I prefer them to the cramped ones from high school. I can disappear in a crowd here—well, as much as my Cheeto-head allows.

My childhood disorders lecture finishes fifty minutes later and my paranoia creeps back in. I exit after the other students have left and find Liam leaning against a bank of lockers outside of the classroom.

"Why are you here?" I'm unable to mask my surprise.

"Well, I figured you could use a friend. I knew you'd be panicking to leave your class, so I thought I'd come walk with you."

"What about your class?" The thought of him skipping out on his class to cater to my delusion sends me into a tailspin.

"Chels, it's okay. I'm ahead in my class anyway, and it wasn't important." His lips curl into a smirk. "Campus security recommends we not walk across campus alone."

"Pretty sure they meant late at night." I take a breath, calming my racing heart and sweating palms. Some things warrant panic, but this does not. Relax. "I have 'family systems and interventions' now."

"That sounds... interesting. Will you be okay in your class?"

"What are you going to do? Sit in my class with me and hold my hand? I'm fine. Everything is fine." My words are as much an attempt to convince myself as him.

"I'll walk you to family systems, and then I'll go to the rest of my classes, okay?"

"Okay." I look down at my feet and start walking toward my next lecture. "My class is in B106, so it's not far. I have two more classes, then I work from three until nine."

"Do you want me to meet you after work?"

"Liam, you don't have to babysit me. I appreciate it, but I'm fine. I was being paranoid."

Maybe if I keep telling myself these things are no big deal, one day my brain will believe it.

A few hours into my work shift, I'm unboxing books, labeling, and placing them on the correct shelves. My to-be-read list is over 300 books long because I inspect each book I come across and find something interesting in most of them—particularly ones about animals. I should be an honorary *Kratt brother*. Unfortunately, college reading takes up most of my dedicated book-time right now, so my list keeps growing.

"Excuse me," a deep voice says from behind me, causing several books to drop from my grip.

I stare down at the mess I've created, praying I haven't damaged any of the books—though it would give me just cause to add them to my TBR collection. The hardcover fantasy novels are strewn about around my feet, so I use them as an excuse to avoid eye contact. I bend over with intentions of inspecting and stacking each one. "How can I help you?"

"I'm looking for a specific book."

"Do you know the title or the author?" I stack the fifth book on top of my mini book tower, knowing once I do, I'll have to converse with this man. Customer interaction is the hardest part of this job.

"*Catch-22* by Joseph Heller."

"Oh, that's easy. It's a classic." I straighten my posture, only to realize the deep voice I was speaking to belongs to the same stranger from the coffee shop this morning. My eyes dart around, looking for a way to escape, but the bookstore doesn't provide much cover with its open-concept layout. Curse this hipster indie bookstore.

The man is approximately my age with tan skin, deep brown eyes, and long dark hair pulled back into a man bun. On anyone other than David Beckham, I would say that hairstyle is ridiculous, but this guy pulls it off. He wears black fitted jeans and a black leather jacket. Everything about him is intimidating.

"Are you okay?" the stranger asks.

I'm panting on account of my rapid breathing, and I struggle to speak. I don't want to let on I am leery of him while there are so few people around.

"Sorry, yeah, I'm fine. The book you want is over there. The shelf along the wall. Look for H; they are organized by author's last name." I hope my directions will get rid of him and I can find somewhere to wait until he leaves. I vomit when I panic, which could result in a less-than-favourable *Yelp* review.

"Thanks. Hey, what's your name?"

Can I give him a fake name? I deflate, realizing I'm wearing my uniform. "Uh, I'm Chelsea." I point to my nametag with an awkward hand flick gesture and notice too late I've given him permission to glance at my chest. He takes full advantage of the opportunity to scrutinize my C-cup, which makes the hairs on my entire body stand at attention. I don't like this.

"Hi Chelsea. I'm Sebastian Puzo." He grins and reaches his hand out to shake mine.

I nod at the books in my hands, thankful I won't appear impolite by refusing. Despite the scenario, I still value my customer service skills. "Puzo, like Mario Puzo?"

"Who is Mario Puzo?" His thick eyebrows creep up his forehead.

"Mario Puzo is the author of the Godfather books. You know, mafia underworld?"

"You're a book nerd, aren't you?" He snickers.

I'm offended by his classification but resign myself to the fact he's not wrong. "I suppose I am. Escaping in books is an easy way to experience adventure somewhere else; to be transported from my own thoughts."

Over-share.

"Do you ever go on real-life adventures, Chelsea?" He steps closer while he stares into my eyes, making me internally cuss out my boss for telling me sunglasses are not allowed as part of my uniform. "Would you let me take you on an adventure?" He beams at me and, as much as my intuition is screaming at me to get away from him, he is sinfully handsome. He is at least eight inches taller than me, so with each step he takes toward me, I'm craning my neck further.

Despite his good looks, I'm itching to create more personal space between us; I take a step backward until my back is against the bookshelf. Ted Bundy was handsome, too. "Real-life adventures aren't my thing."

His smile grows wider—like a dingo that just spotted his dinner. More dangerous. "You never know what you'll miss out on. You should have some adventures, Chelsea."

Why does he keep saying "Chelsea" as if he's tasting my name on his lips?

"I don't have a fear of missing out, Mr. Puzo."

"Well Chelsea, if… no, when you *are* craving an adventure, I work across the street at *The Tipsy Bull*. Come find me."

"Don't count on it. I'd be more inclined to run and hide from adventure than crave it." I'm looking into his eyes, trying to fake confidence, even if my words sound cowardly.

"That's too bad. I'd enjoy making you scream... with joy, of course." His smile looks more wicked than ever.

Stranger danger. He cannot be trusted.

"Let me know if you can't find your book, Mr. Puzo. I'll get back to work now."

"Are you normally this formal?" He lets out a husky laugh.

"You're a customer, and I am treating you as such. Your good looks don't result in special treatment." Ah, shoot. Now look what I've gone and done. I struggle to backpedal and escape this conversation. "If you don't mind, there's plenty of work for me to get done."

Please go away.

"You think I'm good looking?" He smirks as he leans a shoulder on the bookshelf my back is pressed into.

I turn to face this confusing, beautiful enigma beside me, not wanting to be surprised again. "I shouldn't have said that. But something tells me you didn't need me to inform you. Please let me get back to work, Mr. Puzo. Again, you'll find your book over there." I point toward our wall of classics.

"See you around, Chelsea. Hopefully sooner than later." He pushes off the shelf, taking a step past me in the opposite direction I pointed to.

Without responding, I turn toward the bookshelf and pretend to work, ignoring the fact my skin feels like a hedgehog—every hair standing on end. I'm listening to Sebastian's steps as he walks away to make sure he is putting distance between us, but my trepidation does not subside.

Our interaction was strange, and I can't ignore the fact I saw him in the campus coffee shop this morning. Twice in one day is too much to be coincidence.

Once I have a clear escape to the employee room, I walk past the checkout counter and tell Esme, my co-worker, I'm taking a washroom break. She looks up from her book and nods. She's not much of a talker either, so I enjoy working with her. I hide out for five minutes, and once I hear the bell on the door ring, I hope that means Sebastian left. I peek my head out, listen for any voices or footsteps, and once the coast is clear, I return to stocking the shelves, wishing I had eyes on the back of my head.

The rest of my shift passes by with nothing of note occurring. This day has been long and taxing, so I am looking forward to getting into bed and reading—even if it is a textbook detailing the effects of family dynamics on children—I'm basically a case study myself. As the clock strikes 9:00pm, Esme and I have already cleaned the store to prepare for tomorrow since it was a quiet night, and because it kept my mind distracted from obsessing over the day's events.

I let her leave while I close out the cash register because she takes the bus home; I don't want her to travel later than she already is.

By 9:20, after I'm done with the accounting and dropped an envelope of cash in the office safe, I grab my purse and head for the exit.

After scanning the surrounding area beyond the sidewalk, I convince myself it's safe to secure the door, and insert the key, engaging the lock. Apparently, my scouting skills are terrible because I hear, "Chelsea?"

I let out a pathetic yelp, startled by the harsh voice. Had I known who I'd see when I turned around, I would have screamed a lot louder.

My instincts tell me to run, but my feet are solidified to the ground. My breathing is ragged; my entire body is rigid.

"Chelsea?"

The hairs on the back of my neck are standing on end, but I'm not ready to face the man behind me. "What are you doing here?"

"You're difficult to find."

"Maybe because I didn't want to be found." I force myself to turn, and the sight knocks the air from my lungs. "You need to leave!"

"That's no way to welcome your dear old dad after all these years." The ginger man in front of me, with graying hair at his temples, is of average weight and height. He's aged a lot since I last saw him. I hate that when I look at him, I see my nose and eyes reflecting back.

"The only thing you got right in that sentence is 'old'. Now leave before I call the police." I never thought I would come face to face with my father, Kevin Wells, again. He might consume my thoughts more often than I'd like, but being in his presence is a different kind of fear. He has been the source of most of my nightmares since I was a child, and now I am living another one I can't wake up from.

"Come on. Don't you think I deserve another chance? We can have a normal father-daughter relationship. I've changed."

I wish I could believe that. If only I could envision a life where my father wouldn't wrong me. "Kevin, your heart is as cold as Upis beetle." I ignore his confused expression. Of course, he would have no clue what I'm talking about. "Do you even realize what you did to me? We will never be normal father and daughter. Now LEAVE!" I scream so loudly, people across the street take notice. It should make me relieved, but I know from experience, most people don't want to get involved in stranger's tiffs.

Kevin takes a few steps toward me. "I'm not going to leave. You are *my* daughter." His eyes narrow.

"Take one more step and I cannot be held accountable for my actions." My warning would be a good line if I sounded more intimidating than a guinea pig.

He laughs. "Little girl, I spent fifteen years in prison with the worst kinds of people. I was there because of *you*. You couldn't imagine the hell I lived through, so if you think you're going to scare me, you're wrong."

His words void every bit of courage I had built up. I'm reduced to a shaking, feeble coward. I cross my arms over my chest, and my voice comes out far weaker than I intend. "Leave. Please."

"I came here for a reason, and I expect you to listen." He strides toward me, closing the eight-foot gap I was praying we'd maintain. I scream like my life depends on it because I'm afraid it does. Kevin pins me against the wall of the bookstore with his large body and places a hand over my mouth to quiet me.

Being the pathetic person I am, I stand with my back pressed into the uneven bricks and stay quiet in hopes Kevin will release me. It works for opossums. The sharp edges are digging into my back, but I concede. He's in control. He's always in control of me, even when he's on the other side of a prison fence.

Unexpectedly, the hand disappears from over my mouth and the pressure releases from my body, causing me to slump to the ground as a blur rushes past. I hear a familiar voice shouting at Kevin as I look up to see Sebastian in his face.

Both men glance in my direction; one with a look of concern, the other with contempt.

Sebastian glares at Kevin with a gaze so intense words are not needed, then rushes toward me. "Are you okay?"

I nod. My eyes are closed again because I can't come to terms with what is happening. I'm seated against the brick wall of the bookstore, folding my head between my knees, trying to steady my breathing. My phone vibrates in my purse, but I don't possess the emotional capacity to answer it right now. I need to get home.

A firm hand touches my arm, and I cower. The hand disappears.

"I'm sorry. I wanted to see if you were okay." Sebastian may be a perfect stranger, but his presence feels like a wall between Kevin and me.

"Get me out of here. I... I need to go home."

"Okay, let me walk you to your car. Are you good to drive?"

"I'm fine." I force myself to stand, and when I glance over, Kevin is no longer on the sidewalk. "Where did he go?" My stomach churns, threatening to empty its contents.

"He took off."

I cringe, realizing how angry Kevin will be now. He'll make me pay for this.

"I have to get out of here. I need to leave." Terror has overtaken my mind and body, and the tempo of my steps demonstrates my urgency to escape as I walk toward my SUV.

"Where did you park?"

"O… over here." It's taking every ounce of strength I have not to collapse on the ground in tears. Once we arrive at my vehicle, I thank Sebastian without making eye contact, jump in the driver's seat and lock the doors. I turn the key in the ignition, give Sebastian an apologetic wave, and speed home.

Thirty minutes later, I pull up to the gate in our driveway and proceed through. I park my SUV in its usual garage space and stumble inside.

It's ten o'clock, so I'm not expecting anyone to be awake, but as luck would have it, Zach is still in the kitchen. My adoptive father, who is only sixteen years older than me, but light-years ahead in maturity, studies my face as I walk in the door. He sets his mug on the counter and rushes toward me. "What's wrong?"

I don't even get a word out before I burst into tears. Zach knows I don't like to be touched, so he keeps his distance, but his presence gives me the impression I'm safer than I was moments ago.

"My… my dad. My dad found me."

Absorbing my revelation, Zach replies, "Did he hurt you? Are you okay? Chels, talk to me. What can I do?"

"He… He… pushed me against the wall outside the bookstore… and put his hand over my mouth. He was too strong. I couldn't stop him." My sobs are loud and unrelenting.

"Are you hurt? Did you call the police?"

I shake my head. Physically, I am not hurt. "A guy who works across the street heard me scream. He made Kevin leave."

"We need to call the police. Or we can go to the police station in the morning. Zara will come, too. You can make a report and there will be a record of his behaviour."

"A record won't help if he kills me!"

"He will not kill you. I won't let that happen. We can hire a bodyguard for you if we have to, but that man will not hurt you again."

Zara comes running downstairs with her hair resembling a Chinese-crested powder-puff—alarm clear on her face. "Oh, my gosh! What happened? Are you okay?"

"She says she's not hurt, but her biological father tracked her down and pushed her up against the wall outside her work."

"I'm going to kill that bastard." She shouts those words out, then cringes, probably recalling the time she was assaulted and killed her attacker in self-defence. "Chelsea, talk to me, Sweetheart." She looks like she's ready for a fight; she's small, but don't underestimate her. I wish I could be that brave. My bravery rating comes in somewhere around a fainting goat.

"I never wanted to see him again." I choke out several sobs. "How did he find me? My name isn't even the same."

"I'm not sure why we weren't informed they released him from prison. I'm going to sort this out. Did he say anything else to you?" Zara is in full grizzly mode.

"He said he found me for a reason, but he didn't tell me what it was. He's going to come back. Oh, God. He'll be back."

"I know you want to earn your own money, and I respect that, but I think for now the best option is to quit your job at the bookstore. We'll give you whatever you need." Zach has this incredible knack for putting anxiety at ease. He's always logical, yet intuitive.

My brain has its own motto: Why be logical when you can panic?

"I don't want to cost you guys more money." My tears are flowing, but my voice has become steadier.

"Sweetheart, we love you more than anything, and right now, the priority is keeping you safe. Zach is right. You can work with me doing administrative stuff or helping Isla with schoolwork. It would make my life so much easier."

I know Zara doesn't need my help—I'm confident she can handle anything life throws at her—but I can't go back to the bookstore. "Okay. Make me earn money, though. I don't want another handout."

"Chels—" Zach starts, but I interrupt him.

"No. I know what you're going to say, but I want to earn my keep. I want you guys to be proud of me."

"We're always proud of you." Zara tries to assure me, but how could anyone be proud of a sobbing mess? She steps in toward me, giving me a hug, and my instincts are a stark contrast to how I responded to Kevin's advances. After a few seconds, she lifts her head to look at Zach. "Well, get in here, would ya?"

Zach joins our hug. "I'll keep you safe, Chels. I promise."

Before going to bed, I check my phone, recalling it vibrated earlier. There are several messages from Liam.

Liam: Hey, Big Red. Do you need me to meet you after work?

I haven't heard from you, so I'm assuming you're working hard.

Chels? Let me know you made it home okay.

I'm freaking out over here.

Please message me.

I should put the guy out of his misery. He's such a good friend and again I've made him worry. I hate when people view me as a fragile child, but they're not wrong.

Chelsea: I'm home. Had an incident after work. Not going to class tomorrow. I'll tell you later. Good night.

I put my phone on silent, plug it in, and leave it on my bedside table. I lie awake in my beautifully decorated bedroom that never gets fully dark and try to convince my brain to stop re-enacting my entire day. It's no use. The events of tonight remind me of things I never thought I would see again.

I have so many questions—my mind offers as much peace as a troop of howler monkeys.

This is hopeless. I thought a good cry would have me sleeping like a sloth, but I lie in bed tossing and turning, replaying my conversation with Kevin for far too long. I forecast every worst-case scenario for close to three hours before I doze off.

He's here. He is creeping into your room. Strong hands grab you while you're sleeping and slam your head on the floor. He drags your limp body to his small car and throws you in the trunk. You're barely conscious, and too weak to fight. The trunk slams shut, and the space around you plummets into darkness. The road underneath changes from the familiar cobblestone driveway to asphalt. Sleep overtakes you and you lose consciousness. When the vehicle stops, you don't know where you are or how long you've been driving. The trunk opens and staring down at you is Kevin and his "friend" Sal.

I bolt upright, drenched in sweat.

My bedroom door is open, as always, and Zach comes rushing in wearing plaid pyjama pants with no shirt. "What's happening?"

The clock shows that it's 4:30am, so I've slept a total of two hours. Once I gather my thoughts, feeling embarrassed, I respond, "Oh, sorry I woke you. Just a nightmare."

"It's okay. I wanted to get up early today." Zach flashes his reassuring smile as he leans against the doorframe. "Do you want to talk about it?"

"Not really. This time it was basically the same as always, but I was watching it all happen like an out-of-body experience. Some kind of twisted reality TV show my brain made up."

"That makes sense after the night you had. Do you think you'll be able to get back to sleep?"

I'm exhausted, but I've been through this many times before. "No, I doubt it. Might as well get up." I pull the blankets back, confident about the decision I made last night. "I'm going to stay home today." I'm ashamed to let my fear win, but I also know I need some time to process everything.

"That's fine. I'll be in the kitchen. Do you want coffee?"

"Sure. I'll need it. Thanks."

Zach turns and leaves my room before I drag myself out of bed to shower. I don't even have the energy to do so, but I'm clammy from my nightmare and I need to wash this feeling off. Perhaps it will invigorate me. That's a funny thought. Pretty sure not even a lobotomy could accomplish that.

I spend my time in the shower leaning against the wall while the steaming hot water rains down on my back. My pale skin turns pink from the heat, but it's a pleasant reprieve to experience something other than fear. I practice mindful breathing, trying to calm my inner demons.

Just kill Kevin. Zara killed that Patrick guy in self-defence. Any reasonable judge would understand.

Breathe. Intrusive thoughts pervade my thinking, and I can't convince myself murder is a bad idea. I'm not a violent person by nature, but I cannot allow myself or anyone else to go through what I did at the hands of my father. There's nothing in this world that could make me okay with becoming like that monster, either. A losing battle either way.

I enter the kitchen a short time later, still overwhelmed by homicidal thoughts I wouldn't dare say aloud to anyone. Zach slides a coffee across the kitchen island when I take a seat at my regular stool. It's almost eerie being awake in this house before everyone else. It's too quiet.

"Thanks for the coffee." I take a sip, allowing the hot liquid to burn as it trails down my throat. "How did you ever live here by yourself?"

He nods, acknowledging my thanks. "It was kind of lonely, but I had Jasmine here until she was about your age. I don't miss the inescapable silence, though."

"I miss Jasmine. It's too bad she lives so far away. I mean, Toronto isn't far, but far enough we don't see each other much."

"I miss her too. Maybe I'll invite her to come up for a visit one weekend soon."

"Really? That would be amazing."

"Sure. I'll call her later." There's an awkward silence as Zach hesitates before he continues, "So, we should go to the police station today. You need to file a report."

"No."

He sets his coffee down and leans over so his elbows rest on either side of his 'World's Greatest ~~Farter~~ Father' mug. "No? Why not? The man assaulted you, which proves he's dangerous. He might be on parole."

"The guy who got Kevin off of me, Sebastian, I don't want the police questioning him and getting him in trouble. It's not fair when someone tries to do the right thing and they end up being treated as if they are the criminal. I also don't want him to be in Kevin's crosshairs."

Zach sips his coffee, but I can tell he was not prepared for this at 5:00am. He continues his attempt to convince me. "I get what you're saying, but the police wouldn't give him trouble because he did nothing wrong. Kevin though, if we can get his behaviour on record, then we can build a case against him if he does anything else."

I stare down at my coffee, swirling it in my mug. "I don't want to cause Sebastian trouble. He didn't have to help me, but he did, and I appreciate that, so I won't make him a target for Kevin."

Zach releases a sigh. I know he doesn't agree with my decision, but he respects my choice. He's not the type to push.

"Let me know if you change your mind. I'd hate for the result to end up the same as it did for Zara. Or worse. We love you and want what's best for you."

"Thanks, Zach." I'm not sure I even understand the concept of love. I don't doubt the wonderful people I call my family love me; and in my own capacity, I love them in return, even if I barely ever tell them. They've proven time and time again they'd do anything for me—I don't deserve it though, so guilt overwhelms me.

By 7:00am, I've been up for two-and-a-half hours. I go back into my room to get dressed because I've been walking around in pyjamas and a robe since my shower. I glance at my phone when it lights up. Again, I have several messages from Liam.

Liam: What do you mean, 'incident'?

Why aren't you going to class? Are you okay?

Can I come over?

I am in the midst of texting him back when my phone rings, and in my text-messaging fury of fingers flying, I accidentally answer. Thankfully, it's Liam and not someone claiming to be from a duct cleaning service, who are the only other people who call me.

"Hey."

"Finally. I've been texting you for hours." He sounds relieved. "Are you okay? What happened last night?"

A few seconds of silence pass. "I don't want to explain it over the phone. It's about my dad."

"Zach? Is he okay?"

"No, not Zach. My biological dad. He... he found me."

Liam is silent for a full count of ten. "Oh no. Did he hurt you? How did he find you? What happened?"

"Wow. Easy on the questions, man. I'm fine. We can talk about it next time I see you. I don't want to get into it right now. I'm sorry."

"No, I'm sorry. Shoot. Sorry. I don't want you to get hurt."

Liam has been such an incredible friend to me, but he has his own life and priorities. Panicking about me can't occupy his time.

"I know. It's fine. Someone else was there and made him leave."

"Well, I owe that person a beer."

I consider telling Liam my hero last night was the same guy from the coffee shop, but I figure it's not worth mentioning. "Me too. I doubt I'll ever see him again, though. Anyway, I'm not going back to work at the bookstore. Now that Kevin knows I work there, I'm not safe. Zara is going to let me work for her for a while, but I think I'll be okay to come back to classes tomorrow. I wanted a day to decompress."

"Yeah, sure. Let me know if you need me to pick up anything on campus. Tomorrow I'll come pick you up and we'll go together. I'd feel better if you had someone with you."

I smile, grateful he offers what I need before I even think about it. He lives five minutes away, but because our classes are on different schedules, we usually drive ourselves. I'd be relieved not having to go alone for a while, though.

"Thanks Liam. You're the best friend a girl could ever have. I'm sorry I'm the actual worst." I try to sound light-hearted in my comment, but I am speaking truth.

"You're more important to me than a friend." He exhales and takes a beat. "You're like family. I'll see you in the morning, but text or call if you need me."

I'm not sure how to take his comment, so I don't acknowledge it. "Thanks Liam. See you tomorrow."

More than a friend? Family? Like a sister? Or an annoying cousin? Now I have more material to replay on a loop and analyze until I'm more confused than ever.

My day at home consists of puttering around, trying to keep busy. I'm so tired, but I know if I stop moving, my train of thought will start running down the track at the speed of a Peregrine falcon. Classic avoidance—keep busy to avoid facing trauma.

Zara understands my intentions because she doesn't question my incessant need for something to do. She's giving me meaningless tasks, but I'm still glad I can contribute something to make up for all the trouble I cause.

Isla is doing her schoolwork. She's in grade six, but Zara has homeschooled her since shortly after adopting us. Zara started her own counselling business out of our house in order to be home and support Isla's needs. Zara provides her services for very little cost to the many clients who come and go. She wants to help those in need, and she doesn't think finances should be a barrier to mental health support, so she tries to bridge the gap as best she can, which I admire her for. Of course, it helps that

Zach won a multi-million-dollar lawsuit after the death of his parents, and he continues to work for himself.

Isla comes bounding around the corner, with Bond on her heels. "Hey Chels. Whatcha doing?"

"Hey, Troublemaker. I'm putting some paperwork away. Are you done with your school?"

"Yeah, finally. Fractions are the worst."

I giggle at her dramatic eye roll. "Just wait until you get to algebra. Did you have any trouble?"

"No, I got it. Mom told me I could ask you if I needed help."

I take a bow. "I'm here to serve you."

Her giggle never fails to set my mind at ease. "I'm going to take Bond to play in the yard. He thinks school is boring."

I look at Bond, sitting dutifully beside his best friend and chuckle again. "Okay. Be careful, you two."

I carry on with my paperwork, mindlessly organizing and filling in missing information. My schoolwork is awaiting me, so once I'm done my tasks for Zara, I go to find her in her office to return the completed documents. She must have slipped out, so I walk around the house to track her down.

She approaches me as I near the kitchen. "Have you seen Isla?"

"She was taking Bond outside to play in the yard."

"I know, but I don't see her or the dog out there."

Zara appears far calmer than my brain is.

"Did you try the dog whistle? Bond always comes for that."

"Oh, good idea." Zara runs toward the back entrance and, after grabbing the whistle from a drawer, blows on it while sticking her head through the sliding glass door. Bond comes trotting around the side of the house, stopping to make sure Isla is following him. Isla saunters along behind him seconds later. "Isla, where were you?"

"There was a man by the fence. He said he was looking for his dog, but I told him I couldn't help. I said I'd come get you, but he was in a hurry."

Zara and I exchange glances and I know she's thinking the same thing I am.

"Can you describe him?" Zara asks.

"Um, he had orange hair, and he was old." She giggles. "Bond didn't like him. He kept growling."

I glance at Zara, but I can't help the urge to be sick. I take off running for the nearby powder room and lose the contents of my stomach. He found me. He found Isla. My family is in danger now.

I can't compete with the fear rising inside me. Tears pour down my face. My breathing is erratic, there is the weight of a hippo sitting on my chest, and I'm paralyzed. How did this happen? How did he find me? I cradle my knees, curled up on the powder room floor.

A gentle knock at the door precedes its opening without an invitation. Zara is all too familiar with panic attacks to bother waiting for me to speak. After a few minutes, once my breathing has slowed, she says, "Sweetheart, it's okay. She's okay, and we won't let him hurt you."

"He was outside. He knows where we live. I'd never forgive myself if he hurt her." My tears are fast and furious all over again, raining down my face in a deluge.

"Don't worry about that. Isla knows not to speak to anyone, and I've told her if he comes again, to run straight inside. I don't doubt Bond would rip his throat out if he crossed over the fence. We're all okay. It's okay."

"He'll never stop. He blames me for his time in prison, and everything else that's gone wrong in his life. It was my fault my mom died giving birth to me, and he had to do everything alone. It was my fault he lost his job. Then he had to work for those men to make ends meet. It's all my fault."

"Chelsea, listen to me." Zara makes me look her in the eyes—something neither of us particularly enjoys, so I know she's serious. "You are not to blame for *any* of it. It's not your fault your mother died. Any loving mother would give her life in a heartbeat to save her child, and that's what she did. That's not your fault—it was her choice. Your dad went to prison because of his own choices. *He's* the one who got mixed up with bad people instead of finding legal work. *He's* the one who asked for more money than he could ever pay back. When good people have other options, they don't choose the bad ones. He had other options, Chels."

"Girls?" Zach shouts from the other side of the house.

"We're in here!" Zara calls.

Zach comes to the door witnessing the condition I am in, still crying and emitting a *perfume de vomit*. "Are you okay, Chels?"

"Yeah." I lie, and I feel horrible for it, but I don't want anyone else fussing over me.

"You sure? Should we go to the police station now?"

"No!"

"I know you're scared, but we should have a record of his behaviour."

"I don't want him to have more reason to be angry with me. Do you know how often women make reports to the police, but they can't do anything until after the offender has done something wrong? What's the point?" Why doesn't he understand? I can't give Kevin more reason to retaliate against me. Against my family.

"Chels, he assaulted you, and it's possible he's on parole. Maybe he'll go back to jail."

"Then could you imagine how angry he'd be? He'd probably send a colony of murder hornets after me. No. Just no."

"I'm not going to push, but I'm going to hire a security company to come and set up alarms on all the doors and windows. You should always have someone with you when you leave the house. At least for a while."

I'm such a burden—not only are these people in danger, but they have to spend a small fortune to keep themselves safe in their own house.

"Maybe it would be best if I found somewhere else to live." I can't stop the tears from falling again as I say those words. This is the only home and the only genuine family I've ever known.

"Not on my life. Chelsea, you are not being driven out of your home, away from your family, by a man who already tried to destroy your life once! You are not going anywhere." Zara is fierce when she cares about something or someone.

"But—"

"No buts. She's right. You're not going anywhere. I don't care what your head is telling you; we are sticking together through this, and I'll do whatever it takes to keep you safe." Zach is looking at me through his intense green eyes; his posture is stiff.

I can't stop thinking about the what ifs. "I couldn't live with myself if—"

"No! Don't go down that road. You are staying here, and that's final." Zara's face says she is not joking. She is not letting me go without a fight.

"I'll stay, but if he comes back again, I am going to re-evaluate. I can't let you guys be in danger."

Zach places a hand on each of my shoulders, which is unusual for him, but I'm aware he's making himself clear. "It's not somewhere we haven't been before, and we always come out on top. We're sticking together."

I am so grateful for these two incredible human beings who brought me into their home and their hearts. I'll do whatever needs to be done in order to protect them. No one is going to hurt them again. Certainly not on my account.

Wednesday morning, my classes don't start until ten, so I stay in bed later than usual. Liam has later classes too—he's not coming to pick me up until nine. Then it's a thirty-five-minute drive to campus. I didn't sleep the greatest, but given the little I slept the night before and the stress of the day, it was an improvement.

I've showered and dressed in black leggings, a long, black knitted sweater, and my trusty slip-on sneakers. The fall weather is creeping into our town and I'm ready to embrace full-coverage outfits. The more I blend into the crowd, the better.

I drink a quick tea with Zara, over which she tries to keep the conversation positive and distracting. I appreciate her, but once Liam arrives, he's going to grill me about what happened, so I'm tense with anticipation.

A car pulls into the driveway and, knowing only a few people have the gate code, it's no mystery who it is. Liam's silver

Infinity G37 Coupe is certainly flashier than my CRV, but he is less obsessed with safety than I am. He is ever the gentleman and will come to the door if I don't beat him to it, so I holler at Zara I'm leaving and rush outside to save him the trouble. Sure enough, he's just stepped out of his car.

"Hey."

"Hey, Big Red. Are you ready?"

"I guess so." I walk toward his car as he opens the passenger door for me. "Thanks."

Liam looks at me with such concern, I'm anxious for the drive. He's going to want the details of the last thirty-seven hours. He walks around the front of the car and hops into his seat. Once he slips the car into reverse, we're on our way to one of the few places someone can go where they have to pay ridiculous amounts of money to be endlessly stressed.

"So, are you going to tell me what happened, or should I beg?"

"I've been in the car precisely twenty-seven seconds. I haven't even adjusted to the temperature yet."

"Don't stall Chels. I've been out of my mind wondering what happened after work the other night. Please, put me out of my misery."

I know he's trying to break the tension and make me comfortable talking about this, but hearing I'm responsible for his misery doesn't help matters. I brace myself by holding onto the seatbelt as if it's going to provide me some sense of security from my mental anguish and tell Liam my recounting of events.

"The same guy? The long-haired guy from the coffee shop?"

"Weird, right?"

"Too weird, Chels. That's too fishy to be a coincidence. Tell me if you see him again, okay?"

"Liam, it's fine. He saved me, but I'm not about to run off into the sunset with him. You know how hard it is for me to trust people."

"But I don't trust him either. Maybe we should alert campus security about your dad. They can keep an eye out for him."

"Don't remind me I share DNA with that man. The last thing I want to do is remember my childhood or anything to do with Kevin. You are so lucky you have the parents you do." I turn my head to stare out the window. "They've raised a good man."

"Thanks. You make being a good man easy." Liam unnecessarily changes lanes, forcing him to turn and check his blind spot, preventing me from seeing his facial expression when I look back his way.

It's easy to do the right thing when your best friend is a perpetual damsel in distress. Helpless Chelsea, making chivalry easy since the dawn of the twenty-first century.

"Anyway, so Zach is having a security system with cameras installed at the house, and I've been instructed not to go anywhere alone for a while. So, you're going to get sick of me."

"I could never. I'll have your back, no matter what. Day or night."

I'm silenced by Liam's comments. I don't trust easily—that's an understatement—but Liam has shown me time and time again I can count on him. That, in turn, makes me want to do anything to protect him.

The rest of our drive passes with no interesting conversation. Liam has me laughing over his karaoke, singing *Overpass* by *Panic! At the Disco*, and it's nice to have a few minutes of light-heartedness. As we near the college campus, my panic returns.

Liam must notice my trepidation because he reaches over and takes my hand. His friendly gesture brings me back to the present. I glance at him and give an appreciative smile, which he returns with one of his own, reaffirming this friend of mine is the best support system I could ask for.

Once we've parked and gotten our stuff, we walk toward the centre of campus.

Liam asks, "Do you want to grab a coffee? There's plenty of time before class."

I'm nervous to go back to the coffee shop because Sebastian was there last time, and I don't want Liam to take exception to his presence if he's there again. "No thanks. I'm going to head to my class and wait."

"I'll come with you."

"It's fine Liam. Go get yourself a coffee and I'll meet up with you after my classes. If I'm done before you, I'll wait in the library."

"Chels, I don't want to leave you alone."

"I won't be alone. I'm in the middle of campus. It'll be fine. Even if Kevin had the nerve to show up here, there are people everywhere."

Liam shifts his weight from one foot to the other as he looks down at the ground. "I don't want to leave you. Let me walk you to class."

I release a sigh. "Liam, I appreciate you wanting to look out for me, but the last thing I want is to become an obstruction to your social life. It won't bode well for you if every girl on campus thinks I'm your girlfriend."

His eyes pop wide open. "I could think of worse things." He glances to his left and shoves his hands in his pockets. Is he... embarrassed?

"I don't want to cramp your style." I'm saying these words, but I wish Liam could stay by my side the entire day. The guilt is too much, though, and I want him to live his life. He doesn't deserve to be sucked into my nightmare.

"Let me walk with you. My class is in the same direction."

There's no point in arguing with him further if he's determined to chaperone me. I just don't want him to feel obligated to act as my private security. "Then who am I to deny you a few more minutes of my company?"

We walk toward my ethics and professionalism course, ready for a lecture on setting professional boundaries. I agree with the material, but I'm grateful my former counsellor, Zara, blurred professional lines five years ago and adopted me. I can't imagine where I would be had I aged out of the foster system. That thought leaves me with a sinking sensation in my stomach because I'm putting my family in danger with my presence. I know they've repeatedly said otherwise, but they're safer if I leave. Not everyone has nine lives, and even if they do, most of them have been used up already.

We arrive at my class and I'm emotionally drained. Recounting the events with Kevin, having a brief, anomalous disagreement with Liam over releasing him from my security detail, and worrying about my family's safety, I've had a full day. I guess it's a good thing Liam drove me here, otherwise I would have gotten back in my car and gone home to hide.

"I'll meet up with you later in the library, then. Just call me if you need anything, okay? I mean it."

"Thanks." I crack a bit of a smile in Liam's direction. I know he'd come running, but I hope he never has to.

Liam walks off toward his global business strategy course, which sounds painfully boring, and I make my way into my classroom for the next hour of my life.

Walking across campus after my classes, I keep my head down. I'm wearing my sunglasses to avoid eye contact, but my other senses are on high alert. The footsteps of other students draw closer and fade away as I travel down the footpath. I can smell the seasons transitioning as the leaves are turning vibrant colours and the plants become dormant. The cool air hits my skin, and if I went into the coffee shop, I could taste the pumpkin spice obsession that plagues the Autumn.

Every few seconds I lift my eyes to make sure I won't run into anyone or anything, and to take in my surroundings. I haven't been on this level of alert since I was a pre-teen. All the progress I have made in confronting my past trauma disappeared the moment Kevin Wells re-entered my life.

While scanning the crowd, without warning, the hairs on my neck stand up as I see the back of a familiar form speaking with another student.

My thoughts are going in one direction, but my body chooses a less-helpful option—freeze. I'm standing in the middle of the pathway, with angry students swerving around me and muttering unfriendly words as they pass.

"Move out of the way, girl!" someone demands, stomping by.

Trust me, I would if I could. Apparently, both fight and flight mode have been deactivated.

"Chelsea?"

Every single synapse is misfiring at this moment. Right now, I am like a ship on an unchartered course, and I can't get back to safe waters. Sebastian is a lighthouse; warning me to stay away, instead drawing me in.

"Chelsea, are you okay?"

His voice snaps me out of my frozen state, and I lock eyes with him, only to look away. Eye contact makes me too vulnerable.

"Hi," I say, continuing to look at the ground.

"Are you all right? You look like you're about to pass out."

"Yeah, I... I'm fine. Just tired." I'm not very convincing. "What are you doing here?"

"Oh." He looks like the cat that ate the canary—feathers floating around his guilty expression. "I'm here for business."

"You're a business student here? My friend Liam is taking business management. You might know him," I ramble off, attempting to establish some common ground.

"No, I'm not taking business. I'm not a student; just had some business to tend to on campus." He takes a step closer to me. His hair makes me envious because it's so thick and looks outrageously soft. It hardly seems fair. "How are you after the other night?"

I shiver at the thought of my encounter with Kevin. "I'm alive, thanks to you, but beyond that, I can't say."

He cannot be trusted.

"Fair enough. I'm sorry I didn't get there sooner."

"It wasn't your battle. You didn't need to step in at all, but I'm grateful you did."

His face softens, but there's still an edge to his words. "Of course, I did. I couldn't stand there and watch him hurt you."

I mutter under my breath, "Not the worst thing he's done."

"What was that?"

"Nothing. I should be going. I have to meet my friend so I can get a ride home. See you around."

"Wait, Chelsea. Can I get your number? I'll text you mine, so if he ever comes back, you can call me."

I'm shocked by his attempt to get my number. Is he insinuating I call him instead of the police if my paternal donor comes back around? Or is it an excuse because he wants my number for other reasons?

He cannot be trusted.

"I don't think it would be appropriate to call you if another problem appears, Sebastian. Thank you for the offer."

"Well, how 'bout you give me your number so I can call you just because?"

"Just because what?"

"Because I like you, Chelsea. You're... interesting." He takes a step closer to me, causing goosebumps to overtake my exposed skin.

He cannot be trusted.

No one has ever asked for my number before, aside from Liam in high school, so I'm not sure how to decline without offending him. After a few seconds, a solution comes to mind. "Why don't I give you my email address?"

"Email address?" A quirk of his left eyebrow tells me this is not a typical response. "Technology has advanced far past MSN messenger."

"I'm sorry. I don't give my phone number to many people, and that's what I'm comfortable with. It's nothing personal." It's totally personal.

"You drive a hard bargain, Chelsea. I guess I'll take what I can get."

I write my email address, which he doesn't seem thrilled about, but that's flirting dangerously with the edge of my comfort zone. Who knows if I can trust him, and while every logical thought tells me I shouldn't, I can't deny I am drawn to him.

My phone vibrates in my pocket, and I remember Liam is waiting for me. "I really have to go. See you around." I turn to leave without waiting for acknowledgement.

"Count on it."

He cannot be trusted.

I stand in front of the library, willing my body to slow its excessive heart rate. If Liam sees me this way, he'll know something is up, and I don't want to tell him about Sebastian. Call me crazy—no, that's offensive—but I don't want Liam to intervene between Sebastian and me. *If* I see him again, I'd prefer to develop a friendship organically and decide for myself if he's someone I want to spend time with. I want to step out from this mask of fear I've been living behind and act like a normal college student. Well, maybe not a normal college student, but at least a functioning one who's not afraid of rain, sunny days, closed doors, Spanish accents, dog cages, or an endless list of other random things. Sebastian saved me, so maybe he's a good person to start with. Liam can't be solely responsible for my social life. Plus, I need to protect him.

"There you are. I've been waiting for you."

I turn to the familiar voice and find Liam walking in my direction. My brain has a unique reaction to Liam—I'm at ease with him. "Hey, were you waiting long for me?"

"Nah, I wasn't waiting, but I walked to your normal spot and didn't see you. Are you ready to go?"

"Anything ending at home, I'm always ready."

"So, you don't want to stop by the gym with me to get a workout in?" He laughs—I'm not sure if it's funny because I've never worked out a day in my life, or because he knows the gym would be right next to *Snake Island* on my list of places I never want to go.

"If you want to get a workout in, I can wait here. You don't have to rearrange your day for me."

"Chels, it was a joke. A bad one, obviously. I'll get you home, don't worry. Was everything okay today?"

What should I tell him? We've always been honest with each other, and he's never given me reason why I couldn't tell him the truth, but something is nagging at me to keep my interaction with Sebastian to myself. I don't want Liam stressing himself over something that, so far, has given him no reason to. "Yep, everything was fine. Boring in my classes, but that's not unusual." I walk toward the parking lot before we can take this conversation any further. If he asks me questions, I'll crumble like a breadcrumb house.

The drive home is quiet and awkward. I keep shifting in my seat while staring out the window. Not telling Liam the truth is just as bad as if I had lied to him, and that makes me feel guilty. I worry he'll give up on our friendship if he knows I'm not being honest.

I'd be lost without Liam, so I'm at war with myself. Finally, twenty minutes into our drive, I blurt out, "Sebastian was on campus again today. The guy from the coffee shop."

Liam whips his eyes in my direction fast enough the car swerves onto the gravel shoulder. He corrects the steering, and glances at me, trying to keep his eyes on the road. "Did you talk to him?" I'm surprised by how calm he sounds, given he nearly drove us off the road eight seconds ago.

"I did. Not on purpose, but he approached me, and I couldn't run away." Literally, I couldn't run—I could barely even blink.

"Were you scared? What did he say? Why was he there?"

Let the inquisition begin.

"Just hi. He asked how I was after the other night, and um… wanted my phone number." I watch Liam's reaction as I say the last part through gritted teeth. Why am I so afraid to tell him this?

"Did you give it to him?" Liam raises an eyebrow that would make Dwayne Johnson proud.

"No, I told him only a few people had my number. I wasn't ready to share it with a complete stranger."

"Good. I don't trust the guy at all. With your dad showing up, the timing is too suspicious."

"I doubt he has anything to do with *Kevin*." I emphasize using his first name because I hate acknowledging I'm biologically related to him. "Sebastian wouldn't have shoved him away from me if he did. Right?"

"You can't be too sure, Chels. But something doesn't add up. I don't want you getting hurt, and with your dad coming to your work and your house, you can guarantee he knows where you go to school. It's suspicious to me."

Liam's words knock the wind out of my lungs. I was aware Kevin likely knows where I go to school, but hearing it out loud makes it more of a probability than a possibility. I hoped I would have one place to go where I wouldn't need to be on high alert—but high alert is my perpetual state of being.

"Well, thanks for putting me at ease." My words are marked with an uncharacteristic sarcasm.

"It's not my goal to freak you out. I want you to be safe, and this Sebastian guy gives me a bad feeling."

"Well, it's not up to you, Liam. I *can* make my own choices."

"Chels, I'm not trying to decide for you. I'm *trying* to keep you safe." Liam's usual soft-spoken voice is atypically loud and determined, which makes me more irritated.

"I don't need you to babysit me, for God's sake. If I'm pathetic and need my hand held all the time, I don't even know why you're my friend!" I'm frustrated I cause everyone in my life so much stress and worry. Anger boils to the surface, and I can't rein it in.

This conversation has gone exactly how I was afraid it would. Liam and I have never fought before, but we've never had reason to disagree. We've always supported each other's differences. This situation feels foreign.

"No, I don't think you're pathetic, but you are vulnerable, and you have every right to be. I'm trying to save you from going down a path you can't come back from."

"I don't even know what you mean. Ugh! I don't understand how, as a consenting adult, giving a guy my phone number would lead me down some mysterious path. You know what? I don't even want to talk about it anymore. What's done is done, and if I'm ever going to live a normal life, I have to expand my horizons at some point."

"You've taken everything I said the wrong way. I didn't mean to make you upset."

"Well, I am. I'm tired of you babying me. We're the same age, Liam! You're not my babysitter." Here I go again with tears of frustration leaking down my cheeks. Few things in my life have made me cry excessively, but it's become my newest hobby these past few days. I don't know if those tears are because of Liam's words or my reaction. I've tried so hard over the years to control my angry outbursts, not wanting to drive people away. Here I am, failing at that, too.

A short time later, Liam pulls into my driveway, and even though I was upset with him, he still waits in the driveway until I am safely inside. Even when I'm the worst, he's still a good friend.

Liam was only trying to help and I pushed him away. I don't feel worthy of his help, and I don't want to continue worrying everyone by being a useless, pitiful little girl—actually, that is offensive to Isla, because she functions better than I do. By government standards, I'm an adult, and I need to behave as such. Now I can't sleep because I'd rather lie in bed, hating myself.

I stare out my bedroom window overlooking our long driveway and spot a car parked outside the gate. I study the shape of the vehicle to see if any shadows are moving inside. It could be someone broken down, but logically, I know that's not the case. We live on a dead-end street in the middle of nowhere. Only a serial killer would drive out here and break down. That would be my luck.

I shut off the lamp beside my bed, so my silhouette won't be seen in the window, then I walk back to peek out from behind the curtain. My phone vibrates, startling me, and I let out a yelp.

Liam: It's me. I wanted to make sure you were safe.
Chelsea: What's you?
Liam: I'm in my car at the end of your driveway. Keeping watch.

I dial Liam to express my opinion on the matter.

"Hey, Chels." His voice comes through the speaker on my phone, sounding like a meek young boy.

"Liam, what are you doing? You can't sit at the end of the driveway. Besides, we have the dog here, and he'll hear anything before you." I'm more scared for Liam's safety than my own. Kevin is a heartless bastard and won't hesitate to hurt Liam, knowing it would hurt me.

"I'll be fine. I can't go home knowing that scum bag is walking around a free man."

"Liam... I'm not okay with you staying out there all night." I try to think of an alternative to please us both. "Why don't you come stay inside?"

"Inside?"

"Yes. You know, on the other side of the walls you're staring at?"

"Where will I stay inside?"

"Um, I don't know. I guess you can stay in my room. Zach and Zara know we're friends, so they won't be bothered."

"Like a slumber party. Awesome." He sounds disappointed. I can almost hear the eye roll.

"Just come inside, you goof. Open the gate and meet me at the door. Then we can paint each other's nails."

He chuckles, but agrees to my strange request. Not the nail painting—coming inside.

Three minutes later, Liam is striding up the few stairs to the front door. I open it wide, and his vibrant smile isn't as wide as it normally is.

"Hey. Come in."

"Chels, who's there?" Zach asks from the middle of the stairway.

"It's me, Mr. Haynes. I'm sorry if I woke you. I was camping outside to keep watch, but Chelsea insisted I come in. I can leave."

"Liam, for the thousandth time, it's Zach. Second, there's no way we're letting you camp outside. Chelsea's right. You are welcome to stay." He turns to go back upstairs, stopping to add, "You're a good man."

"Thank you. Just doing what I felt was right."

"Well, there's a significant shortage of that in the world, so keep it up. I'll leave you two alone, but be responsible."

There's a quick way to make me blush and become defensive in a hurry. "I'm sorry we woke you, but good night!"

Zach chuckles, waving before continuing up the stairs.

Once Liam is inside, I lock the door and check the front gate is closed. "Come on. You can sleep in my room." I stride toward the stairs. "I can't believe you were going to sit awake in your car the whole night." After how I treated him today, I'm blown away he would do that. "And by the way, I'm sorry for how I reacted today."

"No, I'm sorry. I don't want to treat you like a porcelain doll, but you're special to me, Chels."

"I'm sorry for worrying you. That's not my intention. I shouldn't have told you."

Liam reaches out to touch my arm, and I embrace the warmth of his hand. His touch doesn't terrify, nor repulse me, and that alone tells me how important he is to me. "You don't worry me, and I'm glad you told me. Your bio-dad worries me. That's not your fault."

It *is* my fault. If I hadn't made him so angry in the first place, he wouldn't have returned to ruin my life again. I should have accepted reality and lived with it. Everyone I care for could be in danger because I was selfish.

I don't want to talk about Kevin, and I don't want to have this conversation any longer. "Let's go to bed so we're not college-zombies."

There are a pair of pyjama pants and a T-shirt folded on my bed when we enter my bedroom. Zach must have brought them in for Liam. He and Liam have always gotten along famously ever since I introduced them. They have a lot of similar interests, but their greatest common denominator is the fact they're both wonderful men. They give me hope not all men are monsters.

I pass Liam the pyjamas, assuming he'd go to the bathroom to change, but I forget he's a normal, functioning guy and isn't ashamed of himself. He has confidence, and when he removes his shirt, I can confirm his confidence is justified. His time in the gym is obvious. He's not ripped like the unrealistic models on romance novel covers—talk about objectification—but he is fit. When he removes his jeans to change his pants, I turn away, feeling the heat creep into my cheeks.

Is this normal for a sleepover?

He folds his clothes and places them on an armchair by my window. It's almost two in the morning, and we both have to be in class by ten.

"Where should I sleep?" Liam asks.

"Um. I guess you can sleep in the bed... assuming you're okay with that."

"I'm fine, but are you? I can sleep in the chair."

"No, don't be silly. That won't be comfortable. It's fine. I just..."

"What's wrong, Chels?" Liam steps closer to me.

"Ugh. I have to warn you, sometimes I have nightmares."

"I know. It's fine. Let's sleep, and we'll deal with that if the time comes."

I crawl in bed on my usual side, closest to the door, and Liam occupies the spot nearest the ensuite. There's plenty of space in my queen bed, so we aren't touching, but I am still experiencing his body heat. The man is toasty.

"Good night, Arizona. Thanks for looking out for me."

"Always. Good night, Big Red."

I fall asleep, grateful Liam and I have patched things up— meaning he forgave me for my nonsense, yet again.

When I wake, I blink my eyes a few times to make sure they're not playing tricks on me. Why are Liam and I cuddling in my bed? I jolt back, trying to escape his embrace and wake him. He doesn't seem nearly as concerned about the situation as I am.

"Good morning."

"Um. Yeah. Good morning. Sorry. I don't know how we ended up, uh... entangled."

"You were having a nightmare, and you cuddled into me. Once you fell back asleep, I didn't want to wake you by letting go."

I sit upright, throwing my legs over the side of my bed. I hold my face in both hands, embarrassed I snuggled Liam. How many ways can I mess up our friendship?

"I'm sorry. God, I'm so embarrassed. Here I go, making things awkward."

"Nothing is awkward. It was fine. I'm glad you got some sleep, Chels."

Before I travel any further down this path of regret, Zara pokes her head in my bedroom door. "Good morning, you two. I'm making breakfast. Come down in twenty."

"You don't have to make us anything. We can manage." I try to give Liam an escape so he can leave after our awkward slumber party.

"I insist. We don't have company often enough. I'd like for us to all have breakfast together if you're able to stay, Liam."

"I'd love to. Thanks. Can I help you with anything?"

"That's sweet of you. I've got it handled. We'll have something simple." Without another word, Zara leaves.

"You don't have to stay if you don't want to. I know you're probably dying to get away from me right now." I can't look at him.

"Not at all. Do you mind if I grab a quick shower?"

"Make yourself at home. You'll smell like summer rose the rest of the day, but who knows, maybe that will attract some ladies."

Liam's expression is unreadable as he turns and walks into the bathroom, closing the door behind him. I might as well go have a shower in Isla's bathroom so we can get down to breakfast in time.

I'm convinced Isla has a crush on Liam. When Liam first came to our house, she was immediately drawn to him. Five years later, she's got her chair so close to his, she's nearly on his lap. He doesn't seem to mind, though. He enjoys making her laugh.

Zach and Zara talk Liam's ear off—asking how classes are going, what he's been up to lately, his parents. It's been a while since he's been over, which is unusual since he has joined our Friday family dinners for years, so they have a lot to catch up on.

We're finishing up our peaceful breakfast when there is a loud noise outside.

Naturally, I assume it's Kevin. He's here. He's going to hurt my entire family. I can't escape him.

"Let me go outside and check it out. I'm sure it's nothing." Zach is terrible at faking confidence.

"Don't go. Just stay inside. It's safer in here," I plead with Zach because I can't stand the thought of him being hurt.

"I'll come with you," Liam adds.

"Thanks. Bond will come too. Come on, boy."

Ignoring my plea, Zach, Liam, and Bond walk out the front door to investigate. The moments between when they exit until they re-enter feel endless. By the time they return, I've worked myself into a frenzy, and Zara is doing her best to calm me down. I feel horrible for putting them through this.

"We found nothing. Must have been a random noise. Nothing to worry about, Chels. But to be on the safe side, we'll have the security system installed by the end of the week." Zach tries his best to reassure me while Zara rubs my back.

I can't keep putting them in danger.

Zara shouts, "Over my dead body, Chels!" Her fierceness is not unfamiliar, but the volume she's speaking in is.

"Zara, I can't keep putting you all in danger. I could never forgive myself."

"First, *you* are not putting us in danger. You need to stop thinking that. Second, you're safer here with us than you would be off alone in who-knows-where. We'll get the security system installed and everything will be fine."

"I hate that you guys are forced to spend all this money on something to be safe in your own house. It's my fault, and if I leave, then you don't have to stress over it anymore."

"Chelsea, listen closely. The security system is something we wanted to put in for a long time and kept putting it off. Regardless, we would spend our last dime to make sure you are safe, so please stop thinking you are inconveniencing us. That is what love is. We'll protect you until our dying breaths."

That's what makes this so scary.

"I can't let that happen. I can't. This is all my fault."

"Nothing is your fault, Sweetheart. Not a single thing. You're our family, and you're staying here where we can keep an eye on each other. If one day soon, you're ready to move and have your own place, by all means, we support that. But you're not moving out under these circumstances. I won't allow it." When Zara makes up her mind, I've learned there is little you can do to change it.

"Fine. But if Kevin shows up here again, I will reconsider."

"No, you won't, but the decision is made for now." Zara pulls me in for a hug and I believe she would do anything to keep me safe—but I'm not deserving of that kind of sacrifice. I'd never want her in harm's way at my defence.

The subject will remain on my mind until the situation with Kevin is resolved. If or when that will ever happen remains to be seen. He is like a cockroach, popping up out of nowhere, and seems to have the ability to survive anything, including a nuclear blast.

I wish I knew where to find a crocodile. Or a hippo. Oh, or a tiger shark.

What is wrong with me? Why am I thinking of ways for my *father* to meet his demise, using innocent animals to get the job done? My intrusive thoughts are taking creative liberties thanks to the deadly predators book I read the other night.

Liam pulls me out of my mind by reminding me we have college classes to attend. I'm on edge after the morning's events. I don't know how I'll focus, but staying home will only cause more worry.

"We can drive together again. I'll walk you to your classes."

"That's so much trouble for you, Liam. You already gave up a good night's sleep to watch over me, which was unnecessary, by the way."

"I told you, I couldn't sleep without knowing you were safe. But to be honest, I slept better than I have in days."

Having Liam disclose that worrying about me has caused him to lose sleep makes me more stressed about the impact I'm having on everyone. He's going to end up sleep-deprived, fail out of school, and live his life with a string of dead-end jobs, never achieving his full potential.

"I'm not worth worrying about Liam. Please, just focus on your life. You should be out there being a normal college student—not babysitting your sorry excuse for a friend."

He takes a silent beat before responding. "Have you ever considered maybe I worry because you are important to me? I came to make sure you were safe because I genuinely care? You're not an inconvenience to me, and you're not cramping my style. I wouldn't be here if I didn't *want* to be."

I may trust him, but I have little faith those words could ever be truth. "I'll never understand why."

"That's what's so endearing about you, Chels. You don't ask for things. You don't even think you deserve them, but really, you deserve the world." His expression turns serious, and he's staring directly into my soul. There's more meaning in his words than they are expressing, but I can't trust my delusional brain to pick up on social cues.

"Um. Let's get going. I'll ride with you then." I walk toward the door, shouting my regards to my family, hopeful they'll be safe.

An uneventful day of classes goes by, and I'm emotionally drained. I'm waiting in the library for Liam to finish his last class, eager to get home. I texted Zara far too many times throughout the day to make sure they were safe. She says I'm being overly paranoid, but she's one to talk. She doesn't seem to grasp how truly awful my father is.

"You ready to go?" Liam's voice breaks through the silence of the library.

I smile when I see his familiar face. "Yes. Very ready. Please, let's get out of here."

"Are you okay? Why are you in such a rush?"

"I want to get home to make sure Isla and Zara are really okay."

"I'm sure they're fine, but let's put your mind at ease."

As if my mind is ever at ease.

On our drive home, I stare out the window, thinking about my options to find somewhere else to live. I don't think I'll ever be comfortable knowing Kevin could use my family against me. As much as his presence is a nightmare for me, I'd happily give myself over to him to avoid any harm being done to my family. Is that what I have to do? Is that the only way to stop this, short of death?

"What are you thinking, Big Red? You look constipated or something."

I let out a sharp laugh but return to my serious thoughts. I don't wish to engage in another carpool argument with my chauffeur. There's only so much he'll tolerate. "Nothing. Just thinking about my options."

"Options for what? Coffee order? Future career? Dating prospects?" He smirks at me with a sideways glance while he watches the road.

"Definitely no dating prospects. I was thinking about where I should live. It doesn't feel safe any home anymore." I say this matter-of-factly, not looking for any input on the situation.

Liam rounds the corner onto my road, heading to my gated driveway at the end. "I thought that was settled and you're staying at home?"

"That's what Zara decided, but I'm not sure if I'm comfortable putting them at risk. I can't live with myself if—"

"No, Chels. They're safe. The dog is there, and the alarm is being installed. Everyone will be fine. I doubt Kevin would cross that line."

Liam's words infuriate me. Does he really think he knows Kevin and what he's capable of better than I do? He doesn't know what a monster my *dear dad* is, and I don't intend to let anyone I care about find out. "You have no idea what he's willing to do. There's no line he wouldn't cross."

"Listen, I get he did horrible things in the past, but you're not a little girl anymore, and you're not alone. You have a family who wants to protect you. Let them help." Liam puts the car in park and we each step out.

My adrenaline is pumping through my body as my anger level rises and the cool autumn air does nothing to quell my fury. "Thanks for the life advice, Liam. It's so easy to dish out when you were born into privilege, in a stable home with loving parents. You seem to forget where I come from and what I've been through."

Liam's face displays his own irritation. "Chels. I say this with all the love I have for you. You might have come from the depths of hell, but that's not where you are now. You seem to ignore the fact you are *now* living a privileged life with loving parents." He takes a deep breath before continuing. "What I'm saying is, don't throw it away because of your past."

Ouch. He has a point, but he still doesn't understand my perspective. I'm so tired of feeling on edge all the time. I'm tired of being coddled like a child. I'm tired of being a source of worry for everyone around me.

"You should leave. I don't need you telling me how I should feel or what I should do with myself."

"Chels. Don't do this." Liam takes a few steps toward me, worry etched on his face. "I want to be here for you. Sure, having Kevin back in your life has thrown a wrench into things, but you don't have to stress over it alone. We'll all make sure you're okay."

"No. *I* will make sure I'm okay. I don't need other people to be involved. This is my problem, and I intend to keep it that way." I turn to storm inside, expecting Liam to protest, but he doesn't. He gets back in his car and reverses out of the driveway.

I avoid conversation with my family by heading to my room, not even stopping to give Bond an ear scratch like the monster I am.

J ust as I'm finishing up my residual schoolwork for the evening, still reeling from my argument with Liam, I hear my phone vibrate with a notification. Normally, I don't rush to check my messages, but I have this excitement in my belly to see who it is. It's nice to get a notification other than "fully charged."

I click to open the envelope notification which belongs to an email address, *troublefindsme@youremail.com.* Suspish.

I hope you like hot male as much as you like Hotmail. ;)
Sebastian

He can't be serious. I've got to give him points for a successful icebreaker.

Chelsea: I hope you know CPR because that email took my breath away.

I chuckle to myself for playing his game. Maybe I can be a normal girl my age. Another buzz has me jumping for my phone.

Sebastian: I can bring you an inhaler. Might need to keep it handy with me around.

Well, that's presumptuous of him. I'm not even sure how to respond. I decide to leave my reply for a few moments so I can finish up the last of my textbook reading. He's created a problem for me though, because I can't focus on the words on the page—I'm too focused on the words from Sebastian's email.

He cannot be trusted.

There's no point in reading the same paragraph in my textbook over and over, so I might as well call it a night. *Buzz.*

Sebastian: I'm sure you're busy, but can you add me to your to do list?

Chelsea: Sure. Right after plucking my armpit hairs and scrubbing the tile grout.

Sebastian: I'll take what I can get. If you want some help scrubbing the grout, my number is 705-555-1818. I take cleanliness very seriously.

Nice try, Mr. Manbun. I'm not giving you both my address and phone number in one shot.

Chelsea: I'll keep that in mind.

I laugh at our exchange and convince myself there's no reason I can't befriend him. He's been helpful when needed, polite, and he's the kind of dreamy I could never fathom after a lifetime of nightmares. It's about time I branch out beyond Liam, and Sebastian is the first person to pique my interest.

Sebastian: I hope you keep me in mind, because I know I'm thinking about you.

I can't work up the nerve to respond, but I surprise myself by adding his phone number to my contact list. Kevin's intentions are a terrifying mystery, so it can't hurt to have a backup plan should I need it. Sebastian has proven himself capable of handling Kevin, which may be his greatest appeal.

The weekend passes without incident, but that doesn't mean I've let my guard down or relaxed for a moment. I have, however, put a temporary hold on my apartment searching. Kevin is a predator, and he'll wait until his prey least expects an attack before he pounces. I may not have seen him since I was six years old, aside from the other night, but I will never forget what he's done. He's the sludge at the bottom of the society pond—which makes me what, as his offspring? That monster created me, so I must be a monster, too. What if I'm capable of bringing the same harm to others he has?

Even Liam, who's always been good to me, has avoided me for days. It's the first time in our five-year friendship we've gone over twenty-four hours without checking in with each other. He's finally realized I'm the spawn of a monster.

In the silence of my bedroom, tears trickle down my cheeks. I'm convinced I've lost my only friend. My unrelenting state of fight or flight and overwhelming hopelessness have exhausted me, making me more emotional than normal. Why should I battle through this? What's the point? Fight through the pain once more to be back here again in a few months? Weeks? Days? I can never have a significant period where I live like a normal person. No one would live this hell unless they deserved it. I deserve this.

"Sweetheart?" Zara's quiet voice travels through my open door. I glance over to see her head in the doorway. She must have a sixth sense.

I sniffle back my tears, dry my eyes with my sleeve and try my best to fake confidence.

"What's wrong, Chels?" She walks across my room with intention, settling beside me on the edge of my unmade bed.

"Nothing. I'm fine. I was having a moment."

She doesn't need me bothering her with my stupidity.

"Clearly, something. I know you don't like to talk about things until you're ready, so I won't push you, but you have to know I'm here, Chels. Here, loving you when you can't love yourself. I won't let you drown in the darkness I know you're fighting against right now. I've been there before, Sweetheart, and it was you who pulled me out of it."

"Me?" I add an indignant laugh, declaring my surprise. "What did I ever do except add stress to your life?"

"You do not add stress to my life. Your head is telling you that, but I'm here, telling you it's not true. You add so much to all of our lives, and I only wish you could see." She takes a breath to steady herself as though she's about to dive into a hard topic. "After the situation with Patrick, I was in a dark place. I felt like the world was better off without me, and I brought nothing but harm and upset to everyone around me."

That sounds familiar.

"But you don't! You're amazing, and everyone loves you."

"Do you see, Chels? Your brain is telling you one thing, but it's not reality. It's your brain lying to you, not everyone else. In those dark days, when I was wishing Patrick had killed me instead, I didn't know how I'd get through it—and to be honest, I wasn't sure I wanted to. But then, this sweet, fifteen-year-old girl, whom I loved so much, called me, and I knew I had to get help to change my situation, because she deserved better."

"Really? All because I called you to complain?"

"No. Because of all the people you had in your life, you called me for help. You were counting on me, and I loved you enough to be there."

"I don't understand what that has to do with my situation. Patrick was dead. He couldn't hurt you anymore."

"You think because he is dead, he doesn't still hurt me? Chels, I wake up every day knowing I murdered a man. I struggle with the internal battle, questioning whether I am worthy of the life I have—you and Isla, Zach, Jasmine, Quinn, my parents.

Everyone I love. You've been through some terrible things, but you keep fighting because in the end, it's worth it."

"What's worth it? Being an inconvenience to everyone and an endless source of worry? The trees are out there working hard to make oxygen, and I exist to waste it."

Zara looks at me with a contemplative stare. "Do you think I'm a waste of oxygen?"

"Of course not!"

"Why? Why would *you* be a waste of oxygen and not me?"

"Because you do so much for everyone. You're kind, smart, generous, strong—everything I wish I could be." I'll never be able to make a difference in people's lives like she has.

"You are. I don't see those things in myself, but I see them in you. PTSD alters brain chemistry. What you're feeling is not your fault, and it can get better. Just think about how much you've improved since I first met you."

For the first time since Zara entered my room, I cry again. "I don't know how to make it better. I don't know how to make it stop. Kevin is out there and I am afraid of what he will do. Not knowing is eating away at me."

"I know, Sweetheart. I am confident he'll screw up and land himself back in jail. It's only a matter of time. In the meantime, we'll make sure you're never alone, other than at home, and always keep your phone on your person. Not even in your purse, or in the car. Keep it on your body at all times."

She's trying to offer helpful advice right now, but the fact my life has been reduced to being babysat and needing to keep my phone with me is depressing. I go along with her suggestions to put an end to this emotionally draining conversation. "Okay. I will."

"I'm going to make dinner. Do you want to come help?"

Exhaustion has overtaken me after another emotional breakdown. "I'm going to do some reading and then go to bed. You guys go ahead and eat without me."

"I'll put some food aside for you in case, okay? Come down to the kitchen if you need me. I'm always here for you."

"Thanks. I appreciate it." And I do. But that doesn't stop the nagging feeling I have that I'm not worthy of her loyalty.

"I love you, Sweetheart."

The words are on the tip of my tongue. I want to tell her I love her too, but I wonder what value that could add to a person's life. Me. Chelsea Haynes. Biological child of a monster. Hopelessly tragic. Who would even care?

Zach, Zara, and Isla have gone out for the evening to see a movie Isla was excited to watch. They asked me to join them, but I have a lot of schoolwork to catch up on; plus, I wasn't interested in the movie. Sitting in a crowded room with dimly lit exits isn't my idea of a good time. The fact Zach is a millionaire and still insists on going on Tuesday "cheap night" is a testament to his frugality, but it also means it's the busiest night of the week.

I've been slowly marking items off my to-do list, feeling accomplished, which is the only pleasant feeling I've had for the past few days. Laying on my bed with my nose in a textbook, Bond growls. Since Isla isn't home, I've become his surrogate charge.

"What is it, boy?" I sit, trying not to make any noise so I can listen too. I pick up my cell phone to keep it accessible. No one would show up outside of our house at nine on a weekday unless it was for nefarious purposes.

They installed the security system late last week, but if we activate it, they charge us for responding, whether or not there's an issue. I'd rather not cost Zach and Zara more money than I have. It also seems pathetic to have an alarm installed and call for help only a few days later. The drywall dust is still hanging in the air.

Bond rarely growls without good reason; I hope this time he is. I want to go figure out what the problem is, but my fear is preventing logic from having any say. I spend several minutes taking deep breaths, encouraging myself to toughen up.

I'm not brave at all, but I have to determine what the issue is. I'm not sure what I'll do if I come face to face with a burglar; I might give him a hug as long as he's not Kevin. In case it is Kevin, I've equipped myself with a ceramic bulldog from my desk.

I loosen my shoulders and try to embrace my inner bulldog. Rolling my neck, swinging my arms across my chest, then out wide at my sides, and hopping on my slipper-covered toes, I've done my best UFC fighter impression. "Let's do this," I say to Bond.

From the hallway outside of my room, I listen intently for any suspicious noises. I hear nothing, so I walk toward the stairs. After stopping again for a moment to listen, I tiptoe down one step at a time, keeping my back to the wall. This is what cops in movies do, so it must be critical. When I reach the bottom of the stairs, Bond is ready and waiting with his hackles raised, ears at attention. I walk toward the front door through the open concept living room and foyer. The front motion sensor light flicks on and Bond barks like his life depends on it.

In a panic, I pull out my phone and try calling Liam. I hate to bother him, but if he stays on the phone with me, I might feel better. I don't want to call the police because if I'm being paranoid, they might think I'm like the boy who cried wolf and not come in the future. To my surprise, after two attempts, Liam doesn't answer.

The fear I was experiencing is secondary to the defeat consuming me now. I've officially pushed Liam too far, and he no longer wants to speak to me. I can't say I blame him, but I'm not sure I recognize a life without him. Maybe I should give in and let the mysterious evil outside do what they want to me. Liam has near endless patience and compassion, but I made him tap out. If I can't maintain a friendship with him, I'm not worthy of anyone else.

Another clang comes from outside, causing Bond to bark once again.

I call both Zach and Zara, but they must have shut their ringers off for the movie.

There's only one other person I can call who I'm confident can handle the situation. Reluctantly, I dial.

"Hello?"

"Sebastian?"

"Who's this?"

"It's Chelsea. Red hair. Crazy dad."

"Oh, wow. I finally get your number. I'm honoured."

"Yeah, I have a problem. You said I could get in touch if my dad came back around. I think he's outside my house and I'm here alone."

"Did you call the police?"

"No, I'm not totally sure someone is out there. I'm afraid I'm being paranoid, but the security light came on and the dog is barking. I'm just... Well, I'm scared."

"What's your address? I'll be there as fast as I can. Stay inside with the doors locked."

"Okay. I don't want you to get hurt, though. If you see anyone, call the police, please. I live on Simpson Road. You'll see the driveway with gated access, but you can use the keypad and I'll buzz you in."

"Do you want me to stay on the phone?"

"No, it's okay. If I have to call the police, I'll need my phone free."

"I'll take care of it, Doll. I'm on my way." With that, he hangs up.

I consider places to hide because even if someone breaks in and the alarm goes off, given our location, it's fifteen minutes before the security company or police will arrive. I don't know where Sebastian is, so I can't count on him being here sooner. Our attached garage is my best choice, so I can hide in my car. I mean, worst-case scenario, if someone opens the garage, I can drive away. Or drive over them.

Desperate times.

As I grab my keys from the mudroom beside the garage entrance, a loud bang comes from outside. Bond again sets off his intruder alert, barking relentlessly and looking toward the front door.

Once he's quieted, I call Bond to follow me, escaping into the garage. I can't leave the dog here to fend for himself, so he'll come sit in my SUV with me. I pat my way through the garage, not wanting to turn a light on and alert anyone to my presence, but thankfully, my parking space is closest to the entrance. Opening the driver's side door, I realize I overlooked the fact the interior of my vehicle would illuminate. My clandestine skills could use some work.

I pause for a few seconds while I listen if anyone noticed my vehicle lights but don't hear any suspicious sounds. Bond has called shotgun, and he's sitting like he's about to go trolling for ladies. I guess he's forgotten we are trying to escape with our lives.

A loud bang from outside the garage doors causes my heartbeat to speed up like a golden eagle swooping in for the kill, and I quietly pray for help to arrive. Maybe I should take my chances and call 911.

Right as I'm about to dial, my phone lights up with the phone number from the gate. I'm thankful for that handy feature. I check the camera and buzz Sebastian in. He's not alone, which I find concerning and comforting at the same time. He'll have backup should he need it, but it's also another stranger at my house.

The headlights illuminate the small windows in the top panel of the garage doors. I'll give them a few minutes to check everything out. I hear the car doors slam, one after the other, and low voices speaking, but I can't make out what they are saying.

A few minutes later, I hear an unfamiliar voice yell a curse word, and fast steps pounding before the car doors slam again.

Grabbing my phone, I dial 911, finally conceding. Again, right as I am about to hit send, my phone lights up with Sebastian's number.

I answer. "Hello?"

"Chelsea, where are you? Are you still inside?"

"I'm in the garage in my car. What's happening?"

"We found your intruder."

bear? Seriously?

"She looks hungry. She's digging through your trash cans now and wasn't happy with us interrupting her."

"I'm such an idiot. Sorry. I'll call the Ministry of Natural Resources and see what they suggest. We can't leave her around here. My little sister plays outside."

"Well, bear-relocation is out of my element, so I can't help. While I'm here, I'd love to see you, though."

He cannot be trusted.

I war with myself whether to let Sebastian and his friend in the house—I don't know Sebastian well, and his friend is a complete stranger. I'm here alone with no help if something happens. I would be better off if I went outside to cuddle the bear, but I feel guilty asking them to come all this way and then not even inviting them in.

Do you want to be rude, or do you want to be safe? He cannot be trusted.

"Sure, come to the front door. Just let me make a quick phone call." Maybe I'm paranoid, but I'm not stupid. I call Zara again and luckily, she answers. I tell her about the bear and our human guests. They would have panicked if they came home and saw a strange vehicle, especially given that Kevin knows where we live. She said they are on their way home in five minutes, and Zach will call the authorities to deal with the bear. That gives me less than twenty minutes to get rid of Sebastian before an awkward encounter ensues.

I run inside to the front door and open it wide. Standing there is this devastatingly handsome man who has now come to my rescue twice, although I barely know him. Behind Sebastian is another young man, but he's in Sebastian's shadow cast by the exterior lights. I have goosebumps across my skin before I see his face.

"Hi." I look past Sebastian at the mysterious figure cloaked in darkness. He doesn't reply.

From behind a dangerous smirk, Sebastian says, "Hey, Doll. Your knight in shining armour is here."

Heat builds in my cheeks. "I feel like such an idiot. I'm so sorry I called you. Do you want to come in for a drink or something?"

"I can't say no to that." Sebastian turns to the side to look back toward his mysterious friend. "This is Russel, AKA 'Trusty Rusty'. He was with me when you called, so he tagged along as backup."

I have my doubts this man is even a little 'trusty', but I thank him just the same. He came to a total stranger's house and ended up being growled at by a bear; the least I can do is say thank you. When he comes into the light, I see he is a fellow ginger. His red hair, blue eyes, and freckles mirror my own. He looks like a twenty-year-old Prince Harry with a rebellious streak.

Despite my reservations, I gesture for them to come inside. "You better get in here before the bear comes in and cleans out the fridge."

Sebastian laughs, but Russel merely smirks. Bond is on alert, growling at them both, but not making any effort to intimidate them. If he were trying, they wouldn't want to come inside.

Sebastian peers at the growling German shepherd with raised hackles. "Nice dog."

"This is Bond. He's my sister's dog, but since she's not here, he's being my guard dog. It's his fault I got so freaked out to begin with."

"Bond, like James Bond?"

I don't feel like explaining the meaning of his name. "Something like that."

Russel speaks for the first time. "James Bond is a legend." His raspy voice matches his appearance. A little mysterious—tough to decipher.

"The books are classics. Ian Fleming was a very talented writer."

"Wait. James Bond is in a book?" Russel's mouth forms a perfect O.

Is this guy serious? How do you not know James Bond is a literary series? "Yes. Lots of popular movies started as books. *Jurassic Park*, *Goodfellas*, *Fight Club*, *Sherlock Holmes*... even *The Godfather*." I look at Sebastian as I say that since we've discussed *The Godfather* previously. I see a hint of recognition in his eyes and the right side of his lips turn up into a half smile.

"Wow, I had no idea." Russel turns to Sebastian. "She really is a book nerd."

I'm not sure how to take that comment. Should I be flattered because I came up in conversation, or insulted he referred to me as a book nerd? Not that I care about Trusty Rusty's opinion.

I keep checking the time on my phone, counting the minutes until Zach and Zara arrive home. Even though I have Bond here, I don't feel at ease. I walk into the kitchen and ask the guys what they want to drink. I should have been more specific because they both asked for beer. We don't even have alcohol in our house—a drunk driver killed Zach's twin brother when he was fourteen, and Zara doesn't drink anymore because of medication she is on. "Sorry, we don't have any alcohol here. Can I get you a tea, orange juice, water, ginger ale?"

Russel looks at Sebastian as if he's offended by my inability to give him a beer, but Sebastian doesn't flinch. "Water is fine, thanks."

Easy enough. They can drink their water, then leave before I have to introduce them to Zach and Zara. I grab two medium glasses from the cupboard—less liquid means they'll finish drinking it sooner. After I pour their water from the filter jug, I slide the glasses across the kitchen island to Russel and Sebastian, who are seated on the stools on the opposite side.

Sebastian breaks the awkward silence. "So, your dad is a bad character, but is that the only reason you were so scared tonight?"

He literally watched my father attempt to choke the life out of me on a public street and he's asking me this right now? Is that not justification to be scared? "I didn't think it was a mystery after he threatened to kill me a few days ago. Yes, I fear him." I'm not going to clarify I'm more scared he'd take me alive than I am he'd kill me.

"Nah, I get it. What he did was messed up. It makes sense to be on edge, especially when you're home alone. You can call me anytime, Doll." He winks at me, which causes my cheeks to flush again.

I stare at a spot on the counter while I speak; my eye-contact avoidance skills coming in handy. "Thanks. Hopefully, I won't have to again. I'm sure you have better things you could be doing right now."

"It would break my heart if you never called again. I might have to go catch some mountain lions and let them loose in your yard."

I chuckle at his attempted a joke. He wouldn't put that much effort into seeing me again. I have not given him any indication I'm remotely interesting. Our previous encounters should have him running in the opposite direction. "I am sure you have plenty more exciting girls in your life."

The sound of Sebastian's stool screeching across the tile startles me, and I glance up to see him walking around the island. I shrink back toward the counter behind me. He's looking at me the same way Isla looks at ice cream sundaes.

He leans in to whisper, "You are the only woman in my life I find exciting."

My goosebumps are back. I can't match the intensity of his eyes, so I don't hold his gaze. What do I say? Tell him I'm sad for him that the women in his life are so unremarkable? Explain no matter how interested he is in my lunacy, I'll never be girlfriend material?

The front door swings open and I see Zach standing in the door frame, looking as if he's ready to fight a bear with his bare hands. He catches Russel's eyes in the kitchen and comes storming through the house. Once he makes eye contact with me and sees Sebastian's proximity, he looks like he'd rather team up with the bear to take on the young guys in his kitchen.

"Who are you?" His stern voice is more warning than question.

Without hesitating, Sebastian spins and offers a hand to Zach. "I'm Sebastian. I'm a friend of Chelsea's."

"You're awfully close for a friend, mate. What are you doing here?"

The tension in the room has skyrocketed, but Sebastian seems unfazed. "Chelsea called when she heard a noise. I wasn't too far away."

"We live in the middle of nowhere. Where exactly were you that wasn't too far away?"

Zach has a point. I've never seen Zach act like a hot head before, but if he could spit nails, he would. This situation calls for some diffusing.

"I told Zara he was here. He helped me the other day when Kevin attacked me. We met again on campus and exchanged numbers." I know that isn't entirely the truth, but it's easier to explain than saying I gave him my email address, we emailed back and forth like a couple of teenagers in 2002, and he eventually gave me his number.

Once Zach hears Sebastian is *the* Sebastian who fought off Kevin, he reaches out to shake his hand. "Sorry for the third degree. I'm protective of Chelsea. Thank you for doing what you did the other night. That wasn't your fight, so I appreciate you stepping in."

"No thanks necessary. It was lucky I was working nearby and out on my break. I couldn't stand back and watch."

"Well, regardless, we appreciate you looking out for our girl."

Isla and Zara come in from the garage. Zara looks a bit frazzled, and Bond is jumping on Isla like she's been gone for five years. Her giggles cause some of the pent-up tension I'm holding in to release.

Zara stares at Zach. "Was that necessary? Did you have to jump out of the car before parking it? You left us outside with a bear on the loose."

"I'm so sorry, Baby; I wasn't thinking. I wanted to check on Chelsea." Zach's hand comes up to rub his left cheek, his eyes directed at the floor.

It doesn't take long for Zara to ease his embarrassment. "I'm teasing, Honey. I love that you wanted to go all 'Rambo'. Looks like she's in safe hands, though." She glances toward Russel, studies him for a second, then does the same to Sebastian before shooting me an approving smile. She has the wrong idea here. "I'm Zara, and I'm sorry for whatever interrogation my husband put you through."

Everyone except Zach laughs. "He's doing what any *good* dad would do," Sebastian says, and I don't miss what he's implying. Obviously, I have a *not* good dad, too.

Once Zara is told Sebastian saved me from Kevin, she doesn't hesitate to thank the young stranger in her kitchen. You'd never know she spent so many years avoiding physical contact and hiding in her house because of her own anxiety based on how quickly she drew Sebastian in for a hug. The steps she's taken to recover from her own issues give me a glimmer of hope, but I don't think I could ever be strong enough to accomplish what she has. And I certainly will never be in any condition to be married and have a family.

Regardless of what my future holds, this situation is getting awkward, and I regret being enough of a coward to call Sebastian. I don't know how to ask him to leave politely, and at the same time, I don't want him to because then the parental interrogation will begin. I don't even know how to explain to Zach or Zara why I felt inclined to call Sebastian, of all people; they know how close I am to Liam. I wish Liam had answered his phone. My tailspin my life is headed in is more daunting without him by my side. It's what's best for him, though—keeping his distance from me.

I'm retreating into my mind, focused on my deteriorating relationship with my best friend, and coming apart over the situation when I feel a gentle squeeze around my hip. Isla has walked over to me, bringing me back to reality. Seeing her small form take refuge behind my legs makes me realize I need to act brave for her sake. She doesn't need more reasons to be nervous.

"Chelsea, I'm tired. Can I sleep in your room tonight?"

I look down at this sweet girl who has been through so many hard things in her life, yet she's still shining like the sun, bringing joy to everyone around her. I wish I had that ability, but I'm more doom and gloom than rays of sunshine. "Sure, Troublemaker. We'll go to bed soon. You can sleep in my room."

"Yay! Thanks, Chels. I'm going to go get my matching pyjamas on. Make sure you wear yours too!"

I'm embarrassed by her comment when I look at Sebastian and Trusty Rusty, who are both smirking at me. Why do I care what they think?

"Right, well, we better get going," Trusty Rusty says to no one in particular.

"Yeah, you're right. We better go," Sebastian adds.

"I'll walk you out." They don't have time to change their minds before I walk to the door with intention. I need them to leave before they're both convinced I'm a blundering idiot— more than they do currently.

"It was nice to meet you, Mr. and Mrs. Haynes." Sebastian does his best to charm Zach and Zara with manners and a smile, but I see Zach studying him. He doesn't appear convinced.

"Thank you for coming to Chelsea's rescue, Sebastian. We'll be forever grateful you intervened when you did." Zara gives Sebastian an amused look, which is more unnerving than comforting. I love that Zara is just as awkward as I am.

"No trouble at all. I'll see you around." He turns to meet up with me at the front door, where I'm waiting to show them out. Sebastian opens the door, doing his best to act like a gentleman.

We all scan around the front yard, looking and listening for our newest resident, but the coast is clear.

I walk toward Sebastian's car, a Honda Accord, which appears modified to suit his bad boy persona, and turn to face him once I'm by the driver's side door. "Well… um… thanks again for coming to help me. I'm sorry I made you come all this way for nothing."

"It wasn't nothing." He steps toward me and touches my arm. "I got to see you, so I'd say it was a great night."

He cannot be trusted. Don't let him close.

"Why are you being so nice to me? You barely know me."

Sebastian tilts his head to the left and raises his right eyebrow. "Why wouldn't I be nice to you? I like you."

His confession makes me even more confused.

"I don't know what you could like about me, but thanks for coming. I won't bother you again." Sebastian puts his arm out to stop me before I can walk back to the house.

"Wow, Doll. Not so fast." His words make the hairs on my neck stand up. "I think you owe me a date for coming to your rescue."

"A… a date? Sebastian, I don't date."

"Maybe you haven't found the right guy to sweep you off your feet yet. But now you've found me. So, what do you say?"

"I'm not very dateable. I'm awkward, anti-social, not good at conversation. I could go on."

"You only have to be social with me, and I think your awkwardness is cute. I'll pick you up Saturday night."

"Are you not hearing me? You're not going to take no for an answer?"

"Nope." He smirks, displaying his dimples. He is an attractive man, but he is no Shirley Temple.

"Okay, fine. But if I'm horrible, don't say I didn't warn you."

He smiles an alluring smile and slides past me to get in his car. Once he's seated and turns on the car, he rolls the window down. "I'll see you Saturday, Doll." Then he speeds off down the driveway.

I'm in my room, fending off complete panic, trying to get ready for my date with Sebastian. The fact I haven't spoken to Liam for over a week is eating away at me. These are moments a person should be able to talk about with their best friend, but mine has ghosted me. On one hand, I'm relieved he's created some distance to keep himself safe, but on the other, I'm devastated. Liam has been my world for five years. I don't know how to move through milestones without him.

Zara peeks her head through my doorway. "How are you holding up, Sweetheart?"

"I'm fine." I lie, which makes me feel guilty.

"Can I help you get ready?"

I'm out of my element here, so maybe some help would be beneficial. "Um, sure. I'd like that."

She steps inside my room, taking in the mess of my closet that has spilled into the bedroom. "Have you picked something to wear yet?"

"Ah, no. I couldn't decide. It's such a hard time of year to dress for the weather because it goes from hot to cold so quickly and I don't want to be hauling around a big jacket."

"Makes sense. Where are you guys going?"

"He said some place called *The Core*. I don't know what that is."

"Oh, it's near my parent's house. It's kind of like a club slash music venue. It's on the water." She appears contemplative for a moment. "They don't really have a first date atmosphere, though. It's mostly drinking and dancing."

I'm sorry, what? Drinking and dancing? A club? Meaning he's taking me to a place with loads of people and alcohol? What if he gets me drunk because he wants to take advantage of me?

Zara offers some reassuring words to ease my rising panic. "It's not so bad, Chels. Zach and I went there once to see a concert, and I survived. The only reason we never went back is because we were so old compared to everyone else." She laughs. "If you're overwhelmed, go out onto the deck over the water. That's where I spent most of the night, and the fresh air made everything better."

"I don't know if I can do this. I have no clue what I'm doing. I'm scared out of my mind."

"You'll be fine." She sucks in a breath. "Let me give you this advice. If you never branch out of your comfort zone, things will never change, and that means they can never get better. Try it tonight, and if it's not meant to be, then at least you've tried." She steps forward to my closet, trudging through the clothes on the floor. "Focus on going and having fun tonight. If you need to call me to come get you, I'll be there in a heartbeat, or my parents can be there even faster."

Knowing my adopted grandparents are close by is reassuring. Alanna and Fred welcomed me into the family with open arms. They exhibited the same level of excitement I'd imagine people show when a baby is born—even though a troubled teenager with a list of issues twelve pages long is nothing to celebrate in my books.

"Okay. I'll try. I'm just afraid."

Zara stops scanning my clothing and turns to me, grabbing my hands. "What is it you're afraid of, specifically?"

"I'm not sure exactly. I'm afraid Sebastian is going to hurt me. Kevin has me on edge. I'm afraid everything in my past will keep me from ever having a future."

Zara leans in, wrapping her arms around me. "Oh, Sweetheart. I know you're worried about Kevin, but Sebastian has proven he'll keep you safe. I can't predict whether your date will lead to heartbreak down the road, but I know if you never try, you'll never know what you could have missed out on."

"How did you learn to trust Zach?"

She remains silent for a moment. "I don't know what it was, actually. He always kept his word, and he was honest with me. I could tell he was a good man, and he never gave me reason to not trust him. He always understood me and supported me, even when I was being crazy. He made me feel safe." She fiddles with a rogue shirt I threw on my bed earlier after deciding it was hideous. "I think I knew right away I could trust him, but like you, my fear wouldn't let me. But over time, he consistently showed me I could, and the rest is history."

Sebastian and I haven't known each other long enough for me to decide if he is honest with me, and I'm not sure about the "good man" bit. This is all so confusing.

"I'll be back in a second." Zara rushes out of my room, leaving me alone with my thoughts. Awesome.

I don't think I'll ever be able to make myself attractive, so I don't want to try. At least it will look like I'm ugly because I didn't make an effort, rather than I attempted to look nice and still appear hopeless. Usually when I wear makeup, I end up looking like Napoleon Dynamite in drag.

"I'm back." Zara stops my thoughts from going any further down the track of self-destruction. "I have the perfect outfit. Try this on."

I examine the outfit she's brought. Few college students are the same size and close enough in age to wear their mother's clothing. I suppose this is one perk of being adopted by a woman only fourteen years older. "Are you sure you want me to wear this? What if I ruin it?"

"Of course. It's perfect, and it's a Jasmine original. She was upset she couldn't come visit last weekend, so she'd be happy to see you got to wear something of hers for your first date. It would mean a lot to her."

"Um... okay. If you're sure." Jasmine, Zach's younger sister, is closer to my age than to anyone else in our family, not counting my cousins Caleb and Sophie. She's a talented clothing designer, and she always brings new creations for Zara and me when she visits.

I slide into the deep-red suede skirt that hits around mid thigh, leaving my ghostly-white, freckled legs on display. I pull the black cashmere long-sleeve top on, and it's wonderfully soft. I had no idea goats could make such luxurious clothing.

When I turn to face Zara, she's got a pair of black, thigh-high boots in her hands. "Here, these make the outfit."

"Wow. I'll kill myself in those."

"You'll be fine. They're comfy. I have a black clutch for you to use, too. It's big enough for the essentials; not too bulky to carry around."

"I guess you've been on more dates than I have, so I'll take your word for it. Thanks for helping me with this."

"Sweetheart, I'll be here as long as I'm living to help you with whatever I can."

Deflating again, I hate that I create so much trouble for her. I do nothing but inconvenience the people plagued by my existence.

"I'm sorry I'm so much work."

Zara pulls her head back in confusion and blinks rapidly a handful of times. "Work? Chelsea, you are not 'work'. I am familiar with that feeling of being a burden when anyone offers to help, but I can assure you, I *want* to help you. I love this time we've spent together, and I'm so proud of you for taking this step."

"Maybe I'll be as strong as you one day." Tears threaten to escape my eyes, but I already put on mascara, so these liquid emotions better knock it off.

"You're so much stronger than I've ever been."

What can I say to that? I'm not strong—not even a little. Arguing about it is pointless, though. I nod, hoping to move this conversation along.

"How do I look?" I stand with my arms out wide at my sides, showing off my outfit. Now that I have the boots on, I feel better because they cover most of the glow-in-the-dark skin on my legs. Dare I say, I these heels are working for me.

"You look gorgeous. Remember, never take a drink from someone unless you've seen them pour it, and never leave your drink unattended, even with Sebastian, okay?"

"I know. I'll be careful; I promise. Thank you."

My phone chimes and it flashes Sebastian's name. He's at the gate. It's time to get this over with.

I press the button to open the gate and Sebastian drives to the front of the house in his black car. He walks to the front door when I open it and step outside. I take in his appearance of dark slim-fit jeans and a plain black T-shirt. How can someone look so good in a T-shirt and jeans?

His eyes lock on mine, and a smile splits his face. "Wow. Doll, you look phenomenal. No, not phenomenal. Better than phenomenal, but I'm not good with words."

I giggle at his comment, and it sets me a bit at ease. Maybe this won't be so bad after all.

Sebastian and I arrive at *The Core* and park along the side of the road up a small hill from the venue. Sebastian insists this will be fun despite its underwhelming exterior. I don't think he has any concept of where my comfort zone is, because this is worlds away from it.

I'm surprised by how gentlemanly Sebastian is, helping me out of the car and keeping me steady as I trudge through the grass to walk around his car. I am not high maintenance, but I'm struggling to see the appeal in all of this.

We walk along the road, hand in hand, toward the front of the building, but Sebastian's touch does little to set me at ease. There's a lineup of over forty people, and I note how stunning the other women are. I don't compare to any of them. He's going to ditch me.

I slow my pace as I contend with my thoughts and Sebastian takes notice.

"What's wrong, Doll?"

"Um." How do I approach this without sounding totally pathetic? "I feel a little... You'd be... Ugh. You'd be happier with one of those other girls." I look down at the ground, ashamed those words left my mouth.

Sebastian steps in front of me and gently lifts my chin with his forefinger. "Chelsea, you're the only one I see. I want to take you in there and make all the other guys jealous I get to be with the sexiest woman in the room."

I'm sorry. Sexy? Is he delusional? I have as much sex appeal as the Queen of England. Probably Queen Victoria, who has been dead for more than a century. No offence, Your Highness.

"I'm out of my comfort zone right now. I told you I'd be terrible at this."

"Doll, relax. We'll go in and check it out, and if you hate it, we'll leave. I promise. I want you to enjoy yourself."

His words bring me some reassurance. If I hate it, we'll leave. It will be fine. I'll be fine.

"Okay. Let's go."

To my surprise, Sebastian leans in and attempts to kiss my cheek, but because he catches me off guard, I adjust my head and he kisses in front of my ear. The warmth of his mouth on my flesh sets off my alarms.

He cannot be trusted.

"Come on. It will be fun." He takes my hand and leads me to the end of the lineup. People have come prepared—I notice a few are drinking from flasks. Surely a sign of an interesting night to come.

Sebastian and I wait for twenty-five minutes before we're allowed inside. It's dark, loud, and crowded—three of my least favourite scenarios. I squeeze his hand tighter because even though I barely know him, in a sea of unknowns, he's the person I'm most comfortable around. Sebastian gives me an encouraging squeeze in return.

"Do you want a drink?" He's shouting, but I can barely make out his words without focusing on his lips—his really attractive lips.

I surprise myself when I respond, "Sure." I've never had a drink before in my life, but maybe it will help me relax.

"I'll be right back," he replies, but I keep Zara's words in mind.

"No, I'll come with you. I don't know what I want."

We head to the bar on the left side of the building, noticing a matching set-up on the far right side, with a crowded dance floor in the middle and stage along the back. As Sebastian confidently leads us to the front of the line, I realize I am unfamiliar with all the alcohol options. What does a virgin drinker order to loosen up? I need something that tastes decent and won't get me hammered. Most of the other girls in the area have beer. I don't even enjoy the smell of beer, so that's out.

I see one girl who looks like she's enjoying herself, but still standing up straight, and she's holding a pink liquid in a clear plastic cup. I say to Sebastian, "I'll have what she's having."

He nods his approval, shouts something at the bartender, and once our drinks are provided, he pays and hands me my unknown pink concoction. I'm not going to admit to him I don't know what this is.

The burn of the alcohol catches me off guard. I scrunch up my nose and suppress a cough, which elicits a laugh from Sebastian.

"Stronger than you're used to?" He wears a wide grin, dimples on full display.

"Um, yeah. I'm not much of a drinker."

"I figured. Since I'm driving, I'll only have one or two, but you can have whatever you want. If you don't like the vodka-cranberry, I can order you something else next time."

Oh, it's vodka. Makes sense. Isn't vodka made from potatoes? How on earth does potato juice burn so much? And how did anyone ever figure out you could use a potato to get drunk?

"You look lost in thought. What are you thinking?" Sebastian's words snap me out of my internal tangent.

"Just thinking about potatoes." The words come out of my mouth before I even attempt to make them sound somewhat cool, so I'm left standing here staring at the face of a handsome, confused man.

"Potatoes?"

I grumble to myself, annoyed by my awkwardness. "Potatoes—vodka is made from potatoes. I was wondering who ever figured it out."

"Oh, gotcha. I'd put my money on the Irish."

"I think it was a Russian."

"Oh, good point. You're probably right." He stares at me, unable to come up with something else to carry this conversation forward. I down my drink and pray the burn is worth it.

"I'm sorry, Sebastian. You can't say I didn't warn you. I can call someone to pick me up, and you can find someone more… interesting." More beautiful, entertaining, exciting, and fun, too.

We're standing close on account of the noise level, but he inches in even closer to whisper in my ear. "These other girls are all the same. I don't want any of them—I want to be here with you."

Every bit of air vacates my lungs as his warm breath hits my ear, laced with the scent of whisky and man. I'd normally be headed for the exit from having someone in such close proximity, but I give in to the urge to grab his shirt and pull him against me. "How can I make this more fun, then?"

"Dance with me."

Dance? Me? Dance? Is this guy for real?

I remember what Zara said, so I counter with a new suggestion. "Let's go on the deck. Outside." Awkward Chelsea is on a roll. Where else would a deck be?

After grabbing me another drink, Sebastian takes my hand and leads me to the exit at the end of the bar. Walking onto the deck, I see the waters of Bala Bay, and I feel significantly calmer than I did inside. The cool air causes me to shiver, but it's a welcome temperature change.

Sebastian puts his arm around me and starts rubbing his hand up and down my right arm. "Are you okay, Doll? We can go back in if you're too cold."

I don't know if it's the environment we're in or the liquid courage I've consumed, but whatever it is, it has taken over all rational thought—it has numbed my hypervigilance and paranoia. I spin myself so I'm facing Sebastian, but even in my heels, we do not come face-to-face. I lean in to him and say, "Or you could keep me warm."

His facial expression from this angle looks like a mix of excitement and guilt. He reaches his arms around me, and I allow him to pull me into an embrace. My brain is issuing repeated warnings, and even though I'm tense, my body wants to let go.

His voice drops to a husky whisper. "You're so damn sexy, Chelsea." He exhales, blowing a breath across my ear, and it sends another shiver through my entire body.

Suddenly I'm so overwhelmed by our proximity, I drop what little is left in my drink. It makes sense why they give their patrons plastic cups. The cranberry juice concoction splashes onto my boot. Sebastian bends down to clean it off with a napkin he has in his hand. From his position, stooped in front of me, he glances upward. His eyes are dark and predatory as they meet mine. I'm like a baby flamingo—he's a Marabou stork. I question why I am such a nerd, because that's a strange thing to relate to, but this baby flamingo does her best to lift one leg and pull it away from the stork before he catches his prey.

He stands in front of me, grazing his hands along my legs on his way up. When his hands reach the bare skin of my thighs, my brain and body engage in a Civil War. I don't know which one is right. Do I follow my brain and gather my strength to combat the enemy, or do I follow my physical desires to be close to this man and potentially end up heartbroken? Or worse.

My good sense is drunk—but not from alcohol—because I lean into him and whisper, "I need another drink."

After three more drinks, bringing my grand total to five, I feel like the life of the party—aside from the fact I have to pee every twenty minutes. Normally I couldn't bring myself to use a public washroom because I panic when the doors are closed, but the bathroom here has a steady stream of fellow drunks, making it less terrifying. I met a nice blue-haired girl named Gia in the bathroom on my last trip. She goes to my college, but she is taking Food and Nutrition Management. She's not making smart choices this evening based on her area of expertise.

Sebastian has stuck by my side the entire night—minus bathroom trips. We came back inside after my drink spilling incident because it was easier to get to the bar and the bathroom. We've danced, flirted, and gotten to know each other as best we can with music blaring and throngs of people around. Me, Chelsea Haynes, tore up the dance floor. Who knew I had more moves than a can of worms? I look just as attractive, but my thoughts are so inhibited, reality doesn't bother me. Sebastian was right. I have had fun; though I'm sloshed, so a colonoscopy would be tolerable.

When he asks if I'm ready to leave, I realize how tired I am. It's nearing one in the morning, and I've been socializing and dancing—both are draining for me. He takes my hand and leads me out the door and again the cool air causes me to shiver as it hits my clammy skin. Sebastian pulls me close, and we walk back up the hill to his car with his arm around my shoulders. He stayed true to his word and only had two drinks while we were here, so I'm comfortable with him driving. I get the impression two drinks don't affect him as much as they do me.

When we arrive at his car, I have to walk through the grass to get in the passenger side. Given my current state, it doesn't go well. Before I reach the passenger door, I trip on who-knows-what and take a tumble into the shallow ditch. I let out a shriek as I go down. You can't take me anywhere.

Sebastian basically does a *Dukes of Hazzard* move to get to my side of the car as quickly as possible. He's a hunk. "Doll, are you okay?"

I can't answer. I'm too busy laughing. Me. Laughing. Laughing with complete abandon. Laughing until I might pee myself. Oh, no. Please don't pee.

Sebastian lifts me up to stand and, once again, I'm face-to-chest with this olive-skinned Adonis. "Are you okay, Doll?" he asks again.

"I'm great. Thank you for tonight." For the first time in hours, the acceleration in my heart rate can be attributed to nerves. I stare up at Sebastian, and tug at my bottom lip with my teeth. I can't believe this unbelievably attractive man spent the night with me. Even though other girls were eyeing him like mountain lions stalking their prey, his eyes never left mine. I felt safe, and for the first time, desired.

Before scared, rational me can have a say, I reach my hand up behind Sebastian's neck and pull him down to kiss him. I had intended for it to be more like a peck, but after a few seconds, he presses my back against the car and has me forgetting my name. I have never kissed anyone before, and this guy has proven—wow—I have been missing out.

He keeps his hands in place against the car, which I find disappointing because I want him to touch me. How he's broken down my walls so quickly, I'm not sure. I'm conflicted in his presence, wanting to trust him, but afraid of his intentions. Right now, I'm enjoying the thrill of the moment. Thanks to whoever fermented potatoes.

He's the first one to pull away, and I immediately miss his heat against me. "Shoot, Chels. You're making this hard."

I'm confused. "Making what hard?" I look down at his waist, completely misreading the situation.

I might be drunk, but I don't miss that guilty look flashing across his face again.

He stammers, "You're making it hard to be a gentleman."

"Maybe I don't want you to be a gentleman. Maybe I'm tired of everyone treating me like a piece of glass, and for once I want to be wanted—not pitied."

"I don't pity you. You're incredible. I don't want to cross a line we can't come back from. Not while you're drunk."

"Fine. I get it." I scoff. My better judgement is absent and I'm reaching the next stage of inebriation—angry drunk. "Take me home."

"Chels, no. It's not like that." He reaches a hand up to caress my cheek. "I'd stay here all night with you if I could, but I don't want to treat you like that."

"Whatever. Can you get me home? I didn't bring my walking shoes." Drunk Chelsea is sassy. This is new.

"Only if I can kiss you again."

"What, now?"

He smiles his wicked, dimply smile. "Now, tomorrow, next week. All the time."

Gulp. "Okay."

Sebastian dives in for another kiss that has my nervous system ready to combust. It feels like raw passion. We hear the drunken giggles of some fellow patrons stumbling their way toward us, which breaks us apart.

"Sebastian?"

"Yeah?"

"Please tell me you're not playing me."

He hesitates a beat before answering and struggles to maintain eye contact. "To be honest, at first I thought you were hot. I have a history of being a real Casanova. You surprised me by being more than just hot."

I ignore his comment about me being hot. That's ludicrous. I need clarification here. "You know Casanova was a con man, right? He's known for being a womanizer, sure, but he was a con artist, a prison escapee, and a spy. Is that what you're telling me? Or do you mean Lothario?"

He laughs, but he's missing the fact I am dead serious right now. There's a difference between the two. "You really are a book nerd." He chuckles again. "I don't know who Lothario is, so I can't say for sure. Can I be Don Juan instead?"

"Well, Don Juan isn't any better. He disguised himself and lied to seduce women, breaking hearts in his wake."

He laughs again. Why is he not taking me seriously? "Okay, enough with the analogies. Let's just say I was a selfish jerk."

"I think you mean metaphor," I mumble. I'm looking down at the ground, but I turn my baby blues up to meet Sebastian's near-black eyes. He's actually smirking at me. Does this guy think everything is a joke?

"Let's get you home. You're going to need to sleep off your liquor."

"Wait." I hesitate to voice my request. "One more kiss?" This liquid courage does wonders.

Just before 2:00am, I'm trying to disarm our new alarm system and get into the house quietly. The unnecessary beeping is making this task challenging. I finally yell at the keypad to shut up as I enter the correct code. "Ha! I showed you."

I stumble up the stairs, toward my room and the only one awake is Bond. He's staring at me from Isla's doorway as if to say, "Don't you dare wake my kid."

I raise my hands up in surrender. "Okay. Okay. I get it. Go back to bed."

He turns around like an angry neighbour and slinks back into Isla's room.

"Chels?" Zara's voice calls from her bedroom.

"Yeah, it's me. Sorry if I woke you."

"Did you have fun?" Now she's in the hallway, looking directly at me. "Did you drink?"

"I did, and I had a few, yes. I thought it would help me relax."

"Just be careful, okay? I'm glad you had some fun. Get some sleep. You can give me the rundown in the morning. I love you, Sweetheart."

"I love you too." I reply. Once the words are out, they don't feel as epic as I once thought they were. It's not the first time I've told her that, but I don't say it often.

Sleepy Zara pauses in her tracks as she was retreating to her room. Without saying a word, she walks to me, pulls me into a hug, and starts crying.

"Thank you for saying that, Chels. That means more to me than you'll ever know. Good night." She gives my cheek a peck and walks back to her room.

The significance of the words I said hit me, and I realize one thing—tonight, with alcohol in my system, I wasn't afraid. For the first time in as long as I can remember, I just lived. I want to feel that way again.

I'm staring at my white ceiling as the sun's rays invade my bedroom. The curtains aren't closed completely, and a streak of light across my face is a direct assault on my senses. I didn't sleep great because I was up every half-hour to use the bathroom. My excess norepinephrine was absent last night; I could have used an extra surge to keep my bladder in check. I was also lying awake thinking about my time with Sebastian and acting like a Disney Princess who has fallen in love after one kiss. But, I'm not the kind of girl who gets the fairy-tale ending.

As I throw back my duvet, then stand, a wave of pain floods my head. Oh, joy. My very first hangover. A proud accomplishment.

I walk to the bathroom hoping a shower will help, but I'm interrupted when Isla comes running in the room shouting at an excessive volume. "Chelsea. Chelsea. Chelsea!"

"Shh. What is it?" Someday, when she comes home with her first hangover, she will regret this.

"Mommy wants you to come down for breakfast. She made you coffee."

Coffee sounds delightful. "I'll be down in a few minutes, okay? Let me have a shower."

She bounds off without another word, her wavy blonde hair swaying back and forth with Bond trailing behind.

Twenty minutes later, I emerge downstairs to join my family. I walk toward the counter to grab my coffee and notice Zach sitting at the table with a serious expression. Zara is sitting next to him, looking timid. It makes me nervous, but I ignore it in hopes it's nothing to do with me. I hope Bond ate Zach's favourite shoes or something, but judging by the cockiness this dog is walking around with, I don't get the impression it's him in trouble.

"Good morning, Sweetheart. How are you?" Zara asks, without lifting her head. Ah, shucks.

"I'm fine. Sorry for waking you last night." Hopefully, if I issue an apology right away, we can put their anger to rest. I'm struggling not to retreat into defensive mode.

"That's okay. I was having a hard time sleeping, knowing you were out anyway, so I wasn't really asleep. Come, sit. Tell me about your date."

I make my way over to sit at the dining table opposite Zara, and next to Zach, who is at the head of the table. "There isn't much to tell. We went to *The Core*. I was overwhelmed at first, so we went out on the deck. After a while we went back inside, danced, talked, and then we left."

"Did you have fun?" Zach speaks the first words he's spoken yet, still looking serious.

"I did, actually. It ended up being a fun night."

"Did you have fun because you enjoyed the night or because you were drunk?"

I stiffen. I don't like where this conversation is going. "What does it matter? Legally, I'm old enough to drink. I was due to have some fun, so I did. I wasn't irresponsible, and I didn't go overboard."

"No one is saying you did. We're not upset with you for drinking. We want to make sure you're careful and don't let it become a habit."

Now I'm angry and my fight instincts kick in. "Are you kidding me? For years, you both have been telling me to step out of my comfort zone, go have fun, hang out with people my age, blah blah blah. And now that I do—the *one* time I do— you're telling me I need to reel it in? So basically, nothing I do is ever good enough. Good to know." I slide my chair back to get up and don't even bother tucking it back in before I storm off.

It doesn't appear I'll ever be able to live up to their expectations. I can hide in my room, or I could be the first person to Mars, and they'd still question my intentions. To them, I'm fragile Chelsea and I'll never be more than that.

I huff my way back to my bedroom. Part of me wants to stay locked in there all day. A larger, more determined part of me wants to leave. I don't want to talk to anyone in this house right now. It seems unfair to gang up on me because I drank one time. Drinking once doesn't make me an alcoholic.

When I throw myself on my bed, face first into my pillow, I hear my phone buzz. If it's Liam texting me, I'm going to scream. Too little, too late, best friend. He'd probably voice his disappointment in me too.

Sebastian: Morning Doll

I'm surprised by how big I smile after seeing his message. That is, until I question whether he's texting me because he is thinking about me, or if he's telling me he never wants to see me again.

Sebastian: I can't stop thinkin about kissing u.

My memory might be hazy, but I distinctly remember how kissing him felt. For the first time in my life, a combination of the alcohol and Sebastian had me in a euphoric daze. I wasn't stuck in my own thoughts, and I wasn't afraid. I enjoyed the moment.

Chelsea: What a coincidence. I've been thinking about kissing you.

I don't know what possesses me to be so bold with Sebastian, but I need a distraction after my argument with Zach and Zara.

Sebastian: Really? Are u busy today?

Chelsea: Aside from hiding in my room, no. No plans.

Sebastian: Why are you hiding? Maybe we can meet somewhere.

My heart races at the thought of seeing him again—kissing him again. Will it feel the same sober? Am I only imagining it was amazing because I was drunk and uninhibited?

Chelsea: Long story. Sure, we can meet. When and where?

Sebastian: I'll pick u up. I have a plan. Be ready @ 1

I've been through this with him before. I don't like surprises, and I don't like being unprepared. He wants to keep things a secret from me.

He cannot be trusted.

Chelsea: Please tell me. I need to know what to wear.

Sebastian: You can wear the outfit from last night.

That's not happening. That outfit got so sweaty, it smells like a mosh pit—or what I assume a mosh pit would smell like. What even is a mosh pit? Never mind.

Sebastian: Just wear what's comfy

Okay. Comfortable. I can do that. Since I've already showered, and I have two hours until I have to get ready, I dive into a book I've had on my to-be-read pile for months. Nothing kills time better than getting lost in a book.

Two hours later, I'm sobbing into my book pages, not wanting to set it down. Stopping in the middle of a book is painful sometimes. Don't worry, book babies. I'll be back for you later. If I don't get ready now, Sebastian isn't going to want to take me out. The haggard troll look isn't appealing.

Comfortable but cute is a tough combination to achieve. I decide on my favourite medium-wash skinny jeans, a fitted black long-sleeve shirt, and my ankle booties with a one-inch heel. I throw my hair up in a messy bun because I don't want to style it today, nor have it blowing in my face if we're outside. I dump the contents of Zara's clutch I borrowed onto my bed so I can put what I need into my shoulder bag and notice a slip of paper. Gia somehow slipped me her phone number last night. I set it on my bedside table to contemplate later if I'll ever use it. I am in the market for a new best friend. Again, thoughts of Liam create a heaviness in my heart. He made his choice and I need to respect that. Move on.

Once I'm ready, I sneak out my bedroom door. I nearly make it all the way to the front door before Zach's voice calls to me. "Chelsea? Are you going out?"

"I am. But don't worry, I'm not going to get drunk." I walk straight through the main living space and out the front door without even looking back in his direction. It seems no matter what I'm doing, I won't get his approval, anyway. I might as well attempt to have fun.

Sebastian drives up to the gate, but not down the driveway. I walk out to meet him, only opening the gate enough to squeeze through. I'm frightened only by how excited I am to see him. When I climb into the passenger seat, I'm greeted by his smiling face.

"Hi." I tuck a loose strand of hair behind my ear.

"Hey, Doll. Are you ready for an adventure?"

Am I? I told him I was more likely to run *from* an adventure than *to* one, but here I am. What good is living only to die? With Kevin on the prowl, that might happen sooner than later, so if now is my chance to experience something new, I better take it. "I guess so. Even though I hate surprises."

"Do you trust me?"

His words startle me because it's hard for me to trust anyone under the sun, but I have no genuine reason *not* to trust him. Is *that* a good enough reason? No one could make me feel the way he did with a single kiss if he wasn't trustworthy. "I do."

He smiles a killer smile and speeds away from our driveway. He drives toward the highway and heads north. I have no clue where we're going other than somewhere north, but that leaves a lot of potential locations. I clutch my phone in my hand, staring at the blue dot moving across the screen on my map app.

"Where are you taking me?"

"I thought you trusted me." He's the picture of ease, driving with his seat leaned back and one hand at the top of the steering wheel.

"I do." I pause because I'm not sure what trusting someone really entails. "But I don't like surprises. I like to prepare for things."

"It's fine. You'll like it."

I'm mildly annoyed by his refusal to tell me where we're going, but not enough to get angry about it. He got me out of my house, which I'm grateful for because I didn't want to shut myself in my room and obsess over how much I disappoint Zach and Zara. I'm a perpetual source of upset, and they're better off without me.

"Don't worry, Doll. I promised you'd have fun last night, and you did. Relax."

He cannot be trusted.

I war with my brain to block out these warnings that have plagued me since I met him. For once, I want to give in and have some fun. Sebastian can give me that, and he's right—I need some adventure. If there's a chance his distraction can help me feel nothing at all, then I'll go wherever he wants to take me.

An hour later, we arrive at our destination. I'm not sure why he's brought me here, but I've always loved Parry Sound the few times I have been. When he signalled to exit onto Bowes Street, I felt a bit of tension release, confident he wasn't bringing me to a secluded shack in the woods.

"What is this place?" I look around the unfamiliar space with beautiful gardens and few buildings—one appears to be a storage shed, and the other is a museum. Is he taking me to a museum for a date? I didn't see him as the type.

"This is Tower Hill." He points at a metal structure off to the left that must be thirty metres tall. "See that?"

I nod. "How could I not see it, Sebastian? It's huge."

"We're going to climb it. I promise, the views are amazing once you get to the top."

"You want to take me into the giant cage thing? Are you for real?" I guess I brought this on myself because I assumed a person who knows nothing about me—beyond the fact I'm a cheap drunk with a psychotic father—would choose "adventures" suited to my preferences.

"Come on. Trust me." He grabs my hand and pulls me up the slight incline toward the entrance of the tower. My beats per minute are increasing with each step closer. I try to focus on the beauty of the flowers, the smell of the fresh air, but no conscious effort can combat my panic.

He cannot be trusted.

I climb the stairs, one at a time, like a toddler who has learned to traverse stairs for the first time—lifting my foot onto each elevated step with intention. The railing to my right does little to comfort me as we continue up each level.

Sebastian doesn't release my hand—probably aware I am a flight risk if he does. We stop to take in the view at a few different lookout spots along our ascent, and it is beautiful, but I can't get out of my mind enough to enjoy it.

The metal stairs are constructed with the same bar grating as a fire escape, allowing me to see through the many levels to the ground below, so looking down isn't any more comforting than looking straight ahead. The entire structure vibrates with each step. Subtle clanging sounds we make as we elevate from the Earth make my already taxed nerves fire off one warning after another. We're ascending this monstrous ladder and, as we rise, so does my anxiety level.

When we reach the top, it's fully enclosed. Presumably to keep people from jumping—a necessary precaution right now. I am in a giant cage, in the sky, with a man I barely know. There have been few scenarios I have felt less safe in the past decade.

Terror is consuming me when Sebastian pulls me in for a hug. No, I don't want to be touched. I push him away with the meagre strength I have and step backward toward the edge of the structure. I can't speak through my ragged breathing, so I lift my hand up to tell him to stop as I lean against a bench.

"What's wrong, Doll? Chill. Are you scared of heights or something?"

I shake my head with an emphatic no. I am not scared of heights—I fear being trapped, which, in this case, is at a higher-than-normal altitude.

"Relax, okay? You're fine."

When in the history of time has someone telling another person in the throes of a panic attack to "relax" ever helped? Who, ever, has stopped their frenzied reaction and replied, "Gee thanks for the advice, Tips. Super helpful." If I wasn't in such a panic right now, I'd roll my eyes.

"Do you want something to take the edge off?"

Short of a tranquilizer dart, what could take the edge off right now? I take a few deep breaths and steady myself enough to respond, "Take the edge off?"

"Well, yeah. You don't look like you're enjoying yourself very much, and I promised you would."

I shake my head no, in response to his claim I'm not enjoying myself, but he takes it as a no regarding taking the edge off.

He pulls a small clear plastic bag from the pocket of his jeans. It contains a white powder and I know where this is going.

"Do you do it?" I ask him, nervous about his answer.

"Sometimes. If I'm really on edge."

"'Really on edge' is exactly how I feel right now." I take a few deep breaths. "Do you think it would help?"

"It might. It's worth a shot."

I take a few moments to consider the weight of what I'm deliberating. I know right from wrong, yes, but has it ever benefited me? What have I gotten out of always following the rules? All through high school I stayed out of trouble, kept my nose clean—poor choice of words—and left with one friend who has since abandoned me. College friends were a non-starter. I tried working hard to support myself and ended up being tracked down by the one person I never wanted to see again. I've hurt no one, yet end up hiding in my own home, unsafe. My entire life, I tried to be "good" and not disappoint people after being betrayed by the one living person who was biologically invested in loving me. Nothing I ever do will be enough to make anyone happy. I'm looking at a lifelong journey of fear, anxiety, distrust, and disappointment. What have I got to lose?

"Okay. Show me what to do." I'll try anything to be free from the weight of the world resting on my chest.

Sebastian's smile indicates that was exactly the response he was hoping for.

Sebastian's smile does little to ease my nerves. "Have you ever done anything like this before?"

"No, I haven't. I've been a little busy people-pleasing and being afraid of everything," I respond with a hint of resentment in my tone. I've spent my life following the rules, trying not to upset anyone, thinking if I was the smartest, or best behaved, someone would love me. But no matter what I do, I'm not loveable. I'm a disappointment. A burden. The fact my best friend, who promised he'd always be here for me, has written me off solidifies my decision.

"Okay, we'll go easy this time." Sebastian sets up whatever this paraphernalia is. He is very tedious in his setup, checking the wind, scanning around for other people, then pulling out a piece of aluminum foil, a five-dollar bill, and uses his key-chain knife to create a neat line of the powder.

As I consider what I'm about to partake in, I think of the news stories about street drugs being laced with fentanyl.

Overdoses aren't uncommon, and I doubt many people take drugs, knowing they'll have deadly consequences. I can't imagine how disappointed Zach and Zara would be in me if I overdosed. Or how upset Isla would be. I'm questioning the decision I was confident in about thirty seconds ago.

Sebastian must sense my hesitation. "I'll go first to show you how to do it and prove it's safe. I'm not trying to hurt you, Doll. You're supposed to have a good time."

I nod, then I watch him bend over his crude setup, holding his left nostril closed with one hand, and a rolled-up blue bill in the other. In one swift motion, with the sound of a sniffle, the powder disappears. Sebastian stands up and wipes his nose with his thumb.

"Your turn." He hands me another bill, which I appreciate. We may have swapped spit, but I draw the line at snot. "Are you sure about this?"

No, I'm not sure about *this*, but I am sure I don't want to feel like I do anymore. "What does it feel like?"

"Like euphoria. Within minutes, you feel nothing but happiness."

That sounds like exactly what I need. "Okay, let me try it."

Five minutes later, although the back of my throat has gone numb and I'm drooling, I feel wonderful. I'm more relaxed, blissful, and elated than I've been in my life. I'm enjoying the view, wrapped in the arms of this man, and I'm not afraid. People walk around the distant pier like little ants, and I'm in a cage in the sky, watching over them without a care in the world. I turn toward Sebastian, look in his dilated pupils, and pull his face closer so his lips meet mine. The kiss is so intense; he has me pushed into the corner, pinned against the barrier, which is the only thing preventing me from plummeting to my death, but I don't care.

"Doll, you don't even know what you do to me," Sebastian says as he pulls away from me.

"Then come and get it." I'm surprised by this confidence I have and feel like I am the only girl in the world who could make this man happy. I want him to be mine, because I'm his.

Sebastian lets out a low growl and leans in to kiss me once more, this time lifting me off of my feet and my legs instinctively wrap around him. Things are getting heated when we hear the clanking steps of at least two people headed up to the top of the tower. We pull away, panting.

"Let's get out of here. We can take a drive to the beach."

The beach? It's October. I am about to question his plan, but I decide at this moment, if he told me we were going to The North Pole, I'd grab my snowsuit.

"Wow. This is beautiful." I scan the shores of *Waubuno Beach*, noticing the landscape beyond the water. I think about what it would be like to live across the channel, with no neighbours, safe from the dangers of the world. But is anywhere really safe? Can any one location provide a semblance of security from the evils of the world? Can another person ever fully be trusted?

Disappointment fills me as I realize my high has worn off, and I am back to the same old Chelsea I was an hour ago—filled with fear, scared to trust, and afraid to let go. Now that I know how it feels to be happy and carefree, I don't want to be *this* Chelsea anymore.

"Sebastian?"

"Yeah, Doll?"

"I want to do it again."

"Do what? Coke?"

I cringe as he says "coke." I'm aware doing it again could send me down a slippery slope, but those few moments of peace were worth the risk. "Yeah. Next time I see you, can we do it again?"

He places his hands on my shoulders to spin me to face him. "Next time you see me? So, you're saying you want to see me again?"

I shouldn't have assumed *he* would want to see *me* again. "Oh, well, not if you don't want to."

"If it were up to me, I'd never take you home." He pulls me in for a hug and kisses me on the top of my head, which is a show of affection that would have made me run for my life a few weeks ago. My guard is dropping.

We admire the sun setting over the water; Sebastian sitting in the sand, me between his legs, leaning back against his chest. I'm grateful for him showing me how it feels to be alive and to experience something other than uneasiness and anxiety.

My phone vibrates for about the twentieth time today, but I have been ignoring it, knowing it's likely Zara or Zach. I have eight missed calls and a string of text messages. Sebastian turns on his phone so I check my messages.

Zara: Sweetheart, I'm sorry. We only want what's best for you.

Please, let me know you are okay and where you are.

I'm about to turn twenty-one. I am not going to check in every place I go anymore. She can't watch every move I make; I'm an adult.

Zach: Chelsea, please come home so we can talk. Zara and Isla are both going out of their minds with worry.

Oh, so he doesn't want to talk because he cares about me. He wants to talk because it's upset Zara and Isla? Zara probably forced him to message me. No thank you. What is he? Zara's little lapdog? Thinking I owe him my whereabouts at all times, too? I don't need him watching over me.

Gia: Hey gurl! Last night was lit. Looking forward to seeing you Wednesday.

What did I agree to on Wednesday? How did she even get my number? I was drunk, but I'm almost positive I didn't give out my number. I don't even know this girl; other than she likes to drink, and she goes to my college. Now I can stress over that, too.

"Is everything okay?" Sebastian asks, studying my face.

I plaster on a fake smile and try my best to mimic the confidence I had a short time ago. "Fine. Just text messages from Zara and a friend."

"Well, aren't you miss popular?"

"Ha! That couldn't be further from the truth. It seems I've made everyone upset with me."

"Maybe we should get you home, then. It's a good thing to have people checking in on you. Don't take it for granted." His words are directed to the pale beach sand beneath us.

He sounds like he knows from experience. I mean, I do too after spending a decade in foster care, but having lived that way, only worrying about my survival has honed certain instincts I can't shut off.

"If you're ready to get rid of me, I guess I'll go face the music."

In one swift movement, Sebastian hops up from his seated position in the sand and reaches his hand down to help me up. "Never, Doll. But you have a family, and that's something you need to put effort into. I can't hog all of your time."

His words are sweet, but confusing, considering he was saying he never wanted to take me home. His bad boy image gave me one impression of him, but aside from the alcohol and cocaine, he has a sweet side. I feel safe with him—well, safe-ish—and *that* is not something I will take for granted.

I take his hand, letting him pull me up as if I'm a feather, and I brush the sand off of my clothes. We walk back to his car, hand-in-hand, but I can't shake the feeling I'm being watched. My brain is on high alert again, and I want it to stop.

I return home at 10:15pm to be met at the door by Zara and Zach. I'm going to be grilled to death by the question-firing squad. Zara's face is twisted with concern, whereas Zach looks furious.

Suddenly, I fear they'll be able to pick up on my drug use and their anger toward me will increase exponentially. I decide I'm not going to be the one to break the silence. Maybe if I don't say a word, they'll let me pass.

"Finally. Chelsea, you had us worried." Zach is not letting me by without stating his latest issues with me.

"Sweetheart, are you okay? I'm so sorry if we upset you. We only want what's best for you." Zara takes a step toward me, looking as if she aged ten years since this morning.

Scowling in her direction, Zach says, "I'm *not* sorry for asking a question because I'm concerned about your wellbeing, Chels. We want to make sure you're okay. A lot has happened recently, and it's our job to take care of you." He makes his point without removing the angry look on his face. I've never seen him angry. Nor have I ever seen Zara and him disagree—whether they do in private is a different story.

"I'm sorry for being a giant inconvenience in your life. I offered to find my own place. Is that it? You want to keep me here so you can control me? Why not stick me in a cage?" I storm off, letting no one else get a word in.

I can hear the two of them murmuring as I walk up the stairs. They're going to draw straws to see which one of them has to come talk to me first. What do they want from me? Guilt tripping me for doing what they've been suggesting I do for years, then losing their minds over me going out like an adult. I *am* an adult.

I'm overwhelmed and angry. I want to text Sebastian, but I don't want to appear needy. He left eight minutes ago. After a few moments of a typical internal conflict, my fingers slide across my touchscreen, paying no mind to logic.

Chelsea: I wish I was still with you.

He takes a few moments to reply, leaving me pacing around the off-white area rug at the end of my bed.

Sebastian: Do u want 2 come stay with me?

Do I? I barely know him, but I enjoy being around him. He makes me smile, and most importantly, he makes me forget everything else.

Chelsea: Would you let me? Do you live alone?

I realize I've never even asked him these things. He's always been elusive about his work and home life.

Twenty minutes pass before I receive a reply. My carpet will be thread bare at this rate.

Sebastian: Yeah Doll

U can stay with me anytime

I seriously contemplate what he's offering as I hear a knock on my door.

"Chels? Can you let me in? I want to talk."

"I'm fine Zara. There's nothing to talk about."

"Chelsea, none of this seems fine. This isn't like you. Please, let me in."

Who is she to say what is or isn't like me? Maybe all this time I've been putting on an act and this really *is* me. She doesn't get to dictate the person I will be—no one does. I stomp over to the door, but the carpet doesn't make me sound as aggressive as I intend. I abruptly swing the door open and see Zach no longer looking angry; he looks downright heartbroken. I question my sanity because I'm certain I was just speaking to Zara.

"Come in then. Please, tell me how I've disappointed you." I gesture toward the chair near my window.

He ambles inside my room, leaving the door ajar behind him. "You haven't disappointed anyone. I've seen people drink or use drugs when life gets hard, and no matter how much control they think they have, it never ends well. I wanted to make sure you weren't drinking for the wrong reasons. Wanting to have a good time is fine. Using it to escape is another issue."

My eyes widen when he says the word "drugs." Does he know? I try to think of a way to steer the conversation away from that direction. "What are the right reasons, Zach? Please explain this to me. When is there ever a legitimate reason? It's made specifically for enjoyment—recreation. There's never a *need* for it, short of cleaning a wound. So, forgive me if the one time I had a few drinks and enjoyed myself, I got upset being told I did that wrong. Especially after being told for the past several years, I *should* go out and enjoy myself."

"I didn't tell you it was wrong." His voice is getting louder, but he swallows and composes himself. "I was questioning your motives for drinking. Given the return of Kevin in your life, and the fact you were going on your first date, I think the question was justified out of concern. It wasn't an accusation."

Logically, I know Zach is a reasonable guy. We've never had an issue before, but I can't stop this overwhelming need to push everyone away.

"Whatever. I went, I drank, I had fun. Sue me. I'll probably do it again because I can't remember the last time I had fun. It was as if my fears had disappeared. I enjoyed myself. I had my first kiss without being terrified. It was great."

Zach is looking down at the floor, no longer directing his words toward me. "I'm glad you had fun. I want you to be careful, okay? That's all we want. We love you."

He tells me they love me, and my only reaction is contempt for myself. I'm putting them in danger by being here, and that's selfish. I can't say I love him or anyone else when I'm keeping them in harm's way by staying here.

That forces me to push back instead of making amends. "I don't know what to tell you. I don't even know what I did wrong. Everything needs to stop. The feelings all need to stop." Before I can compose myself, tears are flowing down my cheeks, and I rush to wipe them away before Zach notices.

He's far too observant. "Shh. It's okay." He steps toward me and gazes into my watery eyes. "I'm going to hug you, Chels." He wraps his arms around me, using his left hand to cradle my head against his shoulder, and he lets me cry.

The way he accepts my mess makes me cry harder because he doesn't deserve this. Not my outbursts, not my frustration, and certainly not the risk I present.

"You can't stop feeling, Chels. Please, just let those of us who love you help you get through it." He releases me, and I take a step back. "We all love you and want you to be safe." He turns to the door. I gather as far as he's concerned, this issue has been resolved. But I still have a major problem to address.

Everything about this hurts. Life is so much easier alone when you don't have to worry about hurting anyone. This entire family dynamic is complicated. According to government documents, Zach is legally my father, but my mind won't let go of the ne'er-do-well responsible for giving me life.

To protect them, I have to create distance. It would be a lot easier if they followed in Liam's footsteps.

"I need everyone to stop babying me and let me make my own decisions. I want to live my own life, which means I'll make my own mistakes. I still don't understand how having a few drinks was such an issue, so I'd like it if everyone stopped making it one."

"You having a few drinks wasn't an issue, Chels. But your reaction to being asked was a concern," Zach says from the doorway, arms crossed. Zara is now standing behind him.

When I look at him, I see a look on his face I'm getting familiar with—disappointment. I may have felt like an utter letdown plenty of times, but he's never looked at me like this.

"Sweetheart, we didn't mean to make you think you did anything wrong. But with Kevin around, Zach was only asking to make sure you weren't using alcohol to numb what you're feeling. I swear, his intentions were nothing but good, and we want you to go out and enjoy yourself, as long as you're safe." Zara rambles on, peeking her head out from behind Zach. She's never been afraid to talk to me face-to-face before.

"Can we talk about this some other time? I'm tired and I want to get some sleep before my classes in the morning."

I can see neither of them are pleased with my request, but nothing good will come of continuing to press this issue tonight. They both say good night before walking toward their bedroom—no doubt to talk about me.

I finally text Sebastian back after far too much exhausting conversation. Lying on my bed on my stomach, legs bent and flailing around like a love-struck middle-schooler, I try to find the words to say.

Chelsea: Can I see you tomorrow?
Sebastian: Can't wait

I am woken by my phone buzzing on my bedside table, and I'm cursing the person who has the nerve to message me so early. The name on my screen is one of the last people I expected after more than a week of no contact.

Liam: Hey, Chels. I need to talk to you. Meet me at the coffee shop at 8:30? I'm sorry.

I'm angry he has the nerve to message me after all this time. Like a simple sorry makes up for ditching me. Goes to show, no matter how much you want to count on someone, other people are never truly reliable. Curiosity gets the better of me, though, and I want to know what he has to say for himself.

Chelsea: Fine.

I choose another typical fall outfit after having a quick shower. Charcoal leggings, black sweater, and the same black booties I wore to the beach, which still contain some sandy souvenirs. I dump the remaining sand out of my boots into the garbage can in my bathroom and take a peek in the mirror. For a split-second, I feel beautiful, knowing Sebastian is attracted to me, but with a slight turn of my head, I catch an angle that looks so much like Kevin, my positive thought morphs into disgust. No one who is born of a monster can be physically attractive.

My escape is well-timed, allowing me to avoid the rest of my family. I'm committed to keep driving a wedge between us. There's nothing they can say to convince me having me around can benefit them in any way. It's not possible.

I climb into my red SUV, reversing out of the garage, and head to meet my current—or former—best friend. I'm not sure where we stand, but if he no longer wants to be my friend, I'm not going to chase him. Not because I don't care, but because I do.

After parking in a suitable spot, I stroll toward the coffee shop. The last time I was there was a few weeks ago when I saw Sebastian for the first time. My life looks a lot different today than it did then. Having things disrupted by the human manifestation of a nightmare will do that to a person.

I stand on the steps near the coffee shop, awaiting Liam's arrival. To my surprise, he arrives only a few moments after I do and I'm thankful I'm not left waiting for long.

"Hey, Chels." He looks terrible. His typical glowing complexion looks dull and stressed. His hair is dishevelled and his clothing, wrinkled. Markedly uncharacteristic.

"Hey, stranger."

Liam blows out a breath as he runs his hands through his curly hair, and I realize that's the reason it looks messy. "Hey. Let's go inside and talk. I have a lot to explain." He walks toward the coffee shop.

Immediately, I retreat into defence-mode. "You don't have to explain anything. I don't want to be my friend anymore, either."

He stops outside the door, looking down at me with his brows scrunched together. "That's not what I was going to say, Chels. I'd never..." He opens the door. "Please, let me explain."

I'm reluctant to follow him, but I should hear him out. I can't fault him for wanting to keep his distance, but it stings.

"What do you want to drink? Did you eat?"

I'm not interested in a pity bagel to ease his guilt for ghosting me. I can't blame him. "Just a coffee, is fine."

He nods and waits in the lineup with the other caffeine-addicted students while I go find our regular table. The seat reminds me of my first encounter with Sebastian, and I still find it odd he was here, but given that I've seen him on campus otherwise since then, I guess, like everyone else, he was here to get his fix.

Liam slides into the seat across from me, passing me my drink and a paper bag.

"What's this?"

He takes a sip of his coffee, making a pain face, signalling the liquid is still too hot for consumption. "A croissant. I figured you hadn't eaten."

How he knows that, I'll never understand. I leave the bag untouched on the table, waiting for Liam to drop whatever bomb on me he called me here for.

"I'm sorry I haven't been in touch the past few days."

"Few days? Liam, it's been closer to two weeks than a few days." My accusatory tone doesn't help my case to remain his friend, but it helps him discontinue this friendship that's always had one-sided benefits, anyway.

"I know exactly how many days it's been. I could tell you how many hours it's been since I dropped you off and went home feeling sorry for myself, walking in to find my dad unconscious on the floor, Chels. I know *exactly* how long it's been."

That's not the bomb I was expecting. Not even close.

I snap my dangling jaw shut. "Is he... Is he okay? What happened?"

With tears pooling in his eyes, Liam continues, "He had a heart attack. A serious one. It was lucky I got home when I did, and my mom had drilled her medical knowledge into me since I was a kid. I knew I never would have made a good doctor, but I wished I was." He takes another painful sip of hot coffee. "I called an ambulance, and they arrived ten minutes later. It felt like an eternity. I thought... I thought he was dead. I was sure I was doing chest compressions on my father's dead body."

Tears are forming in my own eyes. I know how much Liam looks up to his dad. "I'm so sorry."

"Thanks." He rips off a piece of a napkin, rolling it between his fingers, watching it instead of looking at me. "When the paramedics said he was still alive, I don't know, Chels. I shut down. I was so relieved but afraid if I left his side again, he'd die."

I don't know what it feels like to love someone so much, but it sounds painful.

"My mom got him into *Sunnybrook Hospital*, and he was there until yesterday. They transferred him back to *Soldier's Memorial*, and he'll hopefully be home in a few days. I've been back and forth to Toronto more times in the past ten days than I have in my life."

"You saved his life."

Liam nods. "Well, he gave me mine, so it seems like some kind of karmic balance or something." He gives a wry smile, but his eyes are still sad. "I'm sorry I didn't reach out. After our last conversation, then my dad... I don't know. I had tunnel vision, and I wasn't able to focus on anything else. But..." Releasing another big breath, he says, "I thought about you a lot. All the time, actually. I guess I was afraid to call because if I did, I'd have to tell you about my dad, and I didn't know if he was going to pull through. Saying it out loud made that possibility too real."

I want to say I understand. I do sympathize with him, because that must have been a hard situation, but it's hard for me to put myself in his shoes. If I walked into somewhere and found Kevin collapsed on the floor, I don't know how I'd react. Would I be sad? Would I be relieved? Would I be happy? What kind of despicable human being would be happy?

I don't know what to tell him, so I say the only thing I can think of. "You're lucky to have him as your dad." I don't mean for that to come out sounding resentful, but it does, and Liam notices.

"How are things with your dad? Have you seen him?"

The last thing I want to discuss is Kevin Wells. I'd rather talk about my menstrual cycle. I'd rather have diarrhea. And a sneezing fit.

I shake my head. "No sign of him since the house."

"Hmm. Weird. Why would he make so much effort into tracking you down, just to disappear?"

I shrug my shoulders. "No idea. He's biding his time. Waiting to make a move. Which is why you shouldn't be around me."

"Chels—"

"No, Liam. You have enough going on in your life. I'm not dragging you into mine. A lot has happened since we talked last. I'm seeing Sebastian now, and he's already proven he can handle Kevin. I don't want you putting yourself at risk."

Liam's face forms a grimace, and he chokes on his coffee. "Seeing Sebastian?"

That was all he heard? "We went out on Saturday and again Sunday. I had a good time." I will neglect to tell him about the drugs and alcohol.

"Wow. Wow. I... um. Wow."

"Yeah. Anyway, it's best you keep your distance from me." I get up from my seat, grab my coffee and prepare to make a beeline out the door. "I hope your dad gets better quickly. He's a good man."

Liam reaches up, grabbing my arm. "Chels, wait." He stands, releasing my arm and flashing an apologetic look. "There's nothing that can keep me from my best friend."

He's not understanding what I'm saying, so I'm going to make him see things from a new perspective. I need to force him to leave me alone. "The situation with your dad kept you away. You couldn't even call, Liam. I thought you dropped me as a friend. Do you know what that did to me?"

"Hey, that's not fair. I was in a tough spot." He looks genuinely hurt.

"Well, so am I. You wanted space to handle things, and I'm asking for the same thing." I need to keep him safe. "Just go back to your dad, Liam. And leave me alone. I'll handle things myself."

I walk out of the coffee shop on the verge of tears. I hope I'm doing the right thing.

For the last two weeks, I've been distancing myself from my family, dodging Liam's calls, and meeting Sebastian in secret—usually when I'm supposed to be in my classes. Because he lives in Orillia, it's easier for him to come to the college campus. I've fallen behind on my schoolwork, but I know I can catch up if I don't let it slide any more.

Liam has been MIA, and I'm assuming he's still helping with his dad's recovery, but since my presence adds no value to his life, I haven't reached out.

I'm skipping my family systems class this afternoon so I can go out with Sebastian. He's taking me on another date tonight—to see a concert at the casino. The weather has gotten cool, but inside the casino will be warm, so my outfit required some thought. I tossed some clothes in my bag before leaving the house this morning so I could get ready on campus and not need to go home. Before I meet Sebastian, I go into the bathroom on campus to change.

My hair is down in natural, loose waves, and I've glammed up my face with eyeliner, mascara, and a bright red lipstick. I put on a black bodycon minidress, the same black thigh-high boots I wore on our first date, and a burgundy open thigh-length cardigan—courtesy of Jasmine—I'll be able to take off when I get warm. Sebastian makes me feel good about myself. I want him to like how I look.

I inhale a line to help myself relax, wipe my nose with the back of my hand, straighten my dress, and exit once the euphoric high I've come intimately familiar with over the past few weeks kicks in. Something I never thought I'd consider has become my lifeline.

As I walk through the bathroom door, I crash into what feels like a solid wall. My senses are dulled, but I'd recognize that scent anywhere.

"Chels? I'm so sorry. Are you okay?" Liam steps back to give me distance, familiar with my many quirks. He doesn't know that right now I don't have a care in the world.

I giggle. "I'm fine. Texting and walking again?"

"You caught me." He stares at me for a moment, which makes me look away, unable to take the intensity of his stare.

"How's your dad?" I might try to push Liam away, but I'll always care.

"He's doing better. Hey… Are you all right? You look…" He takes a few more seconds to inspect my face. "Your eyes look different. Why are your pupils the size of the moon?" There's a visible change in his face when he draws his own conclusion. "Oh, my God, Chels. Please tell me your eyes don't look like that because of what I am thinking."

I lift my head to look at him. "I couldn't possibly know what you're thinking, now could I? You should focus on your own life, Liam, and not worry about what I am or am not doing."

The coldness in my tone makes him shrink back. His reaction is what I'd expect if I struck him. "Chelsea, listen to me.

I'm not asking because I'm trying to be some control-freak. I don't know how many ways I can try to make that clear to you. God." He runs his hands over his hair—not exasperated enough to mess up his curls. "I hate that you think so little of me." He pauses, taking a deep breath, and steadies his gaze on mine. "I'm asking because I'm worried about you, and from where I'm standing, it looks like you're headed down a dangerous road."

His little speech only serves to irritate me. "Listen to me. *I'm* not some damsel in distress who needs you to come to her rescue. We've been over this before. You need to get your own life and stay out of mine." Why can't he see it's for his own good? He doesn't deserve to have me dragging him down or putting him in danger. I storm past Liam and continue on my way, looking more forward to seeing Sebastian than ever.

I'm crestfallen by the time I make it outside of the commons building, my heartbeat has tripled in both speed and intensity. My interaction with Liam annihilated my euphoric high, and now I'm searching for another source of calm.

With my back against the brick wall, I survey the immediate area. I can't shake the feeling I'm being watched, but I can't find the source. It's as if someone's eyes are burning the back of my neck every time I turn around. I want it to stop. I'm clawing at the skin on my arms to distract myself from my own thoughts. Physical pain seems to be the only way to make my brain stop for a moment.

I've turned my wrists red from scratching and squeezing, so I slide my cardigan sleeves down to cover the damage. I do another scan of the vicinity—not convinced I'm safe, but not wanting to stand against an icy wall any longer—forcing myself to walk to my vehicle with my head on a swivel.

Sebastian and I meet for a quick bite, then spent the day driving around, walking the streets hand in hand, going in and out of shops, and talking about everything and nothing. He's still closed off with me, but I hope he'll believe he can trust me enough to open up soon. It doesn't help that I'm not any better.

When he returns me to my car, which I parked near the restaurant we ate at, we drive individually to our next destination so I'll be able to get myself home. We live in opposite directions, and I didn't want to leave my vehicle on the college campus overnight. I'm not about to call Liam for a Wednesday-morning pickup.

We walk into the concert via the rotunda after having our ID checked. I glance into the casino area, and it appears that's the room where dreams go to die, judging by the expressions on people's faces. The house always wins.

Here I go, into another enormous crowd with loud music. I gather Sebastian is more of a music buff than a reader. If it were up to me, we'd have a quiet date somewhere and be able to talk, like our day at the beach in Parry Sound, but I don't want to offend him by suggesting his date ideas aren't good. I need him in my life, so I can't risk making him think like I don't appreciate his effort.

The crowd in the venue is filing in as Sebastian holds my hand and leads me to our seats. I'm not even sure who is performing, but it doesn't matter. Having my hand enveloped in his generates confidence in me, so I feel like I can survive the evening.

We make our way to our seats in the 'J' section, front and centre, but not directly in front of the stage. These are fantastic seats. To my dismay, however, we are in the direct middle of the section, meaning if I have to get up, I'll need to climb over everyone on one side or the other to make my escape. At least we've arrived before our aisle-mates, so I can get in without disrupting anyone. Maybe the concert isn't sold out and we'll have the aisle to ourselves.

Wishful thinking. Within fifteen minutes, not only our aisle, but every seat in the venue is full of people eager to see the show. I'm overwhelmed with no means of escape, and my breathing speeds up.

"You okay, Doll?"

Breathe in. Breathe out. Breathe in… "I'm fine. Just excited." I lie because I don't want him to think he can't bring me places anymore. I want to be normal. "Maybe we can get a drink?" My eyes are pleading with Sebastian, and I try to force my fear down.

"The usual?" He winks at me, and heat rushes through my body.

"Please," I choke out, trying not to let on that I'm so attracted to him it makes me stupid. Keep it together.

Sebastian stands and slides past me, facing forwards so his butt is right in front of my face. I'm not ashamed to admit I take advantage of the opportunity, but feel guilty ogling him like a piece of meat. It's unfair that men are berated for sexualizing females if women do the same to them. My eyes follow Sebastian down the aisle, and I notice several other ladies take advantage of his roaming derriere the same as I did. Okay, cougars. You're embarrassing yourselves.

Sometime later, as the lights dim in the concert hall, Sebastian still hasn't returned. I sit in my seat and focus as I see some images flash on the screens on either side of the stage. Is that what I think it is?

I'm. Blown. Away.

don't even know how to function right now, because what I'm looking at is the logo for *Panic! At the Disco.* How could Sebastian have known I liked them? Maybe he didn't, and he likes them too. I never thought they'd play a small venue like this, but I'm filled with so much anticipation. I am no longer worried about where Sebastian is.

Liam introduced me to *Panic!* when we were in high school, and I'm guilt-stricken being here to see them without him.

Fifteen minutes later, I'm fully immersed in Brendon Urie singing *I Write Sins, Not Tragedies,* and I'm so distracted wondering why anyone would want a door closed so badly, it's only then I realize Sebastian hasn't come back. When lyrics pour out of the speakers encouraging some champagne, I think that's exactly what I need.

I contemplate whether I should go look for Sebastian, but in a crowd of five thousand plus people, chances of finding him are slim. I decide to stay put and hope he returns soon.

I pull out my phone to send him a quick text message.

Chelsea: Where are you?

I turn my attention back to the captivating singer before me, mesmerized by his smooth voice and his exceedingly high energy level. If ever there was a man born for a specific job, I'm sure I'm looking at him. Brendon Urie is the epitome of a seasoned performer.

My phone vibrates, causing my heart to skip a beat.

Sebastian: Can't bring drinks in. Having a drink in casino

Is he for real? He knew I wanted a drink, and without saying a word, he left me here to go drink elsewhere? Some romantic date. As if on cue, "Death of a Bachelor," permeates my ears and I think to myself, spot on Brendon. Spot. On.

Chelsea: Are you coming back?

Sebastian: OMW

What does "OMW" mean? One mean whore? Open my window? Over maniac women? I'm being too needy and now he's done with me. That has to be it.

The song lyrics taunt me. I may not be seated at a table for two, but I've been alone for a large portion of what should be a two-person date.

My excitement over the performance happening fades, and I feel deflated. Liam would have sat with me through the entire show and we would have fan-girled so hard together. Fan-boyed, whatever. But there's a reason I'm here with Sebastian and not Liam. I have to keep reminding myself of that.

I glance down the aisle in both directions. To the right is a group of rowdy girls little older than me who forgot most of their clothes, and to the left, the cougars—no, pumas, as I don't suspect they're older than mid-thirties. The excitement on their face isn't directed at the epic entertainers in front of us, but at the handsome olive-skinned Adonis making his way through the aisle.

As he gets close, he shoots me a smile, making his white teeth glow against the flashing lights. He looks a bit dishevelled with his shirt twisted and his belt buckle partially undone. He must have stopped in the bathroom on his way back and been in a rush. I smile in return, hoping I look convincing. I'm certain he's coming to tell me he's so over me for being a maniac woman.

"Hey, Doll. Sorry." He drops in the seat beside me with a grunt. "You not enjoying the show?"

"I am. *Panic!* is my favourite band of all time. I was just wondering where you had gone. Sorry if I sounded too needy."

Sebastian looks at me, a smile playing at his lips. "You missed me?"

"I... uh... well, I thought this was a date. So, it was my understanding that usually involves two people."

He throws his head back with a laugh. "Why are you always so formal? How do I get you to loosen up?"

"Well, you were supposed to bring me a drink." I glance at him from the corner of my eye after turning back to watch the show.

"Sorry. I tried. Do you want to, uh... take a trip to the bathroom?" He pats his chest pocket.

The soundtrack of my evening is blaring through the speakers when appropriate lyrics radiate through the large space. "Champagne, cocaine, gasoline..." Brendon gives me permission.

"Okay. I can get a drink while we're up. Maybe some champagne."

"Anything you want, Doll." Sebastian reaches over to take my hand before standing. He leads us through the row of seats, saying, "Excuse us, ladies. Sorry. Excuse us. Thank you." He appears to be an average, overly polite Canadian, but nothing about this man is average.

I notice the scowls sent in my direction by the thirsty pumas. Eat your hearts out, ladies; he's here with me. Sebastian is unfazed by the attention and swiftly gets us to the aisle where we can make our escape.

We walk through the chaos that is an alt-rock concert, with intentional steps—we are on a mission. Mission: Chill Chelsea Out. I don't want to look up and see the size of the crowd because that's like pulling the trigger on my anxiety gun and the night will be ruined. One step at a time, holding Sebastian's hand and allowing him to lead me, we make our way to the washrooms.

Sebastian surprises me by pushing me up against the wall and planting a kiss on me so fast and furious, my knees buckle. I'm trying to enjoy the moment, but I can't ignore the surrounding chaos. Without removing his lips, Sebastian reaches a hand into the pocket of my cardigan, then pulls back with a wicked smirk on his face.

"Go get yourself sorted, then we'll get you a drink."

I stand with my back to the wall, dumbfounded by what happened. I can never get a read on what his intentions are, and I wish I had telepathic powers—or at least the ability to read unconscious body cues. Maybe there's a book about that. It could be helpful someday for other reasons besides trying to decipher the thoughts of the handsome man in front of me.

I'm getting lost in my thoughts, as I often do, when Sebastian leans back into me, grabbing a generous handful of my… ahem… gluteus maximus, and asks, "Do you want me to come in the bathroom with you?"

Why would I need him to come into the bathroom with me? I'm a big girl. I mean, I hate public washrooms because the stalls are small, and I hate closing the door, but it's not like I need his help. I'm well past that stage of life.

"Thanks, but I think I'll be okay."

He chuckles as he holds his hand out to the right, directing me to the bathroom door. "I'll wait here for you."

The washroom is lush and opulent as far as public rooms for voiding your bladder go. I do a half-bent-over walk down the row of stalls, looking for one as far away from another set of feet as possible. Thankfully, it's not very busy in here. I choose my bathroom stalls like I choose my parking spots—with a lot of thought and consideration. Once I've settled on the best option, I enter the stall, take a seat so it appears I'm in here to do what is intended, and line up the white powder on the back of my hand. Sebastian has taught me a few tricks over the past few weeks, and I've gotten the hang of it now. I take my hit, wipe my nose with a tissue, flush the toilet for appearance's sake, and walk out to wash my hands. Mission accomplished.

The brunette woman beside me at the sink flashes me a grin, which I try to return. Keyword: try. Glancing in the mirror, I see an awkward grimace on my face. I'm afraid she's onto me.

My heart rate increases, and my blood is thumping in my ears. I have to get out of here. I can't go to jail. I can't. I would not survive in a cage again.

I run out of the bathroom, grabbing Sebastian's hand without a word, and head toward the casino. I need a drink. I need to look like I belong here and not like a random criminal doing illegal activities in their bathrooms. How could I have been so stupid?

"Woah. What's the matter?" Sebastian digs his feet in, refusing to move. He's firmly planted on the circle-patterned carpet of varying colours, probably chosen to hide the amount of spilled drinks and vomit the floor is likely to absorb on an average day. Gross. No, don't think about that.

I don't even know what to say in response to Sebastian, because I don't want him to be annoyed with me. "I want a drink." Perhaps the power of seduction can work to convince him. I step toward him, running my fingers along the waist of his pants. I bite my bottom lip, and even though I am sure I'm as charming as Homer Simpson, I roll with it. "Please. Can I get a drink?"

Sebastian sucks in a breath, which gives me a confidence boost. I think my pathetic attempt to seduce him is working. "Let's get you liquored up." He smirks. Despite my instincts, my prevalent thought is that I can't lose him.

He cannot be trusted.

Now that I'm good and drunk, we're standing in front of our seats, watching the band perform as if they're having the time of their lives. I'll never understand how people can stand up in front of a crowd and not only entertain using their talents, but sing their own songs. The vulnerability in doing that is so far out of my comfort zone, it might as well be Kuwait.

Regardless of my reluctance to stand out in a crowd, I'm happy to be here watching someone else do it. Sebastian is smiling wider than I've ever seen him, but his smile isn't that of a man having the time of his life—it belongs to a bad boy with something on his mind.

My stomach churns when I question what Sebastian is going to want in return for concert tickets and champagne. In my experience, most people don't do nice things without expecting reciprocation of some sort. There are spots in my field of vision. I'm enjoying listening to *LA Devotee*, watching the performance, but suddenly, I'm going to hurl. I drop into my seat, trying to suppress the urge to vomit. Without consulting my brain, I put the carpet's stain-hiding abilities to the test and send everyone in our row scrambling as if I let a colony of tarantulas loose.

Sebastian steps a few feet to the left, leaving me seated and hunched over. I am afraid to move for fear I will vomit again, so I stay as still as possible. The music continues playing, and if I didn't know better, I'd swear he was providing a curated soundtrack to my evening.

I turn my head to see where Sebastian has gone. He's still standing a few feet away, staring at me like I'm the most disgusting creature he's ever laid eyes on. I can't say I blame him.

"Uh, Chelsea? Are you all right?" He asks with his hand over his nose so I can barely hear him.

There's no point in faking anymore. He's disgusted by me. I shake my head. He surprises me by tiptoeing around the pool of vomit, sits in the seat next to me,and rubs my back. The logical part of my brain is on alert, cautiously accepting the contact. My champagne-cocaine cocktail has not made me uncomfortably numb as I had hoped.

He leans down closer to my ear. "We should get out of here, Chelsea. Let's get you cleaned up."

Chelsea. I'm not "Doll" anymore. I have to admit, that hurts—I love his pet name for me.

Swallowing my emotions and residual vomit, I try to proceed with a sense of poise. I want to avoid eye contact with everyone in the immediate area, knowing I'll be the recipient of their glares for ruining the evening. As I stand, Sebastian loops his arm through mine so he's supporting me by my armpit. I think I'll cry if the deodorant marketing department sold me lies. That's an issue for another time, though. I'm in no position to take on a Fortune 500 company for false advertising right now. What I need to be concerned about is getting out of here in a hurry.

With Sebastian's help, I walk back in the direction we came from a short time ago, familiar with the direction of the washroom. With each step, despite Sebastian's strong arm holding me up, I'm struggling to keep myself upright. I need to make it to the washroom. Once I splash some water on my face, I'll be okay.

One. Step. At. A. Time.

Water splashing on my face provides the cool relief I need, but guilt is overwhelming me for killing tonight's entertainment. Sebastian will never want to see me again. Not to mention the lynch mob likely forming in the parking lot with all the pumas and scantily clad college girls.

I lift my head up to look in the mirror, and even I don't want to see myself—all I see right now is a reflection of my father with smudged eyeliner and mascara. I look away, ashamed of myself and my appearance. If I wasn't in an opulent public washroom, I might be inclined to break the mirror so I don't have to face the reality staring back at me.

Get a grip.

After emptying the contents of my stomach on the floor of the music venue, which some poor, low-wage-earning maintenance person has to clean up, I'm feeling better physically. I gather champagne and cocaine were not an ideal combination for me. Thank God I didn't try gasoline like the song implies.

I rinse my mouth out at the sink, splash more water on my face, dabbing it dry with a paper towel, wiping away my ruined makeup, and adjust my outfit. I want to return to the safety of my bedroom walls and forget this night happened.

When I exit the bathroom, I interrupt a conversation Sebastian is having with a gorgeous, dark-skinned woman standing much closer than necessary. He notices I've reappeared and steps back with concern etched on his face. "Uh, Skye, this is Chelsea."

I'm unsure how to proceed, so I choose the civil approach. All of my instincts are telling me there was something more than innocent conversation happening, but I don't want to make an issue of it. "Hi, Skye," I greet while extending my hand.

"Hey." Her clipped tone tells me we're not exchanging pleasantries. I leave it alone. "Guess I'll be seeing you around, Sebastian." Skye purrs his name. I think she's in heat. I can practically smell her pheromones from here.

Taking a few steps forward to stand next to Sebastian, I'm curious how he'll handle the situation. Should I be surprised when he steps to his right to avoid touching me? Probably not, but I am.

When Skye turns to walk away, he backtracks toward me, but instinctively, I step back to keep distance between us. I'm still nowhere near sober, though I feel better, and right now I can't trust him or myself.

"Come on, Doll. Let's get out of here."

He cannot be trusted.

"No, I need to take my own car, so I have to wait around for a bit to sober up." As I say those words, I expect Sebastian to offer to wait with me, wanting to make sure I get home safely. He surprises me for a second time in as many minutes.

"Okay, then. I'll head out." He leans in to kiss me, but this time, I am not a willing participant. He settles for a kiss on my cheek before spinning around and leaving me, drunk and alone, in a place I've never been before.

After watching Sebastian strut away, I'm left standing outside the washrooms like a lost dog. I must look out of place because a blond man, who I'd guess to be mid-thirties, speeds past me before doing a 180 and asking if I'm okay. When I try to play it off and insist I need a moment, he offers to show me how to play Texas Hold 'Em Poker. I decline, because stranger danger is a principle I've adhered to my entire life. After speaking to me for a few moments, I learn his name is Kenny, and he's at the casino with his wife, so I figure he is likely a safe bet—no pun intended. I might as well make use of my time before heading home. I just won't follow him into any closets or outside.

After two hours, I've gotten the hang of poker, and Kenny has done well. His wife, Sherry, is so sweet; I find myself at ease with her. Even if I never see either of them again, I'm grateful they kept me company while I sobered up. I doubt I could have felt more lame sitting on a bench, alone in the lobby. When I arrived, I didn't think I'd need a book for entertainment.

I'm safe to drive home now, so I thank Kenny and Sherry for keeping me company before I walk into the parking lot. Trying to find my SUV, I have an uneasiness taking over my sobering mind, despite the well-lit parking lot. I'm scanning my surroundings while I walk, again feeling as though someone is watching me. When I click the unlock button on my key, watching the lights of my CRV blink in all directions like a homing beacon, a familiar face steps out from the shadow beyond the hedge at the side of the parking lot.

Kevin Wells.

I come to a halt, blinking my eyes rapidly, trying to convince myself this is a mirage. I conclude this is not a drink of water in a desert, and his form is not appearing in front of me because of the right combination of atmospheric conditions.

"Hello, daughter."

I let out a scream with the volume and intensity I wished I had the first time Kevin appeared outside of the bookstore. The parking lot is deserted, and inside is loud, so I'm not hopeful my cries for help will serve a purpose, but I'm not allowing Kevin to think he's taking me without a fight. I'm not a helpless child anymore—I'm a helpless young adult.

"You think that's going to scare me away, stupid girl?"

My voice will betray the fear I am feeling, so I remain silent and focus all of my energy on making my stare as daunting as possible. I'd give Bambi a real run for his money in the intimidation rankings.

"Why do you insist on making this difficult, Chelsea? You owe me for what you've done. I'm coming to collect."

What *I've* done? Being born to a man with a dead heart? Pretty sure I've paid for that already—I'm still paying for every moment of every day, consciously or not.

I'm walking backwards, one near-negligible step at a time, placing distance between my "father" and me. For every inch I move, he gains a foot, but it's all happening in slow motion. Scanning the distance back to the casino door, I know I can't make it inside fast enough.

With my blood-alcohol level barely above zero and the effects of illicit narcotics in my system, my senses are dulled— including fear—even if it is a negligible difference. Since I don't have the option to run, my only logical choice is to stand my ground. Like when you run into a bear in the woods; because I'm not about to play dead.

Not today, Satan. Kevin. Whatever his name is. I don't have to be this helpless young adult. If I don't stand up for myself, who will? My vision is focused on the human version of Mephistopheles ten feet away, but my mind is playing out every scenario on how to get out of this predicament. I hear nothing but the rustling of Kevin's dull brown loafers' movement on the pavement, and my heartbeat pounding in my head.

"Back off!" My words articulate one sentiment, but my shaking hands express another.

Judging by the smirk on his face, my demand amuses Kevin. A declaration that is total bull. "Oh, really? Why would you be afraid of your dear father, Chelsea? You're alive because of me and only me. You're breathing because I allowed you to."

It's unfortunate he did.

"I notice you forgot the word old this time. You must have forgotten. I guess memory fades with old age."

My words intensify Kevin's rage, and his Irish heritage betrays the cool demeanour he is trying to maintain. The redness in his face, magnified by the reflection of the overhead lights on my cherry-red SUV, confirms he's at his boiling point.

I'm inching my way backward in the direction of the driver's door in what I would describe as the slowest Chinese fire drill ever executed. Kevin works his way closer, gaining more ground on me with each movement. I'm tired of being his meek little prey. I do not want to spend the rest of my life looking over my shoulder with my brain on high alert. I'm exhausted.

"Now, you listen to me. I know some rich family adopted you, and if they're smart, they can make me go away." His eyes bore into mine with the intensity of laser beams.

So that's what he wants. I should have known. "They won't give you a dime. I won't let them."

"That proves how stupid you—"

Like an actual oasis in the desert, my prayers are answered as a large group of rowdy twenty-somethings exits the casino and walks in our direction. I'm assuming one of them won some money, because they're all far too happy to be losers. I take the split-second Kevin looks away to dash to my open door, knowing I only pressed the unlock button once, meaning it's the only one accessible. I make as much noise as I can in doing so, sounding like a—I don't know what. The situation is too stressful to come up with an animal analogy. I grab the handle, yank the door open, jump inside and slam it shut, immediately pressing the lock down. I don't take a second to look away from what I'm doing to see where Kevin is, knowing I have a brief window of opportunity to escape.

As my car roars to life, I'm grateful I backed into my spot. All of my years of parking spot scouring might have finally paid off. I lift my head and see Kevin standing in front of my vehicle in some deranged game of chicken.

Giving him a last opportunity to move, I lay on the horn and allow it to blare for a steady five seconds. At the very least, I'll make him nervous by attracting attention.

With the car still in park, I rev the engine to show him I mean business. He doesn't budge. Unfortunately for him, the chicken needs to cross the road, or he's going to be McNuggets.

I pull the gear shift down, confirming the 'D' is lit up in my dash, and I don't hold back. I mean, it's a mom-car, so I am not taking anyone off the line, but it lurches forward fast enough, Kevin has to jump to his left to avoid a date with sweet and sour sauce. I turn to my left, speeding toward the exit as fast as mechanically possible—within reason. I'm not a parking lot renegade.

Once I've put enough distance between myself and the casino, with all the chaos of the night, I want to call someone. But who do I call? I doubt Liam will speak to me after our last encounter. It's well after midnight, so Zach and Zara are probably both asleep, and I doubt they'd want to hear from me. I wish I could call my mom. My *real* mom.

I never got to meet her, and I know nothing about her. But I can't help but think if she hadn't died giving birth to me, my life would have been completely different. I don't know how any reasonable person could end up with a man like Kevin Wells, but I often dream up ideas of what she was like, and how drastically different my childhood would have looked.

Without so much as a picture of my mother, I'm left guessing everything about her. I know nothing of the woman who sacrificed her life for mine. Did she have long, blonde hair? Freckles? Pale skin and light eyes like mine? Or was she a striking brunette who effortlessly pulled off a pixie cut? Was she average height like me? What was her favourite song to listen to while she was driving? Did she prefer the big hits, or did she seek indie artists who coloured outside of the industry lines? I want to know these things and more, but I have no one to answer my endless questions.

I merge onto highway eleven after what felt like a million miles along Rama Road, daydreaming about the sights and sounds of the mother I never knew. I'm rapidly blinking the tears from my eyes, but like high-speed windshield wipers in a monsoon, having little success. Regret for being born and starting the domino effect of problems that have followed my entire life plague my mind. My mother didn't deserve to die. Maybe Kevin was a decent man while they were married, and it was losing her that sent him over the edge. Grief can make people do irrational things.

Maybe it *is* all my fault.

I arrive home before one o'clock and find Zach or Zara have left the exterior lights on for me. They've left a light on in the kitchen as well, but I hope that's because they don't want me tripping over things and waking them up, not because they're still awake.

I pull my vehicle into its regular parking space, close the garage door behind me, and give myself a pep-talk to work up the courage to go inside. I'm utterly exhausted from the events of the evening. The crowd, the toxins, the vomiting—but most definitely the encounter with Kevin.

Walking through the door—which I took a full twenty seconds to turn the knob so it wouldn't make a noise—I am rewarded by an empty, sparsely lit kitchen.

I make a beeline for my bedroom as silently as possible, and once again Bond is there to greet me from Isla's bedroom doorway. His glare is so human like, I can guess what he's thinking. I issue a silent plea, trying to tell him I won't wake Isla. He understands, turning back into her bedroom to resume his sleep-guarding duties.

When I strip off my dress, boots, and bra, exchanging them for tie-dye pyjama shorts and a white T-shirt, I crawl into bed, grateful Zach and Zara weren't awake to grill me upon my return. Settling into my plush mattress, I wonder why. Do they not care anymore if I arrive home safely? Have I made them so angry, they don't love me anymore?

It seems the only success I have in this life is driving away people who love me.

I don't deserve their love, anyway.

My determination to move out has reached an all-time high. My recent confrontation with Kevin has not come up with Zach or Zara because I will not allow them to give that red-haired demon man one red cent. On account of my stress level, I'm so far behind in my classes, I doubt I'll be able to catch up. I'm not ready to launch that disappointment at everyone yet, so I head to campus.

After my first class, I'm waiting in the courtyard outside of the campus coffee shop for Sebastian. I'm nervous to see him for some reason, but I chalk it off to normal, everyday nerves. I've been overtired and restless since leaving the casino six days ago—the never-ending cycle of anxiety exhausting me, but not letting me sleep.

I'm standing in the grassy area, scrolling through my phone to avoid eye contact with passersby, but scanning my surroundings every few seconds as my paranoia has trained me to do. Despite my hypervigilance, I'm startled by a hand grabbing my shoulder from behind. I jump and drop my phone in the grass, then spin to defend myself from the offender.

"Woah, Doll. Relax. It's me." Sebastian places his hand back on my shoulder now that I'm facing him.

"You scared me to death! You can't sneak up on me like that."

"Relax, okay. Noted. From now on, I'll whistle when I walk."

I'm not pleased by his mocking tone, but I overlook it because he isn't familiar with my past—whether I'll ever tell him, I don't know. Since he's the one person who doesn't coddle me like a child, I don't want him to see me as a victim too.

A few deep breaths help calm me, so I'm able to lean in to give Sebastian a kiss. He doesn't seem as receptive, which makes me self-conscious.

"I'm sorry. I shouldn't have done that."

"No, it's just that your friend is watching us, and I get the impression he doesn't like me."

I turn around and see Liam standing in the parking lot, staring at Sebastian and me. Should I wave at him? Acknowledge I've seen him? Then he might come over. He might come over regardless, though, and then he'll think I was rude. I lift my hand to give a meek wave while he's still maintaining eye contact. Sure enough, he walks toward us.

My recently decreased heart rate is on the incline again— progressively picking up its pace with each of Liam's steps in my direction. I only hope I'll be able to hear what he says with the sound of blood pumping through my ears.

"Hey, Big Red. I didn't see you earlier." Liam scans Sebastian, not able to hide the disapproval from his face. "Hi. You must be Sebastian. I'm Liam." Liam reaches his hand out to Sebastian, which I appreciate.

"Hey, man. Yeah, I'm Sebastian. It seems you've heard of me, but I have no idea who you are."

Oh boy.

"Liam has been my friend since high school. He's like a brother to me." I stare down at my feet, avoiding the gaze of both men, but can't stop the flush creeping up my cheeks.

"Right. Liam."

We need to get this over with. It's not pleasant for anyone.

"I thought I'd come over to introduce myself since a friend of Chelsea is a friend of mine."

"I hope that doesn't mean because I'm her boyfriend, I'm supposed to be yours too."

Liam and I have matching expressions after hearing Sebastian's words.

"Boyfriend?" Liam looks at me for confirmation.

Sebastian grabs me by the waist, pulls me beside himself so our bodies are pressed together, and I instinctively place my arm around his back, securing myself next to him. "Yeah, man. We just made it official. I'm a lucky guy."

From his side, I look up at Sebastian, eyes wide, wondering when he thinks we made this official, but I play along so Liam doesn't get the wrong impression upon their first meeting. "Right, we're officially a couple now."

"Wow. Um. Wow. That's... Congratulations, I guess." Liam is shifting his weight, avoiding looking anyone in the eyes. I know he's uncomfortable, so I need to put an end to this little meeting before it becomes any more cringeworthy.

"Thanks, Liam. I'm happy. Sebastian and I are going to grab a coffee before my next class, so I'll see you around."

"Oh. Sorry if I held you back. I'll talk to you later, Chels."

I grab Sebastian's hand and start dragging him toward the coffee shop; my heels digging into the ground with determination. Once we've gotten enough distance to ensure Liam is out of earshot, I ask Sebastian, "Why would you say that in front of Liam?"

He stops walking, causing our arms to stretch to their limit, but he doesn't release his grip on my hand. I come to an abrupt stop.

"Do you not want me to be your boyfriend, Doll? Are you embarrassed?"

"No, of course not. I just… I didn't think that's how it would happen. It felt like you were claiming me."

"And is that a problem? I want you to be mine."

"No," I whisper. "I want to be yours."

"It's settled then. You're mine." He bends down until his lips meet mine and moves his hands around to grab my butt.

I'm uncomfortable, but I won't make an issue of it. I try to release myself into his hands and relax for a moment—an unfamiliar feeling. At least, an unfamiliar *sober* feeling.

"So, boyfriend. What are we doing for the day?" I ask once we've disconnected our lips, but he's still got his arms wrapped around me.

"I could think of something I'd like to do right now." He growls, which results in goosebumps up both of my arms.

I didn't think that far ahead. "Oh. Um. Sebastian…"

"It's okay, Doll. I know you have classes."

That's not the problem, but I let it slide. That's a discussion for another day. I was going to skip my classes to spend the day with him, but it's best if I let him think that's the issue and actually attend them.

"I better get going. I'm going to be late."

He leans down to kiss me again. "When can I see you again?"

"When do you want to see me again?" My insecurities suddenly overwhelm me, and I'm reminded I barely know this guy. I've trusted him enough to invite him to my home, take me places alone, and give me illegal drugs, but based on what? The fact he beat up my father?

He cannot be trusted.

Sebastian doesn't do much to set my mind at ease. "Why don't you come to my place after your classes today?"

"I... Um... I don't know if I'm ready for that."

"Ready for what, Doll? Coming to my place? I promise I'll be a perfect gentleman." He gives me a smirk that screams trouble.

My nervous system is lighting up like a firefly squid, spotting my entire body with reluctance and fear. My lifetime of instincts are flooding my mind, telling me not to be alone with him. But at the same time, I'm afraid that if I upset him, I'll lose my lifeline to the only thing bringing me any sense of relief.

"Okay." I don't know what I'm getting myself into or what the evening will have in store for me, but I'm going to find out because I am tired of the constant alarm bells in my mind dictating my choices.

Sebastian pulls into a driveway belonging to a muted green craftsman-style home on a street running parallel to the main road. I've followed him in my car, parking beside the curb out front. When I check my mirror to make sure it's safe to open my door, I step out and walk toward Sebastian, who is now waiting on the walkway, looking like a beautiful manifestation of trouble.

"You live here alone?" It surprises me he has a house, rather than an apartment. I'm unsure how a twenty-one-year-old man can afford something like this on his own. I examine the low-pitched roof, patterned windowpanes and covered front porch. There is little for landscaping, but the house, in its simplistic style, is exquisite on its own. Understated elegance.

"Yes, and no. I saved through high school to buy my own place, but I rent out the basement."

"You own this house?"

"I do. Free and clear. I got a good deal." His expression makes me think there's more to the story than he's saying, but I'll avoid asking where he got the money from. I don't want to know.

I didn't figure him for the responsible type, and having a permanent address seems quite domestic for Sebastian. Maybe I should stop making assumptions about him.

"Let me show you inside." He grabs my hand, and we walk toward the large arched oak door. He doesn't unlock it before walking inside—I guess he's not concerned about criminals breaking in.

We walk into an entryway that opens straight into the living room. There is a dining room to the left and an L-shaped kitchen at the back of the house next to the dining room. From the right of the living room, there are four stairs leading up to a hallway, which I am assuming is to the bedrooms and bathroom. It's a beautiful home, and not what I'd expect of Sebastian.

"This is cute." I take in the simple décor, surprised it doesn't look like a motorcycle club.

He doesn't reply. In swift movements, he pivots, lifts me, and carries me to the black sectional sofa. As he sits down, I instinctively straddle him, and in this position, our faces are at the same height. He kisses me with a growing passion, but I pull myself back.

"Sebastian. You promised you'd be a gentleman."

A playful grin appears on his face. "My bad. Do you want a tour of the place? I can show you the bedroom." He waggles his eyebrows over his darkened eyes.

"Sebastian."

"Keep saying my name, Doll." He attempts to stand up, still holding onto me, but I dive to the right, free of his grasp and settle myself on the couch.

"Sebastian, I'm not ready."

"Come on, Chelsea. I'm your boyfriend. What's the problem?"

What *is* the problem? He's right. He's my boyfriend. There are certain roles a person has to fulfill in order to be a girlfriend. Right? I'm not ready to take that step with him yet. I like the idea of being "old fashioned" and waiting until marriage, but I doubt that's ever going to happen for me. Not to mention, with my drug habit, it's not like I can claim moral high ground.

"I'm sorry. I... I..." What can I say? I'm short on excuses here. Not being ready doesn't seem sufficient.

With a frustrated groan, Sebastian stands up and walks to the kitchen. Like a sad pet, I follow. I've been his girlfriend for a few hours and I'm already ruining things.

"I'm sorry." My embarrassment is on full display—my freckled cheeks flush, and my hands fidgeting with anything within reach. "Do you... Do you have something to help me relax?"

He walks back around the kitchen counter to come face-to-face with me. "What did you have in mind?"

"I don't know. You seem to be the expert. Help me relax. I don't want you to be upset with me."

He gestures with a head nod to follow him. We walk up the few steps in the living room and his bedroom is to the right, with two more bedrooms to the left, along the back of the house.

The room is painted a charcoal grey that appears black until he switches on the ceiling light. The bedding is black, and hastily thrown across the bed. Otherwise, he only has a small end table and a dresser in his room and the black curtains are closed halfway. When I look at the artwork over his bed, I'm not surprised—a motorcycle, a personal jet, and a yacht, all in black and white.

"Is this your inspiration board?"

He's rummaging around in his dresser drawer but looks back over his shoulder to see what I'm talking about. "Living here isn't my long-term plan, Doll. A guy's got to have some dreams."

I don't know what is so wrong about living here forever. It's certainly better than where I grew up.

"Here. This should be enough for another hit." He passes me a little baggie with the white powder I fantasize about multiple times a day. The effect isn't long, but it's enough of a break to keep me from spiralling. I need that again. I need to relax so I can keep my boyfriend happy.

Five minutes later, Sebastian and I are relaxing on his bed, waiting to experience the sought-after euphoric stupor I love.

He cannot be trusted.

When the feeling hits me, a rush of confidence that is so foreign to my guarded personality overtakes me. I turn to Sebastian, who has his arms behind his head and his eyes closed, reach over to the hem of his shirt that's currently exposing his bare stomach and trace along the waistband of his jeans. My touch surprises him, but judging by the smile on his face, it's a pleasant surprise.

"Doll, be careful what you start down there."

"Sebastian..."

He rolls onto his side to face me, head propped on his bent arm. "What do you want, Chelsea? Tell me." His husky voice is sensual, but hardly relaxes me.

I'm not ready, but I hope the high I am experiencing will negate these feelings of doubt. I've let everyone down lately, and I can't bear to do that to Sebastian, too. "You," I say with no conviction.

His eyes light up with recognition, understanding what I've said. He doesn't take a second to ask if I'm sure or to reassure me. He takes what he wants. I can't blame him for it, but I quickly realize we did not want the same things. He wanted a release. I want to escape.

A few hours later, when I return home, I'm anxious to run into anyone on my way through the house. I don't want them to know what I've done, and my shame is clearly displayed across my face.

"Sweetheart, are you okay?" Zara peeks out of her bedroom door as I try to sneak into my room.

I don't make eye contact, nor stop to offer any conversation. "I'm fine. Good night." I pull my bedroom door closed behind me; a new habit.

There has never been a time in my life when I needed a shower more. No matter how hard I try, I can't scrub myself clean. I stand under the water for far too long, turning my alabaster skin a solid pink shade, but I can't burn away my regret.

Sebastian didn't make love to me how I always imagined. He screwed me and sent me on my way. He was eager, rough, and distant. I didn't feel cherished or even attractive. The romance novels I've read all lied to me. It was nothing how I dreamed my first time would be.

I put on my cotton pyjama T-shirt and panties, crawl into bed, and cry. Waves of heartbreak flow in a steady rhythm. Each time I catch my breath and start to forget, I imagine his hands roughly running across my bare skin and I'm overwhelmed by disgust.

Once it was over, I thought I would feel like I made the right decision for once in my life, but I couldn't have been more wrong.

Sebastian has been radio silent since Monday when I did the walk of shame out of his house. I haven't been to my classes either. I didn't want to explain to Zara why I wasn't going, so I dragged myself out of the house and spent the day wasting time. Tuesday, the sun was shining, so I went and sat by the water at Muskoka Falls Beach, reading and trying to escape my own thoughts. It's harder than it sounds.

Liam has tried calling a few times, but I can't even handle speaking to him. I know if he asks how I'm doing, I'll break down and confess everything, then he'll never look at me the same again. He still hasn't given up.

I'm going to meet Gia on campus today, even though I have zero desire for social activities. She's been texting me non-stop to meet since I cancelled our initial plans two weeks ago. I had no recollection of what I agreed to, so I was hoping if I avoided her, she'd forget about me. I have to give her points for her persistence.

Today isn't the best day for trying to embark on a new friendship because I feel completely dead inside. It's Halloween, and I hate the holiday with the intensity of a thousand burning suns, but it could be beneficial to help me blend in today. Chelsea, from the cast of *The Walking Dead*.

Once Sebastian got what he wanted, he became distant, and now I want what he provided more than ever—an escape. I want that feeling back, and I don't know where else to find it, meaning Sebastian is my lifeline.

Chelsea: Hey! What's the plan for today?

I finish getting ready while I wait for a reply. I put my hair back into an I-don't-care ponytail, throw on my black hoodie over top of my black T-shirt with black skinny jeans, and that's as good as I'm going to get today. My outfit is as black as my soul.

Gia: Meet me on campus after your first class
Can't wait 2 see u gurllll

That still didn't answer my question. I don't know why people insist on making things a surprise. Is it normal for a majority of the population to agree to things they don't know about? If that's the case, I don't want to be normal.

At least I'm giving another friendship a chance. Liam has been my only friend for so long, and he became afraid to befriend other people because he was always busy babysitting me. Since I've been trying to create space between us, I miss having someone I can call at random hours. I miss him more than I ever imagined possible.

When I arrive on campus and settle on an appropriate parking spot, I make my way to the building that holds my first class. I hadn't made plans to meet Liam, but for the first time in his life, he's arrived early, and there he is waiting for me.

"Chels. Chelsea. Hey. I'm glad I caught you."

I haven't seen him since the awkward encounter with Sebastian on Monday, but I don't want to let on that anything is wrong. I'm certainly not going to admit what I did, nor the fact Sebastian has ghosted me.

"Hey Liam. How are you?" Formal is good. Formal indicates no personal details are to be shared. I'd like to know how his dad is recovering, but asking would open the door to a conversation more intimate than I can allow right now.

"I'm all right. How are things with your boyfriend?" He says "boyfriend" as if he gagged out the word.

"Oh, Sebastian is great. He's fine. Yep, everything is great."

Liam stops walking. "What's wrong? You don't look like everything is fine. You can talk to me." Concern is plastered on his face. He told me Sebastian couldn't be trusted. I am not giving him the satisfaction of being right.

"Everything is fine; honest." I try my best to lie, but I'm not very good at it. I used to think that was a good thing, but some more practice might be beneficial.

"If you say so, but you don't look okay. Only a few more days until you're legal drinking age in the States." He laughs, turning up the left side of his mouth into a goofy grin.

The last thing I want to be reminded of is the fact I've had a full twenty-one years of this miserable life. I'm desperate to end this conversation.

"Yeah, thanks. I've got to go to my class," I lie, again. If I stay here any longer, I'll expose my countless mistakes. At this moment, I can't handle being a disappointment to anyone else.

After my first class, which was so mind-numbingly boring, but not in a good way, I decide it will be my only class of the day. I walk to our predetermined meeting spot to find Gia. When I round a corner nearing the place I'm supposed to meet her, I'm shocked by what I witness. Sebastian and Gia are speaking in close proximity. Do they remember each other from the night at *The Core*? Did they know each other before? They didn't say they knew each other, so why do they look so friendly? He's not that funny, Gia.

I'm torn between walking over to them and running away, never speaking to either of them again, but my brain is only thinking about one thing—euphoria. I don't know where else to find it, and it's the only reason I have any hope of surviving the day.

My feet are moving without thinking my actions through, and Gia looks startled to see me walking their way.

They cannot be trusted.

"Hi." My approach feels awkward. I'm interrupting a private conversation.

"Hey, Doll." Sebastian leans in to give me a kiss, and I don't want to embarrass him, so I oblige, but it doesn't feel the same. My body tenses, and I hesitate at his touch.

Gia looks at me with a phony grin. I can spot a fake smile a mile away because I've been practicing them my entire life. It's one thing kindred spirits can always recognize.

"Hey, Girl," Gia chimes in. "Are you done your classes?"

"Yeah, I don't want to go any more today." I look toward Sebastian. "I already made plans with Gia today. I hadn't heard from you, so…"

"That's cool. You girls go have fun. I'll text you later, Doll." Sebastian plants a kiss on my cheek and walks away with a swagger that is both sexy and infuriating. Why am I so conflicted toward him? He's my boyfriend!

Gia stares at him as he saunters away, and I'm certain it's not to make sure he doesn't trip. When he's out of sight, she turns to me and says, "You're all mine now!" She cackles like a hyena, which causes me to stiffen.

Alarms blare in every inch of my body. The panic I am feeling can't even be numbed with narcotics. Without giving her the chance to say anything else, I shout, "Sorry, I have to go!" I take off toward the parking lot, climbing inside my SUV and lock the doors. My safe place.

While sitting behind the steering wheel, the dread eases, and my hypervigilant instincts take over. I put the car in reverse and leave the scene of my panic behind.

I return home for the day to be questioned by Zara about why I'm home so early. My response is that I'm not feeling well, so I'm going back to bed.

As soon as I reach my doorway, I strip away my clothes. I'm so embarrassed by my reaction. Bed is the only place that welcomes me.

A short time later, I hear Isla come to the door, knock gently, and ask if I'm okay. I grumble at her to go away with a sting in my voice I hadn't intended. If I wasn't so desperate to be alone, I would apologize, but that's out of the question.

Eventually, I doze off with an overwhelming desire not to wake up again.

"You're mine, now." Sal sneers.

A door closes in my face, and I'm left inside with nothing but a crack of light at the bottom, and the sound of voices on the other side. I knock as hard as my weak, sleep- and food-deprived body will allow.

"Please, let me out," I cry. "I promise I'll be good. I promise."

Nothing. No one is coming for me.

I wake up to a person sitting at the edge of my bed, leaning over me with hands on my shoulder. I'm drenched in sweat, unable to comprehend my surroundings and push the hands off of me with a force I didn't know I had.

"Chelsea! It's me!" Zara's voice invades my conscious thoughts.

"I… I'm…" I look at her down on the floor beside my bed, bringing herself back to her feet.

She dusts herself off as she stands. "It's fine, Chels. I shouldn't have tried to wake you."

"I'm sorry." Guilt pushes away the panic I was combatting. Zara didn't deserve to be assaulted. Another thing I've done wrong.

"Really, it's fine. I should have known better. I was worried about you."

My guilt morphs into anger. I'm beyond tired of everyone fawning over me. So, I had a bad dream; nothing new. I lived a bad dream for half of my life. The only reason anyone cares now is because it inconveniences them.

"Sorry if my nightmare disrupted your afternoon," I snap. "How inconsiderate of me."

Zara cocks her head to her left, raising one eyebrow, and studies me for a moment. "What is going on with you? You've been so combative and hostile these past few weeks. Tell me what's going on so we can work through it."

Perfect, missus-fix-it Zara, to the rescue again. She's always acting like she can swoop in with her magical counselling skills and heal the world. Doesn't she realize talk therapy isn't going to fix what's wrong right now? Kevin isn't going to stop to chat and try to work through our issues.

"I don't have to work through anything. I want to live my life and make my own choices. I'm sorry if they don't always match up with what *perfect* Zara, or *perfect* Zach would choose." My level of anger is irrational, and I am aware, but I've just been roused from a traumatic nightmare, and all I can focus on is saving them from living the same thing. I want to be left alone. "Leave me alone."

Zara vacates my room, looking wounded.

I deserve to be alone.

I don't even know myself. This person, cocooned in my bed, unable to function or interact with humans. What is this life I'm living? I'm sure this is supposed to be the prime of my life, and here I am, hiding in my bedroom.

Pathetic.

My phone buzzes, which is surprising. I find it hard to believe anyone still wants to speak to me. The question is, will I want to speak to them?

Liam: Chels, can we talk? I'll meet you somewhere after your class.

Well, joke's on you, Liam. I'm not in my class and have no intentions to be in the near future.

After several minutes of contemplation, I decide I won't return Liam's message. I don't know what to say. Tell him I've skipped classes all week, and don't know when I'll go back? Tell him all the ways I've screwed up lately? Tell him how badly I crave the high I have come so familiar with? Or how the only way I can tolerate myself now is if I'm buzzed or completely numb. I'm sure he'd love to hear all of that.

I have no one to talk to about everything going on, and I'm overwhelmed by how quickly my life has turned upside down. It was never smooth sailing, but since Kevin's return, it's been like trying to swim my way through a swarm of piranhas.

Zara keeps telling me I can talk to her if I need to, but if I was genuinely honest with her, she'd hate me. She'd never understand, and I'd merely be Chelsea, the perpetual letdown. That should have been my name on my birth certificate. Mother: Delilah Dixon. Father: Heinous Monster, AKA Kevin Wells. Child: Eternal Failure.

It's best I keep my issues to myself right now. It's not like anyone else can fix anything. This is my life—my problems. Meaning it's up to me to find a solution that doesn't involve Zach giving Kevin money.

I watch movies. You can't negotiate with terrorists, and that's all Kevin is. He'll keep coming back for more.

When my phone buzzes again, I assume it's Liam. I'm not sure if reality is better or worse.

Gia: What was up with you yesterday?

I had to go without you.

Oh, surprise. Another person I've disappointed. Maybe Gia should learn not to imply ownership of people in casual conversation. Common sense is subjective, but that seems like a simple concept to grasp. I don't even know where she was taking me, so if she's trying to make me feel like I've missed out, she's way off the mark.

I haven't even gotten out of bed yet and I'm already over this day. Is Thursday too early to start the weekend? Hopefully not, because it's happening. What do I do on weekends now that I'm unemployed and not doing any schoolwork? I'm not entirely sure, but it's going to include a lot of sleep, assuming my nightmares don't ruin that for me too.

Instead of facing reality, I read a book I picked up at my old job a long time ago. It's outside of my realm of what I'd normally pick up, but it had a cute dog on the cover, so I couldn't resist. It's a funny story and I appreciate it's not a romance. I can't tolerate cheesy, unrealistic expectations of the opposite sex right now. Honestly, how many billionaires with six packs really exist? And don't even get me started on the girl who is a meek virgin with supposed integrity and self-respect, unlike me, but as soon as her BDSM-obsessed boss gives her a wink, she turns into a sex kitten. I suppose I'm being bitter because these fictional stories always end up with happy endings, and I don't see that happening for me.

After a few dozen chapters, I've actually laughed a few times. It must look like I'm in a good mood when Isla comes bounding into my room to tell me Jasmine is here and I'm being summoned to make my presence known. I tell Isla I want to have a quick shower to make myself presentable. I have to try to wash away hints of my misery.

Glaring at my reflection, my usual reaction is disgust. Right now, it's anger. I hate the person looking back at me. I hate the physical similarities I see with my father. I hate the way my freckles dot my face, reminding me of my heritage. I hate the coppery colour of my hair that is a constant reminder of whom I share my genetics with. Maybe I should dye my hair dark—to match my heart.

Throwing said hair into a wet ponytail, I venture downstairs to greet my adopted aunt, who is only a few years older than me. She's essentially sunshine incarnate and I'm not sure I'll be able to cope with her intensity today.

"Hey, Chels." Jasmine greets me as I traverse down the stairs. "What's new with you?"

Oh, you know. The usual. New boyfriend, drug habit, failing out of school, unemployed, self-loathing—that part's not new. I can't say any of that, so instead I say, "Not much. How about you?"

"Same. Nothing much. I was missing you guys, so I thought I'd come up for a visit. I have events happening all weekend, so this was my only chance. The good news is, I can score you some designer goods at the end of the weekend."

I could ask Jasmine to design me a custom straight jacket. Perhaps that would be more fitting for my current situation than an evening gown I'll never wear. Something else I can't say out loud. "That would be great. Thanks."

We sit around the coffee table, chatting about nothing of substance. I would have preferred to finish my book.

"How are your classes going?" Jasmine asks, out of the blue.

Ah shucks. I thought we'd get through this day without addressing anything relevant. Again, I force myself to lie; practice makes perfect. I must have improved by now. "They're fine."

"You didn't have any classes today?" She's fishing and looks interested in my answer.

"I decided not to go. I only had one lecture today, so I figured I'd stay home and work on other stuff." She doesn't need to know what that other stuff was. Hopefully she assumes I mean a term paper or assignment.

I don't even know how I'm going to go back to classes. I've fallen so far behind; I doubt I could ever catch up. Especially when my mind is not focused on it anymore. There was a time when I put one hundred percent of my effort into succeeding in my classes, trying to block out my endless internal dialogue. Since Kevin's re-emergence in my life, school is not my focus. My future is not even my focus; I'm merely getting through each day.

Maybe if I'm medicated, or at least inebriated, I could function like a semi-normal person, but I doubt that would help my academic pursuits.

I excuse myself from the living room under the guise I have work to complete, when in reality, I'm heading back to my bed so I can finish my book. I've done all the socializing I can manage today. It's like my brain is reenacting Lord of the Flies, starring my very own Beelzebub.

Lying in my cloud-like bed, I text Sebastian because I can't afford to burn that bridge.

Chelsea: Hey. Can I come see you?

It only takes a few minutes before he replies.

Sebastian: Ya Doll. This weekend come over.

I'm not sure what his plans are for the weekend, but I'm not about to confess to him it's my birthday. That's another day I hate with great intensity, because any reminder of the day my mother died at my expense is not something I'm going to celebrate. If she had survived, my life would have been so different.

There's only one thing I'm certain of today: my future's uncertain.

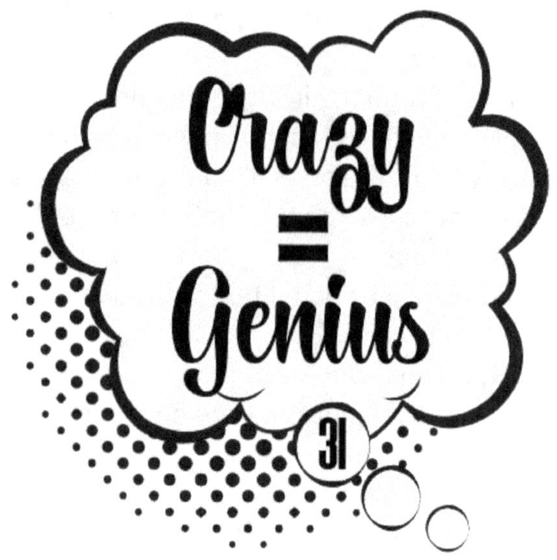

early every Friday night for the past several years, Liam has joined my family for dinner and either a movie or games. We have welcomed him as an honorary family member because his parents work a lot and he's an only child. He fit in seamlessly from his first visit, and that's never changed over the years. With our strained relationship as of late, I'm not expecting him to come tonight. He hasn't been over since before his dad's heart attack.

I keep trying to push him away. I want to keep him at a distance for his own benefit, but selfishly, I don't recognize my life without him in it. Besides the people I share this home with, Liam has been my one mainstay.

Even though it's before dinnertime, it's already dark outside. When I see headlights light up our gated entrance, the conflicted feelings I'm having amplify. I want him here, but I want him far away. I want my friend, but I'm not deserving of his time. I want to feel like I have someone on my side, but I can't justify putting him at risk. It's already eating away at me that Kevin knows where I live, putting my family in danger.

I meander downstairs, but Liam has already made his way inside by the time I get there. Isla is his biggest fan, so she and Bond have welcomed Liam with their traditional song and dance—Isla providing the twenty-questions soundtrack while Bond performs the tail-wagging dance.

"Hey," I greet with a pathetic wave. I don't know how he could even look at me right now. He's so good at reading me, he probably knows everything I'm thinking before I do.

Liam looks up from his position, scratching Bond's ears. "Hey, you." The grin Liam directs at me helps me release some of the tension from my shoulders. "You never answered my text."

Just like that, my shoulders draw back up toward my ears as the tension returns. I don't have a suitable response for him—not a true one, anyway. "I had a lot to get done."

Standing from his optimal ear-scratching position, Liam steps toward me. "That's all right. I was worried you were angry with me again. You kind of ran away from me the other day."

I recall my encounter with Liam before the catastrophe with Gia on Wednesday. Trying to cover up my own mistakes is exhausting, but the last thing I want is for him to know the truth. He'd be disgusted with me.

"Sorry. I'm not mad." To avoid looking at him, I stare at my slippers. "I don't know what to tell you."

"What do you mean? What do you want to tell me?" He steps even closer.

"Nothing. There's nothing to tell," I blurt. There's nothing to arouse suspicion like a rushed denial.

Zach enters the room, interrupting our awkward conversation. "Liam, my man." He welcomes Liam with their trademark back-slap-hug move, distracting him long enough I can evade the discussion that was headed in a direction I didn't want it to take.

I escape into the kitchen, where Zara works to put the finishing touches on dinner. "Can I help with anything?"

Our last few conversations haven't been loving exchanges, so I'm not sure how she'll reply.

"You want to help?" She makes no effort to hide her surprise.

"I can, if you need me to." No, I don't want to, but I'd rather appear like I'm unable to talk because I'm busy than outright avoiding a discussion.

"I don't know how to contain your enthusiasm."

"I don't have to help." My irritation is obvious now.

"Wow, Chels. It was a joke. Here, chop these vegetables." She spins around so her back is facing me. "You don't even have to do it enthusiastically."

After dinner, Liam and Zach finish clean up, as is their custom. I listen to Isla chat Zara's ear off about something to do with a new book she's reading. She's even more of a bookworm than I am, but our tastes are vastly different.

"What do you think, Chels?" Zara asks.

I should have been paying attention, but my thoughts are far away from whatever Isla's reading. "About what?"

Isla sighs like she is embracing pre-teen life. "About me being an author someday."

"Sure. Yeah. Whatever you want."

"Chelsea." Zara directs an uncharacteristic glare at me. "She was really excited to tell you about her dream."

"And?"

"And." She jolts her head forward, shooting me dagger eyes. "You could be a little more supportive."

"She's twelve. She'll change her mind another two hundred times before she settles on a career. I'm not going to throw a party each time." As the words were coming out of my mouth, I didn't mean for them to sound as cold as they did, but making people angry is my specialty now. In order to prevent the conversation going any further, I get up to leave.

"What is your problem lately?"

My problem is, I'm sober. My *problem* is that nothing in the world can compete with the bliss I find at the bottom of a plastic baggie. "My problem is that I can't do anything right, but I'm supposed to celebrate every decision Isla makes. Sure. My apologies." I turn away and walk upstairs, seeking the haven of my bedroom.

Closing my bathroom door, I rummage through the drawer containing my skincare items, removing what I need. Before I can set myself up to chase a high, a knock comes on the bathroom door. For a brief second, I panic, not knowing who is on the other side, but a smooth, deep voice lets me know who's there.

"Big Red. Are you okay?"

Am I okay? Why is he checking on me? "I'll be out in a second." I tuck my vice back in the drawer inside an empty makeup compact, splash some water on my face, and open the door to enter my bedroom.

Liam is seated backwards on my desk chair, and it reminds me of all the times we sat there together, studying and talking about music, movies, books, and life. I miss those days when things were simpler.

"You good?" He pins me with a look that might have worked before I lost all hope for my future. Before I felt anything other than a desire to get high and chase everyone I love away.

"Yeah. Good."

"What was that all about, then?"

"Ugh. Not you too."

"Me too, what, Chels? Asking why you've blown up at your family over an innocent conversation? Was there anything wrong with supporting your little sister's dream?"

"I wasn't unsupportive."

"Really?

"Fine, I'll apologize."

"I didn't come up to tell you to apologize. I came up to figure out what's going on with you, but I think I know."

"Oh, you do? Please enlighten me, because as far as I'm aware, I'm still the same Chelsea."

"How long have you been using?"

I freeze but try to play off my startled reaction. "Using what?"

"Whatever it is, you've been killing yourself with. Pot? No, you're too angry. Coke makes more sense, but I don't want to believe you'd be that stupid."

"Stupid? I'm stupid?"

"I don't know, Chels. Are you?"

"Screw you, Liam. You don't get to come into my room and accuse me of things, call me stupid, and expect me to respond."

He pauses for a second. "I didn't call you stupid. If you recall, I said I don't want to *believe* you'd be that stupid. But your reaction gives me an answer."

He's right. I ratted myself out without saying as much.

"I don't know what you want me to say. I'm trying to survive. I don't even know how to do *that* right."

He stands from his chair, making his way closer to me. "You lean on the people who are there for you. Don't run into the arms of someone who is only making it worse."

It comes back to Sebastian again.

"What's your problem with Sebastian? Why do you hate him so much?"

Liam takes a breath long enough he deflates like a *Loony Toon*. "I don't trust him, Chels. And clearly, he hasn't been a good influence. He's not helping you navigate hard things—he's making things harder."

One thing I have learned in all my years of counselling is that I can't blame anyone else for my choices. Sure, my father may have screwed me up for life. Despite that, my choices are my own. I'm responsible for my decisions, and I'm handling things the best way I can. I need some help to have any joy in my life, and Sebastian is providing that.

"Sebastian isn't making choices for me. I am. You can't hold it against him."

"Chels." Liam takes a moment to lift and inspect the photo of the two of us inside a colourful mosaic frame sat on my bedside table. "I remember this day. You were so happy." He places the photo back in its designated spot. "I respect the fact you want to take responsibility, but sometimes other people are to blame, Chels. When others exploit weaknesses and manipulate people, that's on them."

"I'm not being manipulated!" I retreat into defence-mode. "First, you *imply* I am stupid, and now you're saying I'm weak. If you came up here to give me a pep-talk, you've failed miserably."

"Chelsea!" Liam's firm voice demonstrates his frustration—something that virtually never happens. "I am not trying to pep-talk you, and I'm not insulting you. If you'd listen, you'd hear I care about you, and I'm trying to make it clear you have people in your corner; people who want what's best for you."

"What I need is to forge my own path; even if you don't agree." What I need is for everyone to give me space until they're not in danger anymore.

I might not be making choices everyone thinks are best, but I know what I need to do next.

Liam heads home after our heated conversation, and I prepare myself to do what I think is a logical next step. I am officially dropping out of college. I email the administration office informing them of my choice, hopeful they won't put the effort into calling me to change my mind. I don't know what implications dropping out will have on my future employment opportunities, but at this stage in my life, I'm not capable of handling the pressures of school.

The compounding stresses of attending classes on campus knowing Kevin could appear at any time, the assignments, the study, the financial aspect—I can't do it. My mind isn't committed to it, and I'm convinced this is the right next move.

Tomorrow I'll officially be Chelsea Haynes, the unemployed, cocaine-addicted college dropout. Each day gets me a step closer to hell, and there's no getting out.

It's a good thing I had some practice before now on how to maintain the impression I'm going to classes so Zara doesn't ask questions. It's been three weeks since I submitted my withdrawal from school, and as luck would have it, I received an email stating I will get a partial refund on my tuition for the upcoming winter semester.

There aren't many places to escape to during the day where I can hang out for hours and not look suspicious, so I've been going to the Orillia Library. If anyone checks the mileage on my car, they should still assume I'm going to classes. Until I get that refund, I have little money left, and my "job" working with Zara was short-lived, so I can't justify asking them for anything. The library offers free entertainment, and the building is large enough I feel safe there.

I haven't seen Kevin since our encounter outside of the casino, so I am hopeful he's done something stupid to get himself arrested again.

As I'm sitting in my usual corner on the main floor, my phone buzzes in my bag.

Liam: Can we meet up? I don't like how we left things. I need to know you're okay, Chels.

Nope. I don't want to resolve anything because he'll think we're good, and he'll keep trying to fix things in my life he can't fix. As much as his absence is killing me, I need him to be safe more than I need a friend.

I drift off from the fictional world I had been absorbed in, thinking about the last conversation Liam and I had. His words put a lot of uncertainty in my already doubt-filled mind. I've spent hours analyzing and re-analyzing the initial interactions I had with Sebastian, and he was suspiciously friendly for a stranger. I can't help but wonder if that was because he was attracted to me, or if there was another reason to explain his cordiality.

I don't know if our encounter was typical for people our age. Isn't it normal for guys to hit on a girl and pursue her? Does Liam think I'm not worth Sebastian's pursuit, or *is* Sebastian manipulating me?

This is why fictional worlds are ideal. Even if everything goes to hell, who cares? But James Bond always gets the bad guy. Jason Bourne always defeats the corrupt government. Sandra Bullock always gets the guy. Fiction is easier to navigate.

My phone buzzes again and I'm reluctant to check it, but curiosity wins out.

Sebastian: Hey Doll. You coming over?

I was supposed to go to Sebastian's on the weekend, but I couldn't come up with an excuse to get out of the house without raising suspicion. I need a refill, though, and since Sebastian is my illegal pharmacist, going to see him sounds like a good idea.

Chelsea: Yeah. What time?

When Sebastian replies, inviting me over now, I jump at the chance, so I won't be getting home unreasonably late. Any opportunity to avoid questioning, I'll take it.

Trudging through the freshly fallen snow, I arrive back at my SUV, climb in and drive off to find my fix. The question is, what will I have to do to receive it?

Sebastian greets me at the door with a smile as enthusiastic as Mona Lisa and ushers me inside. "Hey, Doll."

I return his greeting with an equal level of warmth, which rivals the temperature outside. "Hi." I don't want him to be angry with me, so I suck up my pettiness and try again. "Thanks for texting me. Sorry I couldn't come by on the weekend."

"That's all right. I kept myself occupied."

I shudder, thinking about what he did to entertain himself, but I try to move forward.

He cannot be trusted.

Getting to the point, I ask, "Do you have any..."

He sighs, stopping me from finishing my sentence. "I do. But I was hoping you'd give me something first."

That's what I was afraid of. Since I gave in the first time, why wouldn't I do it again? And again? My stomach churns at the thought, and I consider how badly I need a fix.

Badly.

If I have to choose between the lesser of two evils, sex with Sebastian is less bad than being sober. I consider how I can meet my own needs before I meet his. "Can I have a hit first? It makes everything more intense."

He grabs my hand, leading me to his bedroom and after digging in his familiar drawer, he passes me what I need.

I walk into the bathroom, staring at the white powder in front of me, and wonder how I've gotten to this point. Staring at the line on the counter, moments pass before I accept the reality of my life—the never-ending fear and impending danger; the internal battle raging constantly; repeatedly disappointing people. Nothing good. I contemplate flushing the powder and walking out, but the relief I'm craving is too appealing. I don't have the willpower to discard it because I need something good, even if it's fleeting.

Emerging from the bathroom, Sebastian is sprawled out on his bed, and he is gorgeous; yet I feel no attraction to him. I'm drawn to him by necessity.

He pats the bed beside him, calling me over, and a wave of nausea consumes me. I run back into the bathroom, vomiting violently. It does little to reduce the curdled stomach feeling overpowering me, so I stay put for a few moments until my happy dust starts to work efficiently. I know the clock is ticking to get this over with before my high wears off, so I rinse my mouth with water and exit the bathroom again. If my panic-induced vomiting could knock it off, that would be helpful.

"You good?" Sebastian asks, and I'm pleased he's showing a hint of concern. The last time he saw me throw up at the *Panic! At The Disco* concert, he acted like I had the Black Plague.

"Yeah. Sorry. Just too much at once."

"Rookie move." He laughs. "Are you going to deliver?" he asks, licking his full lips.

I hate myself right now. I asked for one thing and agreed to provide another in return. Rationalizing giving my body in exchange for drugs is not something I ever expected I'd do, but here I am. I nod as I slowly walk toward him.

"I'm not crazy about vomit breath, so don't kiss me."

Well, that's setting the mood for romance. I roll my eyes and resign myself to the fact this is happening.

"Wait. You're not pregnant, are you?" The horror in Sebastian's face is mirroring my own. I know I'm not, but I decide to torment him for a few minutes. Maybe he'll give up on sex if he's afraid of knocking me up.

"Oh, uh. I don't know. I mean, I guess it's possible." I sit on the edge of the bed for a front-row seat to his reaction. Cocaine is making this more entertaining for me than it is for him. I've never had the confidence to prank someone before.

"It's not mine, is it?"

"You *are* my boyfriend. Who else's would it be?" I suppress a laugh.

He runs his hands through his long hair, which he has released from the captivity of his manbun. "We never said we were exclusive. I don't know if you're seeing someone else."

Wow. Not what I expected. "If you're my boyfriend—which *you* were the one to point out to me—does that not imply exclusivity? Isn't that how these things work?"

"Not if we didn't say we're exclusive. It's not like I proposed."

Now I'm ticked. My Irish temper rarely hits full throttle, but right now, it's about to. "Are you kidding me? Of course, we're supposed to be exclusive, Sebastian! I'm not a damn whore."

"Are you sure?" He raises his eyebrows at me, and I can't even argue with him.

What do you call someone who exchanges sex for drugs? Someone who runs into the arms of a man every logical part of her brain—of which there aren't many—tells her to run from?

"I'm not pregnant." What was supposed to be a joke backfired horribly.

"You're not? Seriously?"

"Yes, Sebastian. I'm sure. I'm not pregnant."

"Oh, good." His chest falls several inches as he relaxes. "I'm not against practicing, but I'm not ready to settle down or have a kid."

He pulls me back to lie on the bed beside him. As he carries on taking what he expects from me, my mind is a million miles away. If he isn't ready to settle down, why did he want to be my boyfriend? If he doesn't want to be exclusive, why did he give us a title? Had he told me before, I wouldn't have sold my virginity for drugs in order to keep him happy. If he had told me this sooner, I wouldn't be so consumed with shame, I try to burn my skin off in the shower to dull the emotional pain. Why would he do this?

When Sebastian has achieved his own release, my high is disappearing, and my self-loathing is raging. I lie beside him, not as a lover, but as a sinner, and I have no one I can confess to.

After my conversation with Sebastian last week, during the joke that went horribly wrong, I started thinking about what my life will look like in the future. The thing is, I don't see a future at all. I can only imagine the potential for things to go wrong, and how miserable I'll be in one, three, or twenty years. Why would I want to put myself through that?

When I was adopted, I thought things were going to turn around for me. I was foolish enough to think, after a few years of things going well and moving forward, that things wouldn't come crashing down around me at some point.

My former Thursday schedule called for classes until three in the afternoon, so I'm sitting in a coffee shop near Sebastian's house, contemplating texting him or staying here alone. He's my source of euphoria, so I'm trying my best to keep him from having a reason to be upset with me. In order to do that, I try my best to be a girlfriend he'd want to keep around.

Chelsea: Hey. Want to meet me at the café by your place?

I continue reading my book, sipping my lukewarm coffee when I receive a reply.

Sebastian: Not today Doll. Busy with work.

I'm still not sure what his "work" is, but I don't have the guts to ask. I'm confident I know exactly how a guy buys a house straight out of high school, maintains irregular work hours and a steady supply of narcotics. It doesn't take a rocket scientist to draw a reasonable conclusion.

Resigning myself to the fact I'll remain alone, sitting in a booth composed of red pleather bench seats and a wobbly table in the corner of the café, a chime of the door sets me on edge. That's not an unusual feeling, but I know this is different.

Grabbing my puffy coat, which I had taken off and set beside me, and throwing my book in my purse, I ready myself to make a mad dash. I don't get the chance. A body slides into the bench seat beside me, trapping me against the window. I'm frozen.

I read a book about some animals using tonic immobility as a method to escape when they've been captured by a predator. It's essentially playing dead but remaining alert. I consider trying it when my predator speaks.

"Funny finding you here, dear daughter."

This was no accident. He's been following me. How else would he know where I am?

Should I scream? No. I can't. The teenagers at the counter wouldn't be any help, and I'm not about to put them in harm's way. They're working to save up for a college education that will likely land them right back where they've started with a mountain of debt and higher stress levels. Despite that, they deserve the opportunity to try.

"How did you find me here?" I stare at my coffee cup, clinging to it to steady my shaking hands.

"You've underestimated me, Chelsea. The only reason you're still roaming the streets is because I'm giving you the chance to reconsider my offer."

I know what offer he's talking about, but I play dumb. "What offer would that be?"

He swivels in his seat, his khaki pants rubbing against the material of the bench, squeaking beneath him. Even his seat is crying for help.

"Let me talk to your dear 'dad', and I'm sure we can come up with a number to make me disappear. You can go back to living your normal life, playing 'happy family' with *The Brady Bunch*."

I've made some poor decisions lately; I'm aware. But I am not foolish enough to think Kevin would take money one time and disappear forever.

"That's never going to happen, Kevin." I'm facing toward the window, not wanting to look at him. If for no other reason than because I hate seeing how much I resemble him. "You're not getting anything from my family."

"Little girl. You're forgetting *I* am your family. I gave you life, and I can take it away." He chuckles, and it's the most concerning sound he's made, yet. "I won't though, because I can do things that are so much worse."

"I'm well aware. You may have forgotten my childhood, but I haven't." I shouldn't be sassing the man, but I detest his existence so much, it happens without conscious effort.

He leans in closer to me and whispers, "It would be a shame if you didn't cooperate. Your cute little blonde sister would make a decent replacement if you don't want to play my game."

Those words are everything I was afraid of coming to fruition. I knew there was no boundary he wouldn't cross to get what he wanted. I *knew* my presence would put them in danger.

"No. You can't touch her. She has nothing to do with me." There's no hiding the fear in my voice now. The thought of Isla living through what I did, especially after everything she's already dealt with, is too much. I can't catch my breath. Not Isla. I can't let that happen. "Please."

I turn toward the employees behind the counter, and two of them are looking at me. Trying to communicate with them wordlessly through my best pleading eyes, I issue a silent cry for help. I shouldn't expect anything different, but they turn away and resume their regular duties, giggling between them. That's the reaction I've become accustomed to over the years. Strangers don't want to get involved. It's easier to laugh at someone's misfortune than lend a hand, but again, they're young and can't do much to help. It's not as though a middle-aged man sitting next to his female doppelgänger is raising any major red flags.

"It's up to you, Chelsea. Get me what I want, or I'll find another way."

I have to get his attention off of Isla. There's no way I will allow her to pay for my poor ancestry. "I don't even like my family, and I'm sure they hate me, too. You know, since that's how any family treats me. They're not paying anything and hurting the girl won't solve anything." I force those words out, gasping for air, but trying to maintain a modicum of composure to hide my bald-faced lie. I'm desperate to keep my family safe.

"You think I'm stupid? I know more than you can imagine. Your friend, the black guy with the silver car. I don't see him around much anymore. Lover's quarrel?"

This is so much worse than I imagined. I tried so hard to keep Liam away, and still, he ends up in Kevin's crosshairs. I should let him take me. Whatever I have to do, I will do it.

"I'll go with you. Do whatever you want with me, but don't hurt anyone else." I speak my words into the birch-laminate table before me, because I refuse to look at Kevin's face when he realizes he's won. Trading the people I love for someone I hate is the only solution I can think of.

Kevin stands, and I lower my head in defeat. I can't escape the horror that is my life.

"Not today. I'll give you some more time to reconsider my offer." He leans in so his hot, scotch breath blows on my neck. "Don't, for one second, think I'm going to go away. I will get what I need from you. One way or another." He turns slowly, walking to the exit. I'm left sitting in the booth, fighting back tears.

That was all of my worst nightmares laid out before me, and I don't even know how to process it. I want to call Liam, or Zach, or even Zara, but I can't. They'll tell me to go to the police, and I know that's an exercise in futility. Nothing against the police, but what exactly are they going to do if I tell them my biological father came and sat beside me in a coffee shop? I have no way to prove what he said.

Getting up from my seat and gathering my belongings, I steady my jelly legs and approach the same exit Kevin used moments earlier.

I parked in the lot as near to the doors as possible, so I scan my surroundings before running to the safety of my trusty SUV. When I lock the doors from the inside, I finally break down. This is too much.

Not knowing what other option I have, I seek the only escape I can find. I need a moment of peace in my mind before I can figure out what to do moving forward.

f I'm not high, I'm low, and I don't know how to cope with that anymore. I can't confide in anyone about what Kevin threatened yesterday. I've shut myself in my bedroom, refusing to eat, socialize or function until I can come up with a different solution. He should have taken me. I'd be well and truly living a hell I never wanted to return to, but at least I'd know the people I care about weren't suffering on my behalf.

From my plush armchair by my window, I have my feet up on an ottoman. A coppery tang hits the back of my throat, and when I pull myself upright, I sniffle and swipe my nose with my sleeve, discovering streaks of blood across my arm. It takes a second for my dulled senses to realize what's happening. Nosebleed.

I enter my bathroom, positioning myself over the sink and reaching for the nearest baby blue hand towel to press to my face. I spit the blood that has trickled into my mouth, which causes spatter of blood to cover my white sink and countertop.

In my haste to clean it off, I remove the towel from my nose and the blood pours out. It's no longer dripping. I lift the towel back to hold it in place under my nose with my face tilted forward so I don't have blood running into my mouth.

Isla chimes in from my bathroom doorway, "Chels. Are you okay?"

"I'm fine. Leave me alone, Isla. I don't need you pestering me right now."

The hurt on her face would have once bothered me, but I've become immune to the disappointment I bring to others.

After fifteen minutes, I'm struggling to stay upright, leaning over the sink. My bathroom looks like someone slaughtered a deer.

I hear another set of footsteps striding across my room. I swear, if it's Isla coming back…

"Sweetheart, what's happening? Oh, gosh!" Zara's voice rings in my ears. She's not helping matters.

"Just a nosebleed. It's under control."

"Under control? Chelsea, it looks like you're on the verge of bleeding to death."

Maybe today will be our lucky day.

"I wouldn't be that lucky," I mutter. "It's fine, Zara. I'm waiting for it to stop."

"How did this happen? Did you hit your nose on something? Should I get ice?"

"No. Just let me deal with it. I don't need you fawning over me, and honestly, I'll handle it myself." The harshness I exude makes Zara cringe. I see tears spring from the corners of her eyes. The last thing I want is for her to cry.

"It seems you want to handle everything by yourself lately, Chels. You're doing a bang-up job, huh?" Zara's trademark polite demeanour has shifted to an angry mother.

"What's that supposed to mean?"

"It means you've spent the last few months shutting us out and taking offence at everything we do to help you."

I absorb her words for a moment before my anger spews out. "Leave me alone. I don't need your help, okay? I appreciate what you guys did by taking me in, but I'm an adult now. It's time you treat me like one."

"No, Chelsea. It's time you act like one." Zara crosses her arms as she leans back on the doorframe. A muscle in her jaw tics and I know she's clenching her mouth shut to stop from saying anything else. Unsuccessfully. "You want to be treated like an adult, Chelsea? Then behave like one. Take responsibility for your actions and try to do better. Grow, learn. If you don't like something, work toward changing it. Don't go around making your little sister cry because she was worried about you."

So that's what this is about. She isn't worried about me. She was coming to give me a piece of her mind for making Isla upset. Not surprising.

"Well, forgive me if I don't appreciate people coming into my space uninvited." I offer back a glare to Zara, hoping she will get the point.

Zara shifts her weight forward so she is no longer leaning on the doorframe. I take it as a sign she's understood my message and is going to leave. She does not.

"Whatever is going on with you, you better sort it out. If you don't want to talk to us, or to Liam, find *someone* to talk to. You're slowly pushing away everyone who loves you, and that's not a road you want to go down."

Convenient. "So, you're telling me your love is conditional on how closely I live my life according to what you want? Ha! That's not love. That's forced obligation."

Zara groans and shakes her head. "I'm going to cut this conversation now because you're hearing what you want to hear. When you're ready to talk civilly, without attacking everything I say, you know where to find me." She turns and walks out of my sight.

In the meantime, my nosebleed has stopped, but my nose is tender. I shuffle through my drawers looking for some pain medication and find some acetaminophen. The throbbing in my nose and pounding of my head lead me to take three tablets.

I wipe down my counter and sink with disinfectant, but the smell makes me nauseous, so I decide to leave it for later. It's my bathroom, anyway. It won't bother anyone else.

As I return to my bedroom, I notice I got blood on my white fabric chair. I don't want to deal with that now, so I throw a cardigan over it I had thrown on the floor days earlier. Ignorance is bliss. Not that I'd know anything about bliss.

I pull my bloodied grey T-shirt over my head, tossing it on the floor behind me, and exchange it for an oversized black sleep shirt. Dress for the job you want.

Upon waking, I'm unsure what time it is, nor how long I slept. All I know is I'm still tired and whoever knocked on my bedroom door is not in my good books right now.

"Chelsea, come downstairs in five minutes. We need to talk." Zach's voice radiates authority through the door. I have half a mind to tell him to sod off, but I am well aware of how protective he is of Zara and Isla. He probably wants to express his anger with me for earlier.

I drag my duvet off, immediately assaulted by the cool air outside of my warm bed and brace myself for another grilling. I'm so unenthused about the conversation, I don't brush my hair or teeth, and walk down in the same clothes I slept in—if you can even call them clothes.

As I march down the stairs with a stomp-volume to let my irritation well known, I'm greeted by three faces of the three people I once relied on. Zach, Zara, and Liam.

"What is he doing here?" My question is directed at Zach, but I focus my eyes on Liam.

"Sit down, Chelsea." Zach's words are not a suggestion.

My bravado has disappeared because I know Liam wouldn't be here for Zach to have a family conversation.

It's been a few weeks since I saw Liam last, and after the revelation he had last time he was here, I didn't think he'd want to be around me again. That's what I was hoping for.

Zach and Zara are seated on the couch, so I drop into a chair that matches the one Liam is seated in. We're separated by a small table with a lamp and a family photo. One from once upon a time when we were relatively happy.

Zach starts the conversation once I'm seated. "So, Liam has some concerns, Chelsea. And I have to admit, I'm inclined to believe him."

"What concerns?" Again, I speak to Zach, but I'm trying to burn a hole through Liam's forehead with my eyes.

"He believes you've started using drugs. And based on your behaviour lately, it makes sense."

I scoff. Then sniffle. Not helping my case.

"The question is," he continues, "are you willing to be honest with us and explain what's going on?"

I sit silently with anger burning in my belly.

"Chelsea, we want to help. If you've turned to drugs, we can help you through it," Zara adds, with her typical tears for effect.

Zach uncrosses his legs and leans forward, placing his elbows on his knees, head in his hands. "I know the past few months have been rough on you, Chels. We won't judge you if you've found your own way to cope. But"—he sighs and rubs his hands over his face—"this is not the best way to deal with whatever you're feeling."

He's right, but the escape I get from coke is the only thing keeping me from losing it. This is the opportunity I needed to distance myself from them.

I find my voice to say, "So, that's it, huh? Guilty until proven innocent? You're not even going to wait for me to confirm or deny? Just take Liam's word for it?" No one else is willing to speak, so I do. "It's fine. You've already made your mind up about me. You assume the worst because I *am* the worst. I get it."

Zara tries to interrupt, but I raise my hand and continue saying what I need to say. I need to push them away. "It's obvious I've been nothing but an inconvenience since the day you signed on the dotted line. Let me make it easy for you." I stand from my chair, looking down at each of them. "I'm moving out."

All three of the other participants in this conversation stand in outrage and start talking over each other. They're each telling me to "calm down," or "don't be rash."

This is not a rushed decision, though. I've spent months trying to hit the threshold that would make this decision easier.

It's not clear if by this point, I have to keep them safe from Kevin, or from me.

As I stuff what clothing and essentials I want to take with me into my bag, Zach, Zara, and Liam are nagging, begging, trying to make me reconsider. I made up my mind, and I hate that I can't explain to them why things have to be this way. This is the final straw I've been grasping for. My excuse to push them away for good.

I've already texted Sebastian to ask if I can stay with him. Given that everyone else I know is in this room, my options are limited until I can get another job. My future prospects looked a lot worse once upon a time, and I survived. It's doubtful I'll have the same luck twice, but at least I'll know the people I love are safe.

"Chelsea, please reconsider. We're trying to help." Zara pleads with me from beside my desk.

"I've had enough of everyone's help." I continue to stuff clothing in the large duffel bag that will contain all of my earthly possessions by the time I leave here. It's difficult to pack everything up and fend off the arguments simultaneously, but the sooner I get out of here, the sooner they'll be safe.

"You're being irrational, Chels," Liam adds his oh-so-helpful opinion.

"Liam. I'm making this decision because of you. Because you couldn't keep your nose out of my business. When I walk out this door, I don't want to see you again. Ever." I hate the words as they come out of my mouth. It breaks my heart knowing I might push him to the point we can never return from. But I'd rather he be alive and happy without me than in danger with me.

I zip up my bag with enough force, I'm surprised the zipper doesn't rip off in my hand, and throw the strap over my shoulder, tilting from the weight. It's a mystery how a bundle of cotton can be so heavy. I brace myself to say the last words I'll utter before making my decision final. "I appreciate that you took me in when I had no one. I'm sorry for all the trouble I caused you." Without another look, I walk through my bedroom door, down the stairs, through the garage, and drive into the darkness.

My nerves are on edge as I pull into Sebastian's driveway behind his snow-dusted Honda Accord coupe. I've been sober since I had my nosebleed earlier, and I need to fix that. I'm grateful Sebastian is letting me stay here with him—mostly because he has unlimited access to what I really want right now.

His walkway is snow-covered, so I trudge through toward the door, and before I have the chance to knock, it swings open. Standing there is the handsome face of the man who turned my world upside down. One man, anyway. I don't know where I'd be if he hadn't chased Kevin away months ago or if I hadn't replied to his email. This is one of those moments where hindsight is twenty-twenty. I may have been better off if Kevin strangled me.

This is home now. At least for the time being, until I figure out which direction my life will go in from here. I'm reeling from my blow up with Zach, Zara, and Liam. Right now, I need something to ease my mind and calm me down.

I walk into Sebastian's living room, removing my boots and placing them on the mat beside the door. Like a gentleman—uncharacteristic of him—Sebastian offers to hang my coat and carry my bag for me. I'm reluctant to let him take my belongings because I don't want him to assume I'm moving in and we're going to shack up like a married couple. I was hoping I could have my own room because I often need my space, but I don't want to offend him by articulating that; nor do I want to explain why. He doesn't need to be privy to all of my random quirks.

To my dismay, Sebastian heaves my duffel bag onto his shoulder with a grimace. "What have you packed, Doll? The dog?"

I'm going to miss that dog. I'm going to miss everyone.

"It's clothes and bathroom stuff. No creatures. I promise."

Sebastian nods toward the stairs for me to follow him. He turns right in the hallway, directing us both to the master bedroom. I need to speak up. But I can't.

I worry if I tell him I don't want to share a room, he's going to kick me out, and I don't have a backup plan. I stay silent. Keeping him happy is necessary for my survival.

When we enter the bedroom, Sebastian drops my bag and turns to kiss me, pushing me against the wall. The forcefulness catches me off guard, and I try to pull away.

"What's wrong, Doll?"

"Noth... nothing. Sorry. You surprised me."

"You better brace yourself for a lot of surprises, because with you living here, I'm not going to be able to keep my hands off of you. I own you now."

I stand with my back to the wall, opening and closing my fists at my sides to regain feeling in my numbed hands. My heart is pounding in my chest, my entire body is trembling, and my stomach is threatening to rip its way out of my torso.

"I have to use the bathroom," I blurt, running from the room to the bathroom down the hall. I close the door, which makes me uneasy, but it's the lesser of two evils.

My reflection is unrecognizable as Chelsea Haynes. Staring back is Chelsea Wells. Daughter of a demon. I see Kevin. His eyes, his hair, his freckles, his nose, and his chin. I see the spawn of a monster. A succubus.

I've done the right thing by freeing my family of my presence. They're good people; the best. This is the only reasonable solution to an impossible situation. It's time I accept my new reality.

I need a hit. I'm tired of feeling.

Sebastian isn't in the bedroom when I set out in search of him. I breathe a sigh of relief. His voice directs me to the kitchen, so I tiptoe along, not wanting to interrupt him.

"She's here. I've got…"

I trip over the leg on a dining room chair, drawing his attention.

"I have to go." He looks at me with dark eyes. Those aren't eyes of lust, though. Those eyes look angry. "Doll. Can I help you with something?" The coldness in his tone sends a shiver up my spine. Is he mad I brushed him off earlier? I have to fix this or I'm going to end up homeless. He needs to be happy with me.

"Can you help me?"

"What do you mean, help?"

"I need help to relax, Sebastian. Do you have anything?" I employ my lacklustre seduction techniques to increase my chances of him saying yes. I'm desperate to avoid feeling. Today has been emotional, and I'm ready for everything to stop.

He strides forward, sweeping my hair from in front of my shoulder and cradling the back of my neck with his hand.

He cannot be trusted.

I tamp down the fear rising inside me. This is my overly paranoid brain reacting the same way it always does. He has done nothing to justify me being afraid. I'm being unreasonably skeptical. Deep breath.

All the while I'm having my internal battle, Sebastian has been taking a tour of my body with his hands. I should be appreciating the stud in front of me. The man who wants me. Of all the girls he could choose, he picked me to be his girlfriend and allowed me to live with him. That has to be worth something. I *need* to keep him happy. My internal pep-talk does little to relax me.

"Sebastian..."

He leans in to kiss me and I don't have the option to finish my sentence. But I need a hit. I pull my face away, which is met with a deep groan.

"Sebastian. Please."

His clenched jaw and narrowed eyes tell me I've messed up again. What can I do to make this right? Why do I screw everything up?

"Yeah, yeah. I'll get you some coke. I can tell that's all you really want," he snarls. Dropping his hand from under my shirt, he spins on his heel and stomps toward the bedroom. "Might as well come and get it. You're going to have to start paying me soon. I can't support an addict."

Have I officially reached addict status? What's the threshold? I know I've been doing it every day, but these have been exceptional circumstances. I've had a lot going on in my life, and nothing else helps to numb the big feelings I can't deal with. What else am I meant to do?

Whatever the answer to that is, I don't have it right now. So I go with the answer I'm familiar with. Euphoria.

Two weeks of living with Sebastian, I have yet to contact Zach, Zara, or Liam, although they've each tried calling multiple times every day. Zara's last text message was clear.

Zara: Sweetheart, please answer. I'm never giving up on you. I love you.

That's what scares me. She'll hold a candle for me far longer than I deserve.

My work options are few and the little money I had saved is dwindling. Sebastian has made it clear I can't stay with him for free—not that I'd expect him to support me. It's time for me to get my act together and accomplish something more than making white powder disappear.

I'm forcing myself to get out of the house today and going to the grocery store. Preparing dinner for Sebastian when he comes home might help improve his mood toward me. I'm feeling like more of a burden to him than I ever have in my life—

and that's quite an accomplishment. He's been short with me, spending all day out, doing whatever he does, and coming home to eat and make love to me. Is it still making love if he's not in love with me? Don't be ridiculous. No. He comes home and satisfies his urges and I get to satisfy mine—which are remarkably different.

Getting dressed, I'm struggling to find anything that fits. All of my clothes are too big and my skinny jeans now drape off of me like trackpants. My shirts are about as shapely as a curtain, and I'm not even going to discuss the issues I'm having with my foundation garments. If I didn't already feel like a repulsive creature, looking in the mirror hanging next to the closet confirms I am as appealing as a botfly—but they're more desired than I am. I put on my thick winter coat, hopeful its volume will distract from the lack of my own.

I tuck my self-loathing in the mental pocket I've become accustomed to and prepare myself to get out the door.

The grocery store is a few kilometres away, so I have to drive, but I'm consumed with guilt for using a vehicle Zach and Zara paid for to do so. I don't have another option at the moment; I need Sebastian to be happy with me.

When I walk into the supermarket, I can't help but feel like all eyes are on me. I am aware my appearance leaves a lot to be desired, but the way people are staring at me is unnerving.

The temperature change from outside to in, forces me to remove my coat, which was serving as a wearable safety blanket. I'm exposed, vulnerable, and repulsive.

I weave my way through the aisles, picking up items to make "boyfriend steak", which Google has assured me is a sure-fire way to please any man in your life. I've never cooked steak before, and honestly cruising the meat department brings me to tears, but I have to suck it up and do something nice for

Sebastian. Living with Zach and Zara, Isla and I both embraced vegetarian life, but Sebastian is what I'd call a carnivore. I have yet to see him eat a single vegetable, and the man consumes enough animal flesh, he is probably on PETA's watch list.

Turning down the aisle housing the spices, I see a familiar head of tight curls atop the most perfect golden skin.

I consider abandoning my cart with the items I have chosen, but I spent far too long choosing the perfect steaks, and I do not want to subject myself to the dead-animal aisle again.

"Chelsea?" Liam doesn't provide a greeting, instead seeking confirmation I am who he thinks. Maybe I can pretend I'm someone else. I should have practiced a different accent during all my time warming Sebastian's couch over the past few weeks.

"Big Red. Oh, God. Chels." He strides forward to pull me in for a hug—something uncharacteristic for him, since he knows my stance on physical affection.

"Hey, Liam." My brain is reminding me I need to act angry with him, but my heart wants to stay in his arms forever. My head wins. I take a step back to put some space between us. My next mistake.

Liam scrutinizes my withering frame. The light in his eyes at the sight of me fades and the corners of his mouth droop while his eyebrows draw up the centre of his face. "Are you okay? We've all been worried sick."

Funny, because he looks as good as ever.

I stiffen my posture. My well-being isn't his business anymore. "I'm fine, Liam. No thanks to you."

"Chels. Come on. Don't be that way. I was trying to help. I'm worried about you. You haven't been on campus for a while."

Oh, good grief. No sense hiding it anymore. "I dropped out. But if all I do is bring worry to your life, you should be relieved I'm no longer in it."

Liam's wide-eyed expression indicates those words stung. "Don't say that. I want you in my life. I want you to be okay. Can we go somewhere and talk? The baking supplies aisle isn't the right spot. I was grabbing a few things for my mom before I go to the gym, but I'd rather hang out with you. Chels, I miss you. So much."

I contemplate his offer. I miss him more than I ever thought possible. But I can't. He can't end up back on Kevin's radar. I won't ruin his life by being anywhere in his proximity.

"No, Liam. I can't. I'm making dinner for my boyfriend, and I don't have time to socialize."

Liam would make the worst poker player in the history of time because his expressions give everything away. The pout on his face would be comical if I didn't feel so guilty about causing it.

"Can you promise me something, Chels?"

"I don't know. That depends on what you're asking."

"Remember, I'm always here for you." He reaches his hand out to place on my arm, looking into my eyes. "If you ever need me, just call."

I can't maintain eye contact, and I don't want him to catch sight of the tears welling in my eyes. "I have to go." My obnoxiously heavy grocery cart makes it difficult to spin and leave in the opposite direction toward the checkout. Sebastian is going to have to eat unseasoned "boyfriend steak" because I am not spending another moment in this place.

Hours later, it's 8:30 and I've followed the directions to create the perfect steak for Sebastian. Unfortunately, my head is swimming with thoughts of Liam despite my attempts to numb them with narcotics. I knew I missed him before today, but seeing him confirmed it. Being near him was almost painful. He doesn't deserve the chaos and stress I contribute to his life. Nor does he deserve to be put in danger.

Seeing him made me think of my family, and I realize how much I miss them too. My decisions may not make sense to them, but I'm doing what I believe is best to survive. I want them to be safe and no state-of-the-art security system is going to stop Kevin from hurting the people I care about.

I'm doing the right thing.

My thoughts are halted by an ear-piercing beeping.

"No!" I grab a dish towel from the handle of the oven, frantically wafting the smoke around to disperse it and quiet the smoke alarm. Leave it to me to ruin a "foolproof" recipe. I hope Sebastian enjoys a well-done steak. The char might make up for the lack of seasoning.

At that exact moment, Sebastian storms through the front door. "What's going on in here? Are you burning my house down, Doll?"

Like a chastised child—my area of expertise—I reply, "I've got it under control. Just got a little smoky."

Sebastian enters the kitchen, inspecting the damage before turning to face me. "You cooked?"

"Um. Well, I tried. I wanted to do something nice for you."

"And this is how it worked out?"

His harsh response makes me shrink back. My attempt to satisfy him has failed.

"Luckily, I'm not hungry for steak." He growls, and I know what he's implying.

First things first. "Okay, but let me have a bump first." If I can force my brain chemicals to pretend I'm feeling joy, maybe it won't be so bad.

Survival mode. Even though it looks remarkably similar to prostitution.

I escape to the bathroom to shower and brace myself for what lies ahead, desperate to earn Sebastian's approval this evening. If that means I allow him to use my emaciated frame as his vice, then so be it. I have my own to turn to.

My high has been lasting for less time with each hit I take, so I take more tonight. I want that euphoric daze and not have to focus on everything I hate about my life right now. I want to escape. Feel numb. Apathetic.

My method is successful because thirty minutes later, Sebastian is satiated—not from overcooked steak—and dozing off beside me. I lie awake, coming down from my high, recounting the many mistakes I've made recently.

Tonight's actions were just more things I can add to my list of 'Chelsea's Screw Ups.' If it were possible to trade mistakes for rest, I'd never wake up again.

spend most of my days sitting in Sebastian's house alone. He rarely gets home before eight in the evening, and there's only so much I can clean to distract myself. The good thing is, I've cleared a lot of books off of my to-be-read pile by frequenting the library. Reading allows me to escape reality and avoid thinking about how I can move forward with my life.

As I lie on the sofa, reading my most recent withdrawal from the library, a relatable story about a returning war veteran struggling with PTSD, there's a knock at the door. It's what people refer to as "The Holiday Season", and although I've had nothing to celebrate in my life, I hope it's carolers, and not someone wanting to talk.

Looking out the window from my perch on the couch, the blue hair gives away who the person is, long before I open the door. No Christmas carols for me.

"Hi." I don't greet Gia with a cheerful hello. My raised eyebrows and chilly reception make it obvious I'm questioning why she's here, but her wide-eyed expression makes me think she is confused that I answered. If she came to me, I don't understand her surprise.

"Hey, girl. You look like hell."

Lovely. We're starting with some up-building conversation. "Thanks. How did you know I was here?" I haven't spoken to her since I moved in here. Her spontaneous visit is unexpected, to say the least.

"Oh, uh. I ran into Sebastian on campus, and he gave me his address. He told me you were here." Her cheeks flush, and I realize how cold it is outside. I'm letting all the cold air into the house and Sebastian won't be thrilled if his utility expenses increase because I am irresponsible.

She cannot be trusted.

I can't leave her out in the cold if she came all this way to visit me. She's not even what I'd call a friend, so I'm confused by her effort, but I don't want to be rude shutting her outside.

"I'm a bit busy, but you can come in if you want."

I barely get the words out before Gia blows inside, stomping the snow off of her boots, and removing her coat. Okay. I guess she's staying. "What are you busy doing?" She eyes the book I left open on the coffee table.

How can I survive this awkward encounter? I purse my lips, staring toward the kitchen. I don't want to admit the only item on my to-do list today is reading a book. "Can I get you something to drink?"

"Oh, that would be great. Let me see what you've got." Without hesitation, Gia marches through the house toward the kitchen, and with her first guess, opens the cupboard containing the glasses. She turns, opening the fridge, scanning the contents for something desirable. "Let's get drunk." She closes the fridge, staring at my face, awaiting a response. She made herself at home far too easily.

I wasn't planning on drinking today, but Gia is a relative stranger, and I can't exactly excuse myself to go indulge in my usual coping mechanism. Alcohol is a decent alternative. "Okay."

She claps her hands childishly, which looks alien for Gia's no-nonsense personality. I'm not sure how to feel about her excitement level right now. Dial it back, Gia.

Spinning in place, she turns and reaches for the cabinet where Sebastian keeps his whisky. Another lucky guess. Grabbing a second glass, she pours a hefty amount in the first glass—an amount I would expect if we were drinking wine—and pours about an inch into the other. She hands me the glass she over-filled, clearly stereotyping me for my Irish heritage. She's not going to get any protest from me.

I lead her back to the sofa, sprawling back into my usual seat and throwing my feet up on the glass coffee table. Gia mirrors my actions, making herself even more at home.

She cannot be trusted.

It's strange how comfortable she is, considering she's never been here before. I don't have a lot of social experience, and considering Liam's is the only friend's house I've ever been to, maybe this is normal. I never have done things the normal way, so I would bet her methods are more typical than mine.

"So, what happened to you when you ran off on me on Halloween?"

I guess we're skipping small talk. We jumped right over the awkward discussion about weather and I'm unsure how to proceed. I was planning my discussion about the snowfall accumulation patterns over the past two weeks, and she has gone off script. How do I even explain to a virtual stranger that I ran away when her comments sent me into a panic because of my own complicated history? I know most people wouldn't understand, but Gia should know by now, at age twenty, you can't go around claiming ownership of people. But again, she's a better example of normal than I am. Maybe I can explain my hatred for Halloween.

Sigh. "I realized I had somewhere important to be." I speak into my glass, taking a long pull of whisky, embracing the burn down my throat. My impatience grows, wanting to feel the numbness alcohol provides, so I take another sip.

"Right. Geeze, girl. Are you in a race?"

I shrug in response, taking another drink.

Gia stays for three long, agonizing hours. I don't even remember what we talked about; I'm drunk. I'm slumped in the corner of the sectional sofa, eyes closed, waiting for the room to stop spinning. I was able to clean up the glasses, so Sebastian won't be suspicious I had company when he gets home, but aside from that, I have accomplished nothing since Gia left.

The door opens, and a blast of cold air fills the room. The sensation causes me to shiver, and my bladder lets me know it is alive and well—and full.

Also alerting me to his presence, Sebastian offers a greeting as cool as the gust of air that swept through the room. "Hard at work, I see."

I'm unemployed. What exactly is he expecting? Regardless, I don't want to give him attitude. He doesn't need another reason to be mad at me. "Sorry." I rise from my seat faster than my drunk brain can handle, falling forward onto the glass coffee table. The result is disastrous. My drunken body knocks the table from its base, causing the half inch thick glass to shatter. Sheer panic makes me jump up, and despite my drunkenness, my fear over the scenario overwhelms my senses.

I look at Sebastian, and shock is clear on his face. Waiting for it to morph into anger, I struggle to find something to say. "I... I... I'm so sorry."

"Don't move," he commands.

I ignore his order, afraid he is going to hit me, and make a beeline for the bathroom. I'm not sticking around for him to take his anger out on me. Drunk Chelsea isn't quick though, and Sebastian wins the footrace to the stairs.

"Chelsea, stop! You're bleeding."

"What?" Glancing down, I see my light grey leggings ripped and soaked with blood. The sight makes me woozy, but the alcohol in my system has prevented me from feeling any pain.

Sebastian scoops me up in his arms, carrying me to the smaller of his two bathrooms, sitting me on the counter. "Don't move this time. I mean it. I'll be right back."

The fear I felt at those same words a moment earlier is no longer present. I'm focused on the blood oozing from my thigh. The laceration appears deep.

Sebastian returns with some supplies to clean and bandage my wound. I don't know how experienced he is with first aid, but this won't be the first time I've received medical attention from an untrained caretaker.

"This is going to hurt, Doll. It's bad. Do you want to go to emerge?"

"No!" I shout. "I... uh... Well, I'm drunk, and don't want them to do bloodwork." Truth be told, I don't want drugs showing up in my system and ending up on my medical records forever.

"I figured." Sebastian holds up a small baggie of white powder—my saviour. "Here. Take this."

He doesn't need to tell me twice.

Once I'm well on my way to my happy place, Sebastian lifts me again, placing me in the tub. "I have to take your pants off."

Maybe the horrific, ill-fitting granny panties I am wearing will keep him from getting frisky tonight. That is, if my gaping wound and combined use of vices aren't a turn off already. Sebastian removes my tattered pants, tossing them aside, and for the first time, takes in the severity of my wound. After washing his hands, he rinses the blood away from my thigh, and it's even worse than I thought.

"Are you sure you don't want to get this looked at? You could use stitches."

"No. Just put a bandage on it."

"Chels."

"Sebastian, I am *not* going to the hospital."

Reluctantly, he continues inspecting the gash, making sure there is no glass left in it, washing the area, applying some antibiotic ointment, and finally placing a bandage over the seven-inch-long cut with medical tape and gauze. Every drop of water, touch, or movement makes me wince, able to feel the severity of my injury despite the self-medicating I've done. It stretches from near the top of my inner thigh to above the centre of my knee, and the household supplies are doing little to hold it together.

By the time he's finished, it looks like a drunk pre-med patched me up, but he lifts me to stand and ushers me to the bedroom. When I try to stand, I fall because I can't place enough weight on my left leg. I hobble along and he lifts me into bed before retreating to get me another glass of whisky. I'm going to wake up in my ratty underwear with no liquor left in my system, but for the first time since I moved in, I have been cared for. Even though, in this situation, I required more attention and work than I ever have, I don't feel like a burden.

It took twelve days to regain strength in my leg after the coffee table incident. Since that day, Sebastian has been far gentler and more attentive. I wouldn't recommend slicing your leg with shards of glass as relationship advice, but it worked for me.

An unexpected consequence of my injury is that I'm itching to get out of the house. I've been cooped up ever since, and I ran out of books days ago. I'm looking forward to visiting the library and picking up some new entertainment. Maybe one day in the future I'll look for a job, but it's a new year, and I am struggling to picture a new future beyond my current situation.

Snow has accumulated on my vehicle since it hasn't moved for so long, so I sweep it off and allow the SUV to run for a few moments. Once the engine is warm enough, the vents express hot air and I'm on my way. The two kilometres to the library feel like being liberated from a life of solitude—something I'm familiar with.

I park along the road where the Farmer's Market opens, wanting to walk a short distance and test the resilience of my leg. Marching along the sidewalk from Market Street to the library entrance, the chills I experience are not on account of the early January temperature.

My intuition proves right when I round the corner.

"Funny meeting you here."

My flight instincts activate, and I want to listen, but my leg prevents me from doing so. At best, I'd hobble along a few metres until I ripped open the barely healed gash. Before I can contemplate taking the chance, Kevin's hand reaches out, grabbing hold of my jacket and stopping any efforts to run away. As the feeling of dread is taking over, I surrender to it.

"What the hell happened to you?" Kevin asks through a raised upper lip, exposing his yellowing teeth. "What am I supposed to do with you now? I should have known you'd turn into an addict like your mother."

I've always held my mother in high regard, as if she was some mythical hero who would have changed the course of my life had she been around to do so. That fantasy has been the subject of many daydreams. It's not one I'm willing to give up on.

"No. I... I'm not." I raise my chin. "She wasn't."

The laugh escaping Kevin causes a few blue jays to take flight from neighbouring trees. Lucky buggers.

"The apple doesn't fall far from the tree. I can't say I'm surprised. Nature versus nurture."

Like he'd know anything about nurturing.

I watch as a mother and her two children exit the library. The woman stops to investigate what's happening between Kevin and me. I give her my best pleading eyes, like I did with the young girls at the coffee shop several weeks prior. I can't blame her when she places a protective arm around each of her children and ushers them to their minivan. Those kids do not know how lucky they are to have a parent who shields them from potential dangers rather than being one.

My voice comes out as a whisper, with all my strength being reserved for keeping myself upright. "She wasn't." He can call me what he wants, but I will not allow him to destroy the image of my mother I've clung to my entire life. I won't accept that a monster and a drug addict created me. But my gut tells me he isn't lying this time. If this were a movie, a narrator would utter some cheesy line like, "She couldn't fight her destiny."

"Oh, darling daughter. You have no idea who your mother was. She was even more stupid than you and never could kick her bad habits. At least she was smart enough not to try to run me over with a car."

I have no regrets.

I'm assuming Kevin was one of Delilah's said habits—likely the worst of them all.

A police car rounds the corner from Nottawasaga Street, slowing down to take in the situation I'm trapped in. Kevin's posture stiffens, but his grip on my jacket relaxes. He doesn't release me until the vehicle comes to a stop about ten feet away. When I see the brake lights reflecting on the adjacent snowbank before they shut off and the driver's side door opens, I'm relieved someone has arrived to intervene.

"Is everything okay here?" the policewoman asks. I'm all for women busting through stereotypical gender roles, but I know Kevin has no respect for "the weaker sex." I hope he at least has respect for her badge.

"Everything is fine here, Ma'am." Kevin's words drip with disdain. "I'm speaking with my daughter."

"I was asking your daughter, *Sir*." The officer returns Kevin's tone with an equal amount of contempt. I like her.

He scowls at me while leaning in to make his voice clear. "Get yourself sorted. I'll be back for you soon."

"Sir, I'm going to ask you to put some distance between you and your daughter until I hear confirmation from her."

"It's fine, *Officer*. I'm leaving."

For the first time since the OPP car came into view, I take a full breath. Hot air is expelled in a puff of fog.

Kevin turns away from our one-sided confrontation and heads past the police car toward Mississauga Street. The officer returns his gaze with an intensity I admire. I wish I could face off against him as fearlessly as she does.

Once he turns out of sight, my hero approaches me. "Are you all right?"

I nod. Kevin finds me wherever he goes and I can't figure out how it keeps happening. It's making me fear leaving the house at all. Sebastian was the only person who knew I was coming to the library today, and there's no way he would speak to Kevin after their last interaction. Right?

He cannot be trusted.

I'm exhausted. I'm tired of battling my instincts to figure out what is right or wrong. "Thank you for intervening. My father and I have a strained relationship." To say the least.

"That's not uncommon. I recognized the look on your face." She swivels her head around, scanning the immediate area. "Did you take the bus here?"

"No, I drove. My car is around the corner." I point toward my haven on wheels.

"I'll walk you to your car, to be safe." She relays something through her radio in police jargon I don't understand; essentially saying she's helping a damsel in distress find her carriage.

We arrive at my SUV after a silent walk, when the woman reaches into her breast pocket to retrieve a business card. "I know family relationships can be complicated, so if you need help again, call me. No judgement."

Staring at the card I subconsciously took hold of, I notice her name is Officer Lilian McPherson. Sounds like the name of someone who has her life together. I slide the card into the pocket of by baggy "skinny" jeans, thank her and climb in behind the steering wheel of my trusty steed. I don't have anywhere to call home, and I don't have people in my corner anymore, but I always have a sense of security inside these locked doors. The only closed doors to make me feel this way. I slowly pull away from the curb, obeying every traffic law in existence.

Travelling along Andrew Street, I notice a familiar minivan parked at the side of the road. I glance as I drive past and catch the eye of the protective mother who ushered her kids to safety. Her presence surprises me. I realize she didn't run off to avoid the showdown with Kevin. Rather, she protected her children and still didn't leave me when she knew something was wrong. She's the kind of mother I imagined mine would have been, but I couldn't have been more wrong and the reality of that is a thousand times more painful than the gash in my leg.

After my encounter with Kevin, I climb into bed as soon as I arrive back to Sebastian's and cry until I give myself a nosebleed. That's been happening each time I cry, so I need to keep my emotions in check. If I could stop having feelings entirely, that would be great, but no amount of drugs has made that happen.

The front door opens and heavy footsteps enter.

"Doll? Are you here?"

Sniffle. "I'm in the bedroom."

The steps draw closer until Sebastian is leaning against the door frame like some phantasmagorical being. If only he could grant wishes.

"When you said you were in the bedroom, this isn't what I was expecting."

I look around at the tissues strewn about the room, my baggy pyjamas, and I can only imagine how my face looks. It might be a weird thing to wish for, but I'm hoping my lack of sex-appeal repulses him. I don't want to "earn my keep," as Sebastian likes to put it.

The side of the bed sinks down as Sebastian crawls in beside me. His hand reaches under my oversized T-shirt.

"Sebastian."

"Yeah, Doll?"

"Please, stop. I had a rough day. I can't."

With an exasperated sigh, Sebastian stands up, wiping his hands down the front of his thighs like he's trying to remove the feel of my skin on his hands.

"Maybe if I can…"

"Chelsea, listen. I can't keep paying for your habit."

I've had a lot of moments in my life where I was ashamed of myself, but this moment is in my top five. He's not wrong in what he's saying, though. I can't expect him to pay my way.

He continues, "Can't you ask your parents to give you some money? They're rich."

That was not the direction I saw this conversation going. I assumed he'd encourage me to get a job.

"The *parents* I haven't spoken to for well over a month? Sure, let me call them up. 'Oh, hey Zara. Just wondering if you could transfer some money into my account for cocaine. Thanks.'"

"It was a suggestion. It doesn't look like you're getting a job soon." Without another word, Sebastian exits the room, leaving me to evaluate my options.

I know what I have to do.

I'm not sure why I even exist. I offer nothing to anyone, and my entire existence has been one form of suffering after another. There are no good times. Heartbreak. Heartache. Misery. Despair. Is this all my life has to offer?

Thanks to ease of online sales, my bank account is flush with cash again, which should last me several months. The downside being now I don't have a car. I had intended to return my SUV to Zach and Zara, but desperate times call for desperate measures. They've never made an insincere gesture in their lives, and this is how I repay them.

My ambition to find a job has depleted to zero. After my last encounter with Kevin—between his promise to find me again and the revelation about my mother—I lost any desire to live. However, in true Chelsea fashion, I'm too much of a coward to take that step myself.

Sebastian provides little in terms of emotional support, so I don't talk to him about what's bothering me. He expects me to remain silent and service him as required. Each day I think I can't become more disgusted with myself, but by the time I go to sleep each night, I've hit an all-time low.

My cocaine usage has increased in an effort to have some sense of positivity, but it's an expensive habit to maintain. It's no wonder Sebastian told me he couldn't pay for my habit anymore. Thankfully, I can afford to pay for it myself now, and maybe his requests of me will lessen.

I shower to wash off the contempt for myself that grows each day, but vanilla and shea butter are no match for self-loathing. I could use drain cleaner for body wash, and it still couldn't wash away my shame. Nothing helps except for my beloved nose candy.

Looking at myself in the foggy bathroom mirror, I don't recognize the girl staring back at me. I am losing my hair at an alarming rate. My nose is swollen and red. My previously bright blue eyes are sunken and dull. The skin on my face is dry and patchy. At least I don't look like my father anymore—I look like rock bottom if it had a face.

My phone buzzes with a message for the first time in days.

Liam: Chels. Haven't heard from you. How are you?

Why doesn't he understand? I'm not checking in because I don't want Kevin to use him, or anyone else, against me. I feel more fear for everyone else than I do for myself, but I can't tell him. He'd tell me he can handle himself because he's Arizona and has the ability to survive impossible situations. But this isn't a Disney movie. The prince doesn't always get the happily ever after.

Chelsea: I'm fine.

I pacify him with a message to let him know I'm alive. Hopefully, he moves on and finds a new friend to dedicate his time to. Ever since the day I ran into him at the grocery store, I can't help but think how much I miss him, and how badly I've disappointed him. My emotions are so conflicting and the back and forth is exhausting. To want someone in your life so badly but push them away because you want to protect them, well, it sucks.

Wanting to numb myself, I rifle through the drawer Sebastian allotted to me, seeking my relief. When I find a small plastic bag, I relax even before consuming it. The smooth material between my fingers is a familiar feeling I associate with chasing a high. It would be far more economical if simply touching it could satiate me, but I need more. My intentions are as clear as the cellophane my vice is encased in. I need euphoria.

The dose of narcotics I consumed has given me a jolt of energy to do some household tasks, and, for a short period, a reprieve from my internal agony. I figure if I can keep his house clean, Sebastian will be more inclined to let me stay.

I don't have any previous girlfriend experience, but if this is what it's supposed to be like, I don't understand the appeal. I am constantly walking on eggshells around Sebastian, living in fear he's going to kick me out as soon as I displease him. He'll be happier with me if I contribute something to the house, since I'm not providing financial help. He's one person I have left in my life who can face off against Kevin should the need arise. But Kevin would be stupid to approach Sebastian again. His prison yard conflicts didn't prepare him as well as he let on.

I've contemplated reporting Kevin to the police, but he has done nothing worth reporting and even *if* I could get a restraining order, what good would a piece of paper do me? Like I'm supposed to throw it at him if he comes to repeat history? The man doesn't care about laws or being a decent person, so paperwork is not going to change who he is.

Buzz.

Liam: I miss you. I miss my best friend.

Those words distract me for several moments as I stare at Liam's message. I so badly want to reply. I want to tell him I miss him too, and I'd give anything to go back to how things were, but that's not possible anymore. Things are so different now, and I'm not the person I was a few months ago. If Liam could see what I've become, he wouldn't miss me at all. He'd be relieved to be rid of me.

I tuck my phone back in the pocket of my hoodie and carry on doing mindless household chores. The little things like cleaning countertops and sweeping the floor remind me of times my family and I used to have chore day. We'd crank up music and clean every inch of our home, but we always had fun in the process, even if I was scrubbing toilets. I miss them so much, the thought of them creates a lump in my throat. They'll never know how much being away from them hurts.

Sebastian walks in the door, and it's so far from a *Leave it to Beaver* scene, I'd cringe if I wasn't so depressed. "Wow. You actually did something today."

I can't waste my energy being upset by his words. The past month, I've done nothing but spiral and become more of a burden. If I was a good cook, or anything helpful, I might be worth keeping around, but I provide nothing of substance to this home, or this world.

"You're welcome," I reply with no emotion in my voice.

"What are we having for dinner?" he asks like we're a typical domestic couple and he could expect to come home to a three-course meal.

"I'll order something. I didn't get to the grocery store." Without a vehicle, I have not been inclined to walk in the freezing cold and carry home a load of groceries. As a result, I've been eating only once a day, and even that's only because Sebastian requests something. If it were up to me, I'd be surviving on whisky and cocaine. Well, maybe surviving isn't the right word.

"Surprise." Sebastian rolls his eyes.

I ignore his comment, searching through my phone to find something to order. In the middle of my search, my screen turns black as my battery dies.

"Can you order something? My phone died. I'll go plug it in, but it will be awhile before I can place an order."

"Yeah, whatever. Are you paying for it?"

Chivalry is dead, but considering I live in his house, I know it's the least I can do.

"Yes, I'll pay. Pick whatever you want, but please pick something for me I can eat."

The last few times Sebastian ordered food, he chose meat appetizers with a meaty main course, and I swear if they made steak ice cream, he would have ordered that too. I didn't even know "meat salad" was a thing, but it is. A quick search in the online dictionary clarified that salad is not limited to vegetables. I no longer ask him to "order a salad."

I plug my phone in and lie on the bed for a while, exhausted from the unfamiliar physical activity of the day.

Sebastian walks in the bedroom, and I open one eye to look at him. "I ordered food, but I'll go pick it up. I'm going to shower."

"Yep." I don't bother asking what he's ordered or when it will be ready.

He removes his clothes from the bedroom and walks naked to the bathroom. I think back to the night of the concert when all the women in our row were staring at him. They'd be jealous of my view right now, but if I could trade places with any of them, I would.

As he closes the bathroom door, I close my eyes again, eager to find euphoria. As I line up the powder on the bedside table, I hear Sebastian's phone buzz.

I call out to him, "Sebastian, your phone is buzzing. You got a text." I pick up his phone from the table in front of me, assuming it's regarding our meal. My intentions are to bring it to him until I notice the name on the screen.

Kevin: Are you ready?

Sebastian enters the room wearing a towel and looks startled when he sees me standing near his phone. He sighs and rubs his face with both hands. "I wish you hadn't seen that. It's not what you think."

"And what *am* I thinking, Sebastian?" He *is* a Don Juan Casanova.

"That I've been in touch with your father."

"Don't call him my father. He was never a father to me. But, you... I thought you liked me."

"I do, Doll. I really do. Listen, Kevin approached me before I met you, saying he wanted to make amends with his daughter. We're part of the same street crew and we help each other out, you know? So, when he tracked you down, I agreed. I promise; I thought he was trying to reach out to his long-lost kid. I didn't know anything else."

It's becoming difficult to hear what he's saying because of my pounding heartbeat. I reach down to pull my phone from the charger, sliding it into my pocket, remembering Zara's words from months ago: "Always keep your phone on your person."

"The day I saw you at the café for the first time, I thought Liam was your boyfriend, so I didn't approach you. Your fa… Kevin was ticked I missed my chance, so he told me where you worked. That's when I met you at the bookstore. I swear, the second he laid his hands on you, I knew his intentions weren't good and I wanted to protect you. Believe me."

"No." It takes another moment for me to work up the courage to speak any more words. "I don't have to believe you, Sebastian, because you're a liar. You've lied to me since the moment we met. I've spent my entire life scared to trust people and the moment I let my guard down, this happens? Am I seriously this stupid?"

"You're not stupid. I do care, and I want to keep you safe."

"I think I need to be kept safe from you." I stride to the closet to pick up my duffel bag I arrived with months ago. "Screw you, and screw my father. You two deserve each other." I don't know where I'm going, on foot, in early February, but I can't stay here.

The moment those words leave my mouth, his demeanour changes. His eyes narrow and his expression looks grim. "I'm afraid that's not possible, Doll." The way he spits out the word "Doll" makes every synapse in my body fire off on alert. My amygdala is going to put in for overtime.

The Sebastian in front of me is not the same Sebastian from sixty seconds ago.

I would rather die than live through any life at Kevin's hands again. My hands slide into my pocket to grip my phone, and I try to keep my breathing calm, which takes most of my conscious effort. I fiddle with the smooth screen from inside my pocket, unsure if I'm accomplishing anything. I hope I don't accidentally call Sebastian. After fiddling for a moment, I feel the vibration from ringing. I hope whoever I've called answers. A second later I notice the steady vibrations of a voice, but I can't hear who is speaking—thankfully, because if I could hear it, Sebastian might too. Before this person hangs up, I have to make my point clear. They could easily assume I but-dialled them.

"I want to leave, Sebastian! You can't keep me here. Please, let me leave."

"If you leave, I'm a dead man."

That statement confuses me. "A dead man?"

Sebastian laughs—not a funny laugh—a concerning one. "You really are naïve. I've honestly never met someone so easy to fool. You were a mark, Chelsea. A job. I was told what to do, and you made it easy."

The tears are stinging my eyes. I'm not upset because he doesn't care for me; I'm used to that. What hurts is the reality I fell for his lies and got myself in this position after so many people told me to stay away from him. After every instinct I had told me I couldn't trust him, but I dismissed them as over-reactions. I assumed it was the same as years of my fight-or-flight response reacting to every imaginary danger.

The phone in my pocket is no longer vibrating and I don't know if the person hung up, or if they're listening quietly. As much as I wish I could fight my way out of here, my meager 112 pounds is no match for Sebastian in strength, and if I'm being honest, my will to live is minimal. Why would I want to continue down this path I keep ending up on?

"Whatever you want from me, Sebastian, get it over with, because I have no fight left. Maybe I am naïve, but I'm not a monster." The indignation in my voice waivers as I decide to confess my past to Sebastian. "Before you decide, let me tell you a story." I know explaining this to him is my only chance at him growing a conscience. So, as much as it hurts to talk about it, it's my only shot.

"A story?"

I nod. "As a five-year-old girl, I had spent my life up to that point living with Kevin. He resented me from day one because my mother died during childbirth, or so he said, and that was my fault. I mean, maybe it was." I'm choking back my tears. The life I thought I could have had if my mother survived giving birth to me likely wouldn't have been any different. "My *father* neglected and abused me. He kept me locked in a dog cage in the corner of the living room most of the time. It was to the point I preferred when he left me to starve because at least he wasn't hurting me." I take a deep breath to gather the strength to keep going. "I had started kindergarten when I turned five and my teacher, Miss Jackson, was the first person I had ever met in my life who was genuinely nice. It was so refreshing to have an adult around who didn't beat me, so I became a teacher's pet. I never told her what life at home was like, but I can't imagine it was a secret because I was about twenty pounds lighter than the rest of the kids and had random injuries my father tried to pass off as 'normal kid stuff.'"

"Get to the point! This isn't therapy, Chelsea. I don't want to hear your life story."

The coldness in Sebastian's eyes bores right into my soul, and I no longer care about what happens to me. If monsters like him exist and can make their way into my life so easily, I don't want to live in this world. "Okay, you want to know what happened? My father sold me. Well, not so much sold me as traded me to cover a debt he had accumulated with your beloved street crew. The only problem for them was, they didn't have a hand in human trafficking yet, so they didn't know how to unload me. Sal, your *wonderful* leader, decided the best option was to keep me locked in a closet until they found a buyer. They figured surely a little red-headed girl would fetch top dollar, but they got greedy. They kept me in the closet for months—how many exactly, I'm not sure. I had no concept of day or night, and at five years old, it's not like I could count very high. The only time they let me out of the closet was to hose me down or to beat me for crying. Eventually, the closet became the safest place to be, so I accepted it. So, for almost six years of my life, 'home' was a dog cage and a closet."

Sebastian's face looks grim, but it almost appears there is a hint of guilt. "I remember you." He hesitates to explain further, but continues, "I was at Sal's house with my dad one day and I heard you. He said you were on timeout, so I didn't ask. They made me bring you food."

"Well, it was a long 'timeout' Sebastian. But I guess you know what happened. My teacher, Miss Jackson, fought for me and forced the police to keep looking after I stopped coming to school. My father was investigated, and that led the police to your crew. I was 'rescued'; released from my physical cage, only to spend the rest of my life as a prisoner of my fear. But you know what, Sebastian? I don't care anymore. Death is a better option than going back there, so if that's your plan, do me a favour and put me out of my misery."

He stands silent for a few moments. My heart is beating wildly in my chest, and tears are trailing down my cheeks.

"Chelsea, I didn't know that was you."

Now rage is building inside of me. It's burning in my stomach, desperate to escape. That's probably vomit, too. "Does it matter if it was me, or some other helpless five-year-old girl? Should it matter that you know me? You still worked for and with people who kept a little girl in a closet! Had I known you were a part of them, I wouldn't have given you a second look. You're just as guilty, Sebastian."

I can tell he is warring with his own thoughts right now. Maybe he isn't as bad as the rest of them—maybe he isn't too far gone. He still has a hint of a conscience.

Before my train of thought can travel any farther down the 'maybe Sebastian still has redeemable qualities' track, the front door to his house flies open. I jump at the sound and it doesn't take long for the door assaulters to present themselves in the hallway outside of the bedroom. The first face I see is cloaked with shadows, but once he speaks, his chilling voice is unmistakable.

Kevin Wells.

"What the hell, Sebastian? What's taking so long? You should have texted me back." Kevin steps into the light and right behind him is another face I recognize; Trusty Rusty.

When I make eye contact with him, pleading for him to speak up and offer help, he utters words at me, tipping my entire world on its axis. "Hey, sis."

I'm sorry. What? "Si… Sis?" I glare at Kevin, demanding clarification on that statement. Is this Prince Harry wannabe my brother?

"What? You didn't think your addict mom was the only woman I was screwing, did you?"

Each time I think I can't be more nauseated by this revolting man, he swoops in with something else to lessen my opinion of him. Considering that my opinion lists chlamydia as a more useful entity than Kevin Wells, it's a low bar.

I look at Rusty, AKA 'PHW', and say, "Well, aren't you lucky? You get to share genes with the dregs of society."

He looks down past his crinkled, freckled nose. "I'm not sharing any jeans with nobody," my genetically gifted brother replies.

At this moment, I'm confident I received all the brains in the family tree, so maybe I stand a chance here. I need to be smart—smarter than these three, at least.

"We were stopping in for a bit of fun. I wasn't about to let go of the merchandise without a payoff after all the work I put in," Sebastian finally replies to Kevin as he pulls on a T-shirt to cover his formerly towel-clad body.

Kevin strides across the room to come face to face with me. When I look into his eyes now, I no longer recognize a father—I only see a demon in flesh form. The worst humanity has to offer. It makes me ill to know I share DNA with a man who could be so heartless and hateful.

He reaches up and grips my jaw with his callused hand, squeezing my face, and forces me to look into his revolting eyes. "You keep trying to get away from me, Chelsea. I told you, there's nowhere on this Earth you could go to get away. You belong to me, and I will choose what happens to you. If you had been cooperative, maybe I would have chosen something better. Now, I might even take your little sister to make up for the trouble."

Before he uttered those words, I was content with my only escape being death—either me or him. But now, knowing Isla is in danger, there's no way I am going out like a coward.

"I don't care what you have planned for me, *father*." I spit my words to express my disdain for the man in front of me. "You can kill me, but you will not touch her."

Kevin laughs in my face—close enough his hot breath blows on my clammy skin. "I would love to end your life so I didn't have to look at your face ever again, but what I have planned for you is so much better. I told you I would make you pay for having me sent to prison. You're a fool if you think I'd let that go."

He grabs my hair, dragging me from the bedroom and down the stairs into the living area.

"Does it make you feel like more of a man to punish your own daughter for your mistakes?" I barely finish speaking before Kevin's meaty hand strikes my face. The coppery tang of blood reaches the back of my throat. It's not unfamiliar anymore, but I spit it onto the floor. At least if he kills me, I can leave a DNA trail. It might be my last living act to make a CSI team's job easier. What a legacy to leave.

"You're my mistake. You disgust me."

"The feeling is mutual."

Kevin's rough, sweaty hand strikes me in the same spot for a second time and brings me to my knees. I spit blood onto his pants and shoes. I'm only focused now on leaving as much of a forensic trail as I can.

After living my entire life with fight-or-flight mode activated, I'm ill-prepared for this moment when my instincts could be useful. Isn't that some tragic irony? Shakespeare could have written something poetic about this scenario.

I scan my surroundings, trying to find a sign of hope to give me a chance at taking these bastards down with me. The least I can do is save the rest of humanity from these vulgar vermin. I will give my last breath to make sure they don't touch Isla or anyone else.

I try to recall every book I've ever read; every movie I've ever watched. There's no way to talk my way out of this, because Kevin has no sense of compassion and no morals. There's no tugging at his heartstrings—they're made of electrified barbed wire.

From my knees with a stinging cheek and blood trickling into my mouth, I formulate a plan, but I know I can't physically take all three men. The best I can do is inflict harm.

When the front door flies open, we all turn to see who is there, and for a brief second, I hold a glimmer of hope. That hope dashes as soon as Gia opens her mouth. "You guys don't have her ready to go yet? What the hell are you waiting for? My dad is going to flip."

My eyes widen a considerable margin as I take in the scene before me. Gia strides over to Sebastian, cupping his butt with both hands and planting a kiss on him that would make me blush if I wasn't so shocked right now. What is happening?

"Hey, Babe," Sebastian greets her, without the least bit of surprise in his expression.

Babe? Her dad?

"Do I finally get you back to myself? I'm tired of sharing you." She pats the crotch of his pants like a chihuahua—or a dachshund—and glares at me. "Did you enjoy your ride on my boyfriend, Chelsea?"

My disgust for myself can't be contained anymore. I vomit on Sebastian's sofa, shiny new coffee table, and floor. I'm not leaving here without destroying whatever I can, since the four people in this room have destroyed my worth as a human being. The stupid thing is that Sebastian can replace whatever I ruin with his illicit money, but my self-worth can't be recouped.

"Ew. You're disgusting. Take her outside or something!" Gia shrieks.

I turn to wipe my mouth on my shoulder before I reply, "You're right. I am disgusting. Yet, I'm the only person in this room who isn't a monster."

Gia laughs. "Oh, Chelsea. Poor, naïve, Chelsea. It's about dollars and cents. About power and fear. Eat or be eaten. Fight or flight. You're the bottom of the food chain here."

When Gia says, "fight or flight," my mind goes back to my initial idea. Now I have another person to contend with, but I can still make it work. I eye the lighter tucked on the bottom level of Sebastian's coffee table—an oh-so-handy Zippo.

I calculate a plan in my head. My high has worn off and with it, my confidence. My will to live disappeared a long time ago, but I'm not going out alone.

"I have to go to the bathroom." A few minutes in the bathroom, I can make a fire starter with cleaning products and a toilet paper roll. We're all going down tonight.

"Gia, go with her. Don't let her out of your sight."

That plan backfired already. Plan B.

Since I've already requested to go, I might as well take the opportunity. The norepinephrine coursing through my body has my bladder in check, but anxiety has other plans for the back end.

After following me into the secondary bathroom, Gia sits on the edge of the tub. I've never had the kind of friendship I'd use the bathroom with someone else present, and this is not one of those instances, but now is not the time to be shy.

Once I've relaxed on my throne, anxiety comes to play. To say I'm experiencing gastrointestinal distress is an understatement.

Gia's horrified face is comical.

"Oh. My. Gosh. Why are you so disgusting?"

"Sorry. Your stomach never reacted to stress before?" I roll my eyes. "You're welcome to leave."

"I'm not letting you out of my sight. You heard your father."

I wish people would stop calling him that.

Sitting on the toilet, suppressing a laugh at Gia's expense, I decide on my next plan. Surely all acids are flammable.

Stomach acid is not flammable, even with a decently high alcohol content. I hoped a raging inferno would be my ticket out of here, but upon dropping the zippo lighter into my stomach contents on the carpet, the flame snuffs out. I should have thought of Plan C before I attempted Plan B.

The four savages' backs are facing me as they conspire with each other how best to "deal with" me.

A fractal of light reflects off something beneath the edge of the sofa. I hunch myself over, acting like I'm about to hurl again; hopefully everyone will stay away from me. Glass. More specifically, a four-inch-long shard of broken coffee table glass in amongst the dust bunnies. I leave it where it is for the time being because I need something to wrap around the edge. There's little sense trying to brandish it as a weapon, just to slice my own fingers off.

Like another glimmer of hope, I hear a murmur from my pocket, and I have a renewed sense of optimism—whoever I called is still on the line. That means they heard my performance in the bathroom, which is embarrassing, but this nightmare is ending tonight.

When my captors break from their secret conversation, Rusty heads up the stairs toward the bedrooms, Gia takes a seat on the sofa as casually as she did last time she visited, and Sebastian enters the kitchen. Kevin stands beside the TV, glaring at me before pulling his phone out and walking off to make a call.

Rusty re-enters the living room with a hand towel, tossing it at me. The shock must be clear on my face because he tells me, "Clean up your vomit. No one else wants to smell it."

"Oh, my apologies, dear brother." I try to act annoyed, but never in my life have several things gone right in a row. The odds have swayed in my favour.

I put on a real production "cleaning" my vomit. I gag, heave, fold myself over. Anything I can to keep people away until I grab the glass under the sofa. It's only a few inches from Gia's feet, so I have to be stealthy. That would be a decent superhero name: Stealthy Chelsea.

Slowly, I tear a frayed strip from Sebastian's ratty bathroom hand towel, appreciating his bachelor ways. Gia shoots me a questioning look, so I gag again, using the small piece of cloth to cover my mouth, encouraging her to look away.

Sliding the glass out from its hiding place, I slip it into my hoodie pocket, wrapping the strip of cloth around the wider end of the sickle shape and running my finger along the narrowed end to check its sharpness. It'll do.

"Sebastian, hurry up. We've got to get her to Sal before the buyer backs out."

Taking a deep breath, I look at Gia, who stands, but she's distracted looking at Sebastian through her lust-filled eyes. This is my chance. They think I'm a sheep along wolves, but they're about to learn that when I take the first swing, it's a knockout. It's now or never.

I leap up from my position on the floor, wrapping my arms around Gia and tackling her to the floor; face first in the vomit. Nice touch.

Gia is now distracted by her vomit face as she stands, allowing me to throw her arm above her head, locking her into a half Nelson and placing my makeshift weapon right under her chin.

I didn't think about what I'd do next. It never occurred to me I'd get this far.

Gia squirms, and though she outweighs me by a good twenty pounds, body mass doesn't matter when you have a shard of glass threatening to slice your carotid artery.

"You aren't taking me anywhere. I'm leaving."

Kevin's cackle causes Gia to stop struggling. With one simple sound, he's made it clear she is another pawn in his game. "Stupid girl. Maybe you are as dumb as your mother. You think I care about this blue-haired tramp? Slice her throat. I don't give a damn."

Gia tenses. "My father will kill you."

"Sal is a joke, little girl. He doesn't scare me."

Wait. What? Sal is Gia's father. The man who kept me in his closet for months? He had a daughter my age the entire time? This keeps getting more twisted.

I lost sight of Sebastian while staring at the merciless lowlife who helped bring me into this world. He reappears on the stairs, pointing a gun in my direction, taking intentional steps toward me. So much for Canadian gun control.

"Put the glass down, Chelsea."

Does Sebastian actually have a heart? Didn't see that coming. I guess it's only my life that has no value for any of the people in this room. Maybe they're right. Why am I assuming

Gia's life is worth less than mine or that it's okay to harm her for my benefit? That makes me just as much of a villain.

I'd rather die than be anything like them—I wanted to be my own hero, not an antihero.

My eyes drop to the floor, and I resign myself to the fact I need to release Gia. Saying nothing, I drop Gia's left arm, which she takes as permission to run. The shard of glass slices the side of her neck, and she drops to the floor.

What have I done?

I see the muzzle flash before the sound assaults my ears. I stumble back onto the couch beneath the window. It takes a few seconds to wrap my head around what happened, but the new burning pain in my left arm steals my focus. The ringing in my ears is secondary. Burning flesh was never something I was curious about, but I can confirm the smell is not something I enjoy. I grasp the end of the towel I used to wrap the glass, allowing the shard to unroll and drop to the floor where Gia is no longer situated. I use the fabric scrap to place over the gaping hole in my bicep. It hurts. My blood is pumping in a race to exit my body.

Why is everyone running away? Like ants under a microscope, they're scurrying toward the back door with Sebastian helping a wounded Gia. I still can't hear much, but I see lights flashing through the front windows.

However they managed to arrive at this moment, I'm thankful for. I pull myself to my feet, rushing out the front door.

It hadn't occurred to me my rescuers would view me as a threat, so along with the cold air, I'm greeted with two drawn weapons by the police officers on the scene. I've set a personal record for the number of guns pointed at me today with three. I'd prefer to stop there.

Officer McPherson lowers her weapon as I collapse to one knee.

"They went out the back." I clutch my arm tighter, desperate to stem the blood flow. "Four. There's four of them."

My two-time hero makes her way to me, relaying the information through her radio. When I hear her request the presence of an ambulance, another wave of relief surges through me and I collapse to both knees. Another police car approaches, sirens blaring. I'm happy my hearing has returned somewhat. Everything I'm hearing points to the situation being over. Until I realize it's not.

"Isla. They're going to take Isla."

"Who's Isla?" Constable McPherson's partner asks.

"My sister. She's twelve. You have to stop them."

When the additional officers arrive on the scene, McPherson stays with me, and the three others take off in pursuit of the evildoers. I relay what information I know. Manbun conman. Prince Harry wannabe. Blue-haired proselyte. Mobster with no soul.

"Let me help you." A firm hand reaches up to place pressure on my arm. McPherson removes the towel for a moment to inspect the wound. "You'll be all right. It grazed the muscle. You'll have a nice scar."

I nod, focusing on breathing steadily.

"Do you want to tell me what happened?"

I can't quite wrap my head around what happened in there and struggle to find the right words. "I stabbed her." Not the right place to start.

"The blue-haired girl?"

"I was trying to use a piece of glass to fight my way out. But I couldn't do it. I couldn't hurt them. It was an accident."

"Okay. Shh. Don't worry. We'll get you some help and sort it out."

I nod again, unable to contain my tears. I'm just as much of a monster as Kevin. Genetics don't lie.

When a familiar, silver Infinity comes to an abrupt halt, half in a snowbank, Liam jumps out from the driver's side. Upon seeing him, followed closely by an ambulance, for the first time in months, I have people in my corner. I never should have doubted him.

"Chelsea!" Liam bounds over the snowbank, running through the snow in Sebastian's front yard, and up the few steps to where I am kneeling on the porch. "Chelsea. Come here." He kneels down beside me, pulling me into his arms.

It's safe to call the sound coming out of me now, wailing. Liam's head is pressed on top of mine and his large frame all but consumes me.

"I'm so sorry. I'm so sorry."

"… Here. I'll call you back." Another familiar voice enters the scene, and even through my blurry vision, I can tell it's Zach. He steps up onto the porch, shaking hands with Constable McPherson, and getting the all-clear from her to approach me. Liam skipped that step. "Chels. Are you okay?" His voice is tender and concerned.

I sniffle, wiping my nose with my sleeve and realizing my nose is bleeding again. I'm so embarrassed. The paramedics call for Zach and Liam to clear the way as they approach me with a gurney in tow.

For the next few moments, I'm poked, prodded, and questioned. Zach and Liam stand to the side, watching closely. When the paramedics ask if I have taken any drugs recently, I consider lying, but what good would it do at this point? I've disappointed everyone I love as much as humanly possible, and still they showed up for me. My whispered confession is still loud enough for Liam and Zach to hear. I don't miss the side glance they share with each other.

Whatever is in the IV the paramedics gave me is awesome. I'm not feeling any pain from my arm now, and they've bandaged it tightly. They've wrapped me with a metallic "blanket" that's essentially a giant sheet of tinfoil, and placed a thicker blanket overtop. I hadn't realized how cold I was until I started to warm up.

As I'm being wheeled toward the back of the ambulance, one paramedic speaks. "That was amazing. What you did in there."

The pain meds have made me loopy, so I giggle. "Stealthy Chelsea, to the rescue."

He smirks at me. "Good to see the meds are doing their job."

I chuckle again as I'm lifted into the ambulance and catch a quick glance at Liam's worried face. "Can he come with me?"

"Hop on in," the female paramedic waves Liam over and he wastes no time climbing in beside me.

At this, one of the worst moments of my life, he's the person I need at my side.

A few hours after arriving at the hospital, I've been stitched up, medicated, and tended to by multiple doctors and nurses. I'm alone in a secluded section of the emergency department, aside from the security guard seated outside of the room. Apparently, I need to be guarded until the police can speak with me.

In the early hours of the morning, Constable McPherson peeks her head through the curtain and asks to enter the makeshift room. She's closely followed by her partner, who enters with a toothy grin framed by his facial stubble. He's far too happy to be in a hospital, unless he got a cute nurse's phone number.

"How are you holding up, Chelsea? How is your arm?" McPherson asks.

"I'm fine. Thank you for coming when you did."

She and her partner exchange a look. "Do you know how we got there?"

"Did I call you? They didn't take my phone, so I blindly dialled a number in my pocket."

"Smart thinking. You did good. You actually called Liam. He didn't want to hang up to call 911, but he was driving, so he went to the nearest police station. They tracked your call. It was a coincidence my partner and I got the call."

Liam. He saved me. Of course he did.

"Am I in trouble?" I blurt out, unable to stand the unknowing anymore.

"Trouble? Why would you be in trouble?"

I glance down at my feet, fidgeting with the sheet between my toes. "For what I did to Gia. And for..." I'm ashamed to say it out loud. "For the cocaine."

McPherson sits on the edge of my bed like she's about to deliver bad news. My breathing speeds up and the electrodes I'm equipped with alert everyone in the room to that fact.

"Take a breath, Chelsea. You're not in trouble. My partner has some news for you." She nods at the handsome man with the unreasonable smile.

"We tracked down Gia, Sebastian, and Kevin."

His admission has little effect on my heart rate.

"Gia only had a surface scratch on her neck. Nothing life threatening. But that's not the good news."

That sounds like good news to me. I don't want to possess any similarities to my father, even accidentally.

The man continues, "We searched Sebastian's house and found a significant stash of cocaine and other paraphernalia in the spare bedroom."

I'm not sure how this is good news.

"Um. Did you know who lived in the basement apartment?"

"No, I never saw anyone come or go. I heard movement down there every once in a while." I'm confused by the detour this conversation is taking.

The officer exhales and looks at his partner, silently pleading with her to proceed.

"It was Kevin, Chelsea. Kevin was the basement tenant."

My eyes open so wide, I can see my own forehead. Kevin lived inside the same four walls as me for the last few months and I didn't know? Now I'm beeping like a carnival game. "But… how? Why didn't he take me sooner?"

"Well, we aren't entirely sure. He's refusing to talk; but if I had to guess, I'd say he was biding his time and forcing you to live in fear until he was ready to make his move."

He succeeded. His unpredictable presence forced me to throw away everything I had going in the right direction. The progress it took me fifteen years to make, he undid with his comeback. I hate myself for allowing him to manipulate me that way.

"You're going to let me in!" I hear another familiar voice in the hallway, followed by the security guard telling the person to calm down and wait until the police finish speaking with me.

Sensing the determination of the woman outside, McPherson stands and says, "When you are up for it, we'll have you come to the station to make a statement. But given the amount of drugs found in the house, I don't think you'll be seeing either Sebastian or Kevin for many years." She turns to leave through the curtain with her partner following.

A second later, Zara comes bolting through the curtain like a pronghorn antelope—which is an underrated fast runner. Everyone always talks about the cheetah, but the antelope is doing its thing at eighty kilometres per hour, and no one notices. That's Zara. She's underrated, but she is incredible.

"Sweetheart! Oh, I'm so happy you're okay." She dives on top of me, giving me a hug I couldn't possibly fend off, but I don't want to. I'm surprised she doesn't hate me.

"I'm so sorry. I'm sorry." There's no number of times I could say it that would express how sorry I am.

"No, I'm sorry. I should have tried harder. You weren't okay; I knew that. I'm so sorry."

"There was nothing you could have done. You've given me more than I ever deserved, and I treated you terribly. I don't blame you if you hate me."

"Hate you?" She pulls her face back to look at me and I can see the worry etched on her features. "Why would I ever hate you?"

"I handled everything wrong. I didn't want you guys to get hurt, and I didn't know what to do, so I pushed everyone away. Then I was lost. I shouldn't have trusted him. I should have listened, but I was so scared."

"Chelsea, you listen to me." Her serious voice has been activated. "There is nothing, and I mean nothing, that could make me hate you. You are the first person outside of my biological family who I ever loved. I know what you went through wasn't easy, and it won't be easy going forward, but we want to help you get through it."

"We?"

"Yes, we." She turns to face the curtain. "Come on in, guys. Assuming the brute out there will allow it."

I snicker at her audacity.

Zach strolls in with Isla at his side and Liam behind them.

Isla runs the ten feet when she spots me. "Chelsea!" She dives on the bed like a klipspringer, and I'm impressed by my family's athleticism.

"Hey Troublemaker. You got so big."

She wraps her arms around me, abruptly lifting her head. "You got so small."

"Isla," Zara warns.

"Sorry." She looks ashamed.

"It's okay. I know I got pretty skinny. You got so big."

"I grew two inches. I missed you so much. Bond missed you too."

"I missed you guys too." I realize when I say those words, how I feel; euphoric. The epiphany brings me to tears.

"What's wrong? Did I hurt you?" The poor girl's blue eyes are wide with panic.

"No, Troublemaker. I'm so happy to see you."

She smiles at me and snuggles back in, and I soak in the moments of happiness I have been missing for the last six months.

We all chat for a while, and they inform me what they've been up to since I moved out, which isn't much. I can tell they were all stressed out by my absence, and it seems they mostly stayed at home, aside from the odd outing.

"We should let Chelsea rest. We can come back later if she isn't discharged today. Is that okay with you?" Zach's voice of reason is another thing I missed.

I am tired, but there's something I have to do first. "Sounds good. Thank you, guys, for coming. I am really sorry."

"Stop, Chels. You handled the situation the best way you could. We'll move forward, okay?" Zach reassures me.

I nod. "Before you go, Liam, can I talk to you?"

Zara and Zach look in Liam's direction. He gives a shy smile in return, and I can't tell if he's hesitant to stay and talk to me or if he's furious with me. Either way, I don't blame him.

"Oh, I made this for you," Isla chimes in, passing me a folded piece of paper. "I made one for Liam too." She hops off the bed, careful to avoid my IV.

"We'll see you later. Call if you need anything specific, but I'll bring you some clothes and toiletries when I come back, okay?" Zara blows a kiss, grabs Isla's hand, and they file out of the room.

The silence left is uncomfortable. I guess he's going to wait for me to start the conversation. "Thank you."

"Nothing to thank me for, Chels. I'm happy you're okay."

"No, Liam. I owe you everything. When I called, you could have hung up or hated me for shutting you out. You didn't owe me anything, but you made sure I was safe. You were right about everything." I wipe the tears from my face, unable to make eye contact with him. I'm afraid to see the disappointment on his face.

"Chels. There's nothing I wouldn't do for you, ever. I… I thought you forgot about me."

My heart aches when he says that. I reassure him, "No one ever forgets the hero."

"You didn't need me to be your hero. By the time I got there, you had already saved yourself. You're not just a hero, Chels, you're a legend. From what the police have told me, you were nothing short of amazing; they can't stop talking about you." He breathes out a heavy sigh. "I'm sorry I didn't get there sooner. I don't know what I would have done if something…"

"Stop. I'm experienced in that 'what if' road, and you don't need to travel down there. I'm here, and I'm going to be fine. There's a lot for me to get sorted out, though."

"No matter what, I'll be here for you. You're my best friend and I love you."

I hear his words and want to put more stock in them than he's offering, but I can't go down that "what if" road, either. "Thanks, Liam. I'm lucky to have you."

With a meek smile, he leans over to give me a peck on my forehead, then turns and leaves.

For the first time in months, the high I'm craving is the love of my family; not artificial inebriation caused by an illicit substance. I can't trust myself to maintain that outlook, though. I need more than love.

After a long talk with the doctor who handled most of my care in Emerge, Dr. Weekes, I've got myself sorted to attend a rehab facility specializing in the mental health aspect of addiction. It's in Toronto, which is about ninety minutes from home, but close to Zach's sister Jasmine. She was my first call to tell her what was happening, and she agreed to come pick me up to take me to the site of where my future will begin.

The process will be hard, but I'm ready. My life the past few months is not the life I want for myself. The situation makes me far more sympathetic for people who can't afford to get into treatment because of the costs. I understand it's expensive to run, but that seems to perpetuate the cycle. Inaccessible mental health treatments, self-medicating with drugs, addiction leading to crime or other dangerous behaviours, and then no way to break out of it. It makes me nauseous to think of the thousands of people, on any given day, being held hostage by things they have little control over.

I've dressed in clothes Zara brought. Thankfully, she noticed I've shrunk, so she purchased a few new stretchy items that fit. I'm not winning any style icon awards, but I'm suitably dressed for a Canadian winter.

Jasmine is outside the main entrance of the hospital when I exit after seventy-five hours of receiving treatment. She's parked in her hot pink Jeep. When I hop in, she looks as if she doesn't know what to say.

"Hi." I break the silence, not expecting this to feel as awkward as it does.

"Hey, Chels." She shifts into gear, pulling away from the curb. "Are you ready for this?"

"I think if there was ever a time to be ready for something like this, it would be after hitting rock bottom." I make no effort to sugar-coat the happenings in my life recently.

"Yeah. I guess."

We drive several kilometres in silence before she speaks again. "I wish you would have told me."

The guilt trip. My least favourite trip of all.

"I didn't tell anyone, Jas. I couldn't wrap my head around what was going on, and I didn't know how to deal with it. My solution was to push everyone away." An entire song on the radio plays before I speak again. "In my mind, I was bringing trouble and danger to everyone. I couldn't live with that, so I did what I thought I had to do to protect everyone."

"We're all sorry you thought you had to do it alone. I'm sorry this is how things turned out."

"I'm not." She gives me a side glance, keeping her eyes on the road, so I continue, "I was struggling in ways I couldn't put my finger on. I was trying to be a good student, an exemplary employee, an obedient daughter. But I wasn't happy. If all of this hadn't happened, I would have kept going like that."

Wringing my hands, I make my point clear. "I'm not happy about how things happened. I'm not happy I disappointed everyone. But for the first time in a long time, I feel like I can take steps toward making myself happy."

After my monologue, Jasmine takes a moment. "I'm not happy about how it happened, either. I've never seen my brother or Zara so stressed in all my life. But I can give you credit for doing what you thought you had to do." She looks straight at me to make herself clear. "Just don't do it again."

I nod. We ride the rest of the way in virtual silence, sharing a few benign tidbits to keep it from getting awkward, but the dynamic has shifted between Jasmine and me. She's twenty-five and a successful fashion designer, working in downtown Toronto. She's dating a "handsome Brazilian" man named Rafael who works as an architect, and from what I surmise, things are getting serious. She seems happy. Despite the challenges she's faced in her life—losing her brother, Zach's twin, when she was young, then finding her parents dead from carbon-monoxide poisoning when she was eleven, being put in the foster system and eventually, Zach being granted guardianship over her—she's still thrived.

For the last twenty minutes of our trip, I'm consumed by thoughts that I deserve everything bad that's happened to me. Bad things happen to everyone, and I'm not strong enough to handle them. Where I am and where I'm headed, it's all my fault.

I made Jasmine promise to not tell Zach or Zara where I was going. I couldn't risk getting emotional and deciding not to go, but she will inform them once I am admitted. This next step in my life requires my full commitment. I hope I get my money's worth. Something good has to come out of selling my CRV. Another issue I haven't fessed up to, yet.

The woman in charge of intake is a stout, kindly woman with blonde hair, rosy cheeks and gentle eyes, named Sarah. I don't know what I was expecting, but something more along the lines of *The Shining.* I'm glad it's not.

When Jasmine leaves through the front door, I try to imagine all of my past baggage exiting with her. I know it's not that simple, and I have a long road ahead, but I can pretend this is a fresh new start.

Sarah guides me on a well-rehearsed tour of the remarkably clean facility. Dr. Weekes was helpful in determining this was the right facility for me and assured me I would have freedom to come and go from my room at my leisure, but there are curfews and mandatory programs in place. The important distinction was that I am here voluntarily, and I am not a prisoner. I feel at ease as Sarah shows me the rooms where patients stay, and reminds me there are also out-patient services available should I decide that option will work better for me.

My intake appointments are tedious and exhausting. I had an initial interview, a full physical by one of the in-house physicians, and then a psychological assessment. I didn't dive deep into the trauma I dealt with as a child, or even recently, but I felt Dr. Crawford, the psychologist, was professional and receptive. She will have me confess my deepest, darkest secrets in no time.

As far as addictions go, I was not using for very long, and without cocaine in my system for three and a half days, I have managed okay. Most of that relief comes from knowing Kevin and Sebastian are both locked up, and Constable McPherson promised I would be notified if that changed. My biggest hurdle is overcoming the reason I turned to drugs in the first place, and healing from the betrayal I suffered at the hands of Sebastian.

I have mild difficulties with insomnia, headaches, irritability, and a fever that's impossible to sweat out, but according to the accounts of my fellow addicts, I've been spared the misery of intense drug withdrawal.

On my third day in treatment, I'm scheduled to see Dr. Crawford for our first appointment beyond my initial assessment.

Within the first thirty minutes, she's got me telling her everything short of my underwear preference, and if she asked, I'd disclose that too. The woman has a gift for making people open up.

As we discuss my PTSD and trust issues, she's listened attentively, taking notes, and not cringing with everything I say. Believing she's not judging me is helping me remain at ease—unmedicated. Her acceptance reminds me of my early days with Zara, but here I am, back in the same place, working through my problems with trusting people once again.

"We're all a little guarded, Chelsea. That's normal, and it's okay. What we need to do is train you to trust your instincts, but distinguish between logic and panic. I think we can do that."

"I have my doubts." I huff out a laugh. "My entire life, I've kept people at a distance, afraid to trust anyone, and the first person I let in—the first person I trusted—betrayed me in the worst possible way."

Dr. Crawford's eyes are focused on me. I recognize this look as one where she's trying to determine how to deliver a hard truth. I tense, anticipating I'm about to have my world rocked.

"He's not the first person you trusted. From what you've told me so far, aside from your father, Sebastian was the first person you trusted who betrayed you. But, if you really look, you'll see most people you put your trust in were more than worthy of it. Don't rob them of what *they* deserve because one person didn't."

Somehow, her words have reached into my lungs, robbing them of air. I sit in silence, absorbing what she's said. I have trusted people; worthy people. Zara, Zach, Isla, Liam. They've all been worthy of the trust and love I placed in them. My instincts never warned me they couldn't be trusted, or that they were a danger. Maybe my instincts are more finely tuned than I thought. Maybe the first person I need to learn to trust is myself.

'**ve been in the rehab facility for three weeks, and today I'm having my final in-patient therapy session. I will remain as an outpatient for a few months to make sure I stay on top of my mental health and don't revert to drug use, but aside from the shame I'm experiencing for *needing* treatment in rehab, I'm proud of the progress I've made.

In an effort not to derail my progress, I haven't spoken to my family since I arrived. Jasmine was instructed to tell everyone where I was and let them know I was okay. The staff also has provisions in place so approved family members can call to see how a patient is doing, but they recommend taking a few weeks with no contact. Some people could be triggered to revert to their old ways by those closest to them, so it makes sense. From what I've been told, I've had family members and "a young man who sounds very handsome" checking on me every day.

I sit across from Dr. Crawford, who I have come to appreciate. Her way of telling me how things are in a no-nonsense way, but still honouring my feelings, has been a great balance to guide my progress.

Today we're discussing my future plans, and when the prospect of moving forward comes up, I find myself lost.

"But I don't even know who I am."

"If you don't know who you are, then create yourself."

My face twists in confusion. "I don't know what that means."

She sets her notebook and pen on the coffee table to the left of the colourful fake-flower centrepiece. "Your purpose will never hit you over the head and make everything, Chelsea. You have to make a conscious effort to create the life you want by embracing your strengths and what makes you happy."

I absorb what she's said, but I still don't understand how to move forward.

"If you knew you couldn't fail, what would you do with your life? What would make you happy?"

"I'm not sure I'd recognize true happiness."

"I think you would. And I think it's clearer than you want to make it. Don't worry about what everyone else wants. What makes Chelsea happy?"

Ouch. "You think I've intentionally made things harder for myself?"

"No, not intentionally. I think you've struggled to see your worth and spent many years thinking you didn't deserve happiness. What I'm saying is, your future happiness is likely not as difficult to find as you think."

I have a lot to think about, but I know where I want to start.

When Sarah, the same woman who handled my intake, announced I could leave, there was only one person I wanted to call. Sarah smiles, gives me a nod, and hands me the corded phone.

As I dial the number, I'm filled with anxiety. After a few rings, I hear the recognizable click and breathe a sigh of relief.

"Hello?"

"Hey. It's me. Um… Chelsea."

"Big Red! How are you? Where are you? Are you back home?" Liam resorts to his typical rapid-fire questions.

"Liam."

"Sorry. How are you?" He takes a deep breath.

"I'm good. Really good, actually." There's a brief pause when Liam doesn't speak. "Liam?" A few more seconds pass.

Liam sniffles in the phone, and he sounds choked up when he says, "I'm so happy. I'm so happy to hear that. I've missed you so much."

His emotions are encouraging mine to spill over, but I keep them in check. "I missed you too. That's why I was calling. I was hoping…"

"Anything."

"You don't even know what I'm going to ask."

"It doesn't matter. Whatever it is, the answer is yes."

I giggle at his eagerness. "I was wondering if you'd come pick me up."

"Tell me when and where."

I give Liam the location of the facility and leave the timing up to him and what works for his schedule, but he's determined to come right away. I am nervous to leave, even though the staff have already confirmed with Zara and Zach I can go back home to stay with them. As much as I've made progress, it took little to derail me a few months ago, so I'm worried I'll disappoint them again.

I'm packing my bag of belongings and I come across a folded piece of paper amongst my clothes. Isla gave me this when she visited me in the hospital and I forgot all about it. I unfold the paper to see one of her family-famous drawings. She's always drawing her hopes and dreams as if she can make them reality by putting them on paper. I look at the pencil crayon portrayal of Liam and me, standing hand-in-hand, watching a sunset. It reminds me of a camping trip we took years ago. Only on that occasion, Isla was in between us. That is one of my favourite memories.

After clutching the drawing to my chest for several minutes, I tuck it safely in my bag, zipping up the contents, and make my way to the reception area to sign some final documents. These are all menial tasks, but together, they represent big steps. I can only hope I keep my footing.

With one last smile, Sarah sends me on my way, reminding me to call if, at anytime, I'm overwhelmed with my circumstances. The team I have behind me has grown—even if I had to pay them thousands of dollars—and it gives me a much-needed confidence boost I'll be able to tackle the road ahead.

When Liam pulls up to the front of the building, he doesn't wait for me to climb in. Before his car comes to a complete stop, he jumps out, bounding up the stairs in my direction. He pulls me into a hug, and I can't help but allow his presence to invade my senses; the sound of his breathing, his arms around me, the joyful expression on his face.

"I'm sorry, Chels," he says as he releases me from his arms. "I got carried away. I shouldn't have hugged you."

My countenance displays my disappointment upon hearing his words.

"Sorry, I mean, I know you don't like physical contact, and I kind of... um... forced myself on you. I didn't mean..."

I interrupt his sentence by throwing my own scrawny arms around him, which barely reach behind his back. As my hands struggle to interlock, Liam reciprocates the hug, and we stand there for a moment, lost in each other's embrace.

When I think back over the years of our friendship and how loyal Liam has been to me, I can't help but beat myself up for ever allowing Sebastian into my life. As the guilt consumes me, I remember the conversations I've had with Dr. Crawford. I made mistakes in the past, but the important thing is to learn and move forward. Dwelling on them won't serve me any purpose.

"Let's get you home, shall we?"

Home. There's an unfamiliar concept. I've spent the last several months with no place that felt like home. Knowing I shared a dwelling with two men whose sole purpose in life was to destroy the lives of others, going back to somewhere I am cared for is foreign. I know I'll have to work at regaining the trust and love of Zach and Zara. I don't even know how they feel about me moving back in.

"Aren't you excited to go back home?" Liam interrupts my thoughts.

"Uh, I guess. Just a little nervous."

Liam's furrowed brows threaten to touch in the centre of his forehead. "Why are you nervous?"

I don't have a specific answer for that, so I go with the simplest explanation. "I am afraid they'll hate me for everything I've done."

The same eyebrows that were threatening to form a united force on Liam's face mere seconds earlier are now looking to disappear into his hairline. I've never noticed how animated his facial expressions were before.

"Hate you? Are you crazy?"

I'm not too pleased with his word choice. "No, not clinically."

He takes a second to catch on. "I'm sorry. I didn't mean it like that. I don't think you're crazy. It's just..." Taking a pause, he continues his thought. "Your family loves you, Chels. They were a mess when you were gone, and I'm not saying that to make you feel bad. I know you did what you thought was right, but they… all of us… felt like our world wasn't complete without you. The love they… we have for you isn't conditional on you doing everything right. You need to know that."

"It might not be conditional on me doing everything right, but it could be for doing everything wrong. I don't know how they could ever forgive me."

Liam puts one hand on each of my shoulders, squaring me to face him. "I'll tell you this as many times as you need to hear it, but I'm hoping once will be enough. Every choice you made has been forgiven, because your intentions were clear."

"But look where I've ended up, Liam. I am walking out of rehab! That's not evidence of excellent choices."

"You may have been misguided, Chels, but the fact you're walking out of a rehab place right now proves to me how amazing you are."

Liam has always been straightforward with me, and since we've become friends, I can't say I've doubted a single word he's said until now. Amazing is not a word I'd use to describe myself in any capacity.

"Liam, I think you might be the crazy one here. You're looking at a girl who has the emotional stability of Caillou."

"What's a Caillou?" he asks as we walk to his still-running car parked a few feet away.

I realize not everyone has younger siblings that subject them to the tiny bald tyrant who's the shame of Canadian television. "Consider yourself lucky you don't know who Caillou is," I say as Liam shuts my car door.

When Liam climbs in the driver's seat, the blasting heat causes his cologne to fill the space and the familiar smell helps me to relax. I don't know how things will go when I return home, but now is the time to find out.

As we pull through the gate of my former—rather, current—home, I feel a mixture of excitement to see my family and anxiety, despite Liam's constant reassurance. He reaches over to put his hand over mine as we pull up to park in front of the four-car garage. He gives me a gentle squeeze, releasing my hand to put the car in park. I look at the garage door that previously housed my beloved SUV.

Time to face the music.

I'm greeted outside the door by a tearful Zara, a straight-faced Zach, beaming Isla, and Bond, whose tail doesn't budge. He's obviously not happy to see me.

Zara pulls me in for a hug and for the second time today, I've willingly accepted an unexpected hug. "Oh, Sweetheart. I'm so happy you're home." Zara releases me to take in my physical appearance. "You look so much better."

"Well, to be fair, I haven't been shot today."

Zach snickers, reaching over to place a hand on my shoulder. "It's good to have you back, Chels." Having Zach's approval to come home means more than anything. "Let's get you inside." He has a mysterious smirk on his face.

As soon as the door opens, I understand why. "Welcome home!" a group of people shout. I look around and see Zara's parents, Alanna and Fred, her sisters and their families—minus Caleb, who I hear is studying culinary arts in France—Zara's best friend Quinn, who was a sort of bonus mom when I was younger, along with her husband Tyler, their five-year-old son Leo, and three-month-old baby, Jake. Rounding out the crowd is Jasmine with, who I am assuming is Rafael, the architect. What a wonderful first impression for him to have of me—at a 'welcome home from rehab' party.

Behind everyone is an enormous banner that says "Welcome Home" in colourful letters hanging from the ceiling, and the fact they've put effort into welcoming me home on such short notice is overwhelming. I left the facility two hours ago.

I turn to Zara. "How did you do this?"

Placing an arm over my shoulder, she says, "We've all been waiting for you to come home, Chels. This is where you belong."

A sense of belonging is something I've struggled with my entire life. I've been present in places, but to really belong is an unfamiliar feeling. Even in the five years I lived here before leaving, I don't think I ever felt I belonged—not because of anyone else, but because of what I thought I did or didn't deserve. I don't know if I'll ever belong, but if this is what it feels like, I want to try. Another thing to add to my list of things to work toward.

I glance back at Liam, who gives me a reassuring smile that tells me he knew about this, which was probably why he kept me talking outside of the rehab facility for so long. A delay tactic.

I tentatively make my way around the room, accepting as many hugs in thirty minutes as I have in my entire life to this point. Aside from Zara's sister, Noa, who has always insisted I called her Mrs. McNamara, everyone is very welcoming. I can't say I blame Noa for her reluctance to be around me. I wouldn't want my influence around my kids, either.

Sophie has the opposite reaction as her mother. She welcomes me with open arms. Since I was adopted, although we don't see each other often, we've always gotten along well. I wish I was as put together as her; then again, she rarely smiles. The grass is always greener.

Zara, being aware of the fact I wouldn't be up for a lot of socializing, ushers everyone out the door only an hour after I arrive home, and I'm grateful. Everyone except Liam. He stays to help me get settled back into my bedroom.

When I was first adopted six years ago, I was as unfamiliar with this place as I am now. I moved in late March, all those years ago, and I'm experiencing déjà vu. I'm arriving here after being alone, lost, and hopeless. Once again, I was granted a lifeline by the same people whom I have learned the hard way, *do* always want what's best for me.

One thing that was addressed repeatedly in my therapy sessions was my pride. It's important for me to recognize I don't *have* to do everything myself, and despite the fact I've had people in my life who have disappointed me—there's an understatement—there have also been many people who have proven their trustworthiness.

For so long, I've been determined to prove my worth to people who I thought I had to, in order to make my presence worthwhile. It never occurred to me people can just love. I didn't realize people can embrace you without ulterior motives, or without you earning their affection.

I also had to learn there's a major difference between someone saying something to insult or disrespect me intentionally, and me *feeling* disrespected. Before I recognized what things triggered me emotionally, I took everything as an attack. Looking back on the conversations I've had with people over the last few months, I can finally see things from their perspectives. I can only hope they understand things from mine.

Here I am, I'm in a place I'm able to approach things from a more logical point of view. My PTSD will be a lifelong battle I have to deal with, but I can face it now with people in my corner. I can face it with more tools in my emotional toolbox and have a recourse in place if I'm losing control again.

As I am unpacking my bag, Liam is seated on the edge of my bed. It's nice to be around him and not fear for his safety.

"So." He breaks the silence that keeps building between us.

"So. You knew about the party?"

"I did. It was just a greeting party. Zara knew you'd want to get settled back in."

I'm studying each article of clothing as I remove them, tossing items into the corner of the room. A few items are too small now that I've regained some of the weight I lost. A couple articles are ruined from months of neglecting anything and everything beyond a high, and a few items hold memories I don't want to keep with me. The hoodie I wore when I thought my life was going to end; it can go. It has a bullet hole in the sleeve, anyway. The leggings with a gigantic tear from slicing my leg on table glass; they can go. The pyjamas I wore when Sebastian repeatedly used me to fulfil his carnal desires, and I allowed it to happen; they can most definitely go.

Liam shoots me a questioning look with each item I throw to the floor but doesn't ask me to explain. He makes idle chit-chat while I get myself reacquainted with my unchanged space. The room hasn't changed, but I couldn't be more different.

"So, I graduate soon," Liam adds casually.

"Liam! That's amazing. Congratulations." I am so happy for him, even if deep down I'm kicking myself for falling behind and dropping out when I did. He's moving on with his life, embracing adulthood. What if he moves away for a job? What if he finds a woman who deserves him every bit as much as he deserves her? What if he leaves me behind because I'm Chelsea, the unemployed, uneducated, recovering addict?

"What's wrong?" he asks, stepping forward to place a hand on my arm and stop the frantic folding I'm doing.

"Nothing. Nothing. I really am happy for you. You've worked so hard, and you deserve this. I'm proud of you." I offer a weak smile, trying to convince him I mean what I said, and I do.

"Chels, please don't shut me out again. If something is bothering you, I want to know. You don't have to navigate everything alone, remember?"

With tears welling in my eyes, I confess my new worries. I think I'd be better equipped to handle the reappearance of Kevin again than I would losing Liam.

He's quick to reassure me. "I'm not going anywhere, Chels. The internship I had has paid off, and they offered me a job after graduation. I'm staying right here. Well, I'll get my own place because that's the next logical step, but I'm not leaving town." He places his left hand on my right arm, now holding me still. "I'm not leaving you."

When I lunge forward, I was intending to give Liam a hug, but my momentum drives him backwards and he ends up on his back on my bed with his legs draped over the edge and my diminutive frame lying on his torso. My tears make way for laughter, and soon I'm in hysterics, unable to believe I tackled this man-mountain so easily.

Liam joins in, laughing at the turn of events. When he catches his breath, he props himself up on his elbows and in a low, gentle voice he says, "I missed this. I missed you."

My laughter halts. "I missed you too. More than you'll ever know. I don't deserve you." I squirm beside him and cuddle in, similar to how I did many months ago in my sleep when seeking a safe place.

He kisses the top of my head. "Shh. You deserve everything, Chels. Everything."

I don't believe his words, but I believe him, and come to another realization. If you never find people to trust, then you'll live a very lonely life.

He can be trusted.

The big day has arrived. Not *my* big day; Liam's graduation day. He obtained three tickets for the graduation, so I will attend with his parents. I'm flattered that, of all the people in his life, he considers me to be important enough to share this moment with.

He's been a dutiful best friend ever since I came home from rehab. He calls and texts me every day, comes and picks me up to get me out of the house regularly, and like the complete rockstar he is, he brings me an endless supply of books. Even though he was busy last month studying for exams, there wasn't one day I felt I wasn't on his priority list, and I appreciate his support so much. As much as I hate crowds, he wants me there today, so I'm going to do it for him.

It's not lost on me that I should be graduating too, but I don't think my initial career choice was the right one for me. I'm going to take some time to get myself in a better place, and I will re-enrol in something I'm better suited for in the future. But today isn't about me. This day is about Liam.

It's early May, and the weather is unpredictable, as per usual in our corner of the world, but Jasmine left me an amazing off-shoulder bodycon dress I'm excited to wear. It's been so long since I attempted to make myself look decent; today is a perfect day to try. The dress is a barely off-white colour, with a wide banded section across the top which covers my upper arms, but leave my shoulders exposed. There's a cute bow detail around my waist and a slit to the left of centre over my thigh. My hair is in a relaxed, half-up, half-down style, making me realize how badly I require a haircut in the immediate future.

Liam's parents, Ian and Dola, pick me up at home, and our drive is awkward. Mostly because I am afraid of what they think of me, knowing I was in rehab. I try to keep the conversation focused on Mr. Davis and his recovery, which has gone well. They are polite and kind as always, setting me at ease, as much as another person can.

When we arrive at the venue, we search for our allocated seats. There are thousands of people in the room and I'm on high alert but trying to stay calm so I can focus on Liam and his achievement. His parents are clearly proud of him, and I will not ruin this day for anyone.

Once we reach our aisle, Ian, the perpetual gentleman, stops at the end, allowing me to go first, followed by his wife. Sometimes in the past, I felt envious of how lucky Liam was to have the parents he has for his entire life. But something Liam said a while ago stuck with me—I'm as fortunate to have the family I do now, even if I didn't my entire life.

Seated in my chair, wringing my hands, I'm trying to keep my breathing steady and remember why I'm here. A gentle hand touches my right knee.

"It's okay. You're safe here. Just tell me if you need to get some air, and we'll go," Dr. Davis reassures me with a gentle smile, and I'm more at ease. I'm not going to make her miss her only son's college graduation.

I gulp down the lump in my throat, refusing to cry. Before I can stress anymore, I thank her with a silent nod. The graduates all enter the venue in a neat line, like well-trained sheep, and find their seats in alphabetical order. I can't help but think that must have been a nightmare to organize and now I am glad I'm not in the line-up.

As the graduates make their way on and off the stage, each one receiving a piece of paper and a handshake, my pessimistic mind is focused on the amount of debt strolling across that stage today. Lucky for Liam, his parents paid for his education, so he gets to walk across free and clear. His opportunities are limitless going forward. That thought makes me nauseous—not because I don't want that for him, but because I know of all the opportunities presented to him, I can't compete with them.

I'm choking down my emotions again, afraid of how a future without Liam would unfold. I can't fathom it.

As Liam strides across the stage, his parents stand, throwing their hands in the air and shouting their approval. The way Dr. Davis is beaming makes me regret not being able to give Zach and Zara the same opportunity today. Liam turns, waves toward us, and descends the stairs at stage-right.

We patiently await as the rest of the alphabet crosses the stage, and I don't know about Liam's parents, but with the start of each new letter, I breathe a sigh of relief we're getting closer to seeing Liam in person. He drove himself this morning, so I haven't spoken to him today and I am eager to give him his graduation gift—it is so cheesy.

When the time comes, instead of holding her husband's hand to navigate the crowd, Dr. Davis takes mine. She weaves through the smiling throngs of people, shielding me with her own demure frame. She's the definition of a powerful woman, and I can see where Liam gets his protective instincts from.

When I spot his gorgeous smile about fifty feet away, I refrain from running toward him. I want his parents to have the opportunity to congratulate him first.

Liam spots his mom, then locks eyes with me. He walks to me, stepping past his parents without speaking. He pulls me into a hug. "You look beautiful."

In our years of friendship, Liam has never once commented on my appearance. I always assumed he didn't have an opinion on my looks one way or another, so his words give me goosebumps. "Thank you. Congratulations, Liam. You earned this." I tap the rolled-up paper in his hand.

"This is fake. They send the real thing by mail so they don't risk giving someone the wrong one." He chuckles.

"Oh. Well, you earned the real thing. I'm proud of you." I look behind Liam to see his mom smiling like a quokka, looking every bit as adorable. "You should go talk to your parents. I think your mom is dying to congratulate you."

I expect Liam to say something acknowledging his parent's presence and move to go speak with them. He shocks me when he says, "No. She's happy to see me with you."

I'm sorry. What? I take a second to contend with the surprise-grenade launched at me. "Why would that make her happy? I'm... I'm me."

"That's why, Chels. Because you're you... and *you* make *me* happy."

I stumble on nothing, turning my ankle, nearly spilling onto the ground. Liam catches me with one hand, keeping me upright. "Me... what... I..." I can't form a coherent thought.

"What do you say I go greet my parents, and then we get out of here?"

"I... I thought they were taking you to dinner."

"That can wait. I'll still be a graduate tomorrow."

"Liam, I don't want to come between you and your plans." That sentence has more weight than I intended. I meant dinner with his parents, but it applies just as much to his future.

"Just trust me."

Trust him. Me, Chelsea Haynes, trust someone? I can do that. "Okay."

I watch Liam shake hands with his father, hug his mother, who threatens to never let him go, and the display of love is heartwarming. After years of being jealous of these moments, right now, I couldn't be more appreciative of the love these parents have given their son—because he so readily extends it to others. Our Irish fathers couldn't be more different.

Liam disrobes—to the dismay of the other young female college population, only removing his graduation gown—and hands it to his mother. He's wearing light grey dress pants with a medium-blue button-down shirt and a subtle striped tie. He gives his mom a peck on the cheek, waves toward his dad, and, while stealthily removing his tie, he walks back to where I'm standing a few feet away.

When Liam grabs my hand, gently pulling me through the crowd, it's remarkably different than it was with his mom moments earlier. I feel cherished and protected. Of all the people he could spend this day with, he wants to be with me. Even after everything I've put him through over the past few months, he still chose me.

And I choose him.

Liam opens the passenger door, allowing me to get in his car. As I slide back into the seat, he lets out a gasp. "What the heck is that?"

I expect to see a cobra coiled under my seat or a bear in the back, judging by his reaction. No creatures as far as I can tell. "What is what?"

"Your leg. What happened to your leg?"

I look to see the slit on my dress has exposed a portion of the scar on my thigh. It's been nearly five months since the injury happened, but the skin is raised, pink, and hideous. I grab the fabric of my dress, pulling it to cover myself. "It's nothing. I cut myself."

Liam's gaze is locked firmly on my thighs, even though the scar is no longer visible. "Chels, that's more than a cut. It looks like you almost cut your leg off."

"Leave it, Liam. It's fine. Please." I don't want to talk about it, and the interaction has caused every bit of excitement I was feeling to dissipate.

"Sorry. I just…"

"It's fine. Let's just go." I issue the command, staring forward. I need a second before I look at him.

He closes the car door, walking around to his side and easing in behind the steering wheel. Once he's settled, I try to drive the conversation forward, avoiding all discussions of the past several months of my life. I'm working through it all, but that doesn't mean I want to talk about it today. Today is to celebrate Liam.

"So, where are we going?" I ask, looking at the profile of my best friend.

"I'm not really sure." He reaches his right hand back, cradling the back of his neck.

"I thought you had a plan. You ditched your parents. I assumed it was for a reason." I worry that he's regretting his decision to leave his parents behind, not knowing it was a heat-of-the-moment decision.

"It was… it *is* for a reason. I just don't know where we're going yet."

"If you don't know where we're going, then what was your reason?" I roll my eyes back, trying to fight off the panic and stare at the ceiling of his car. I feel immense guilt that his parents have sacrificed so much to get him through his schooling, and he abandoned a celebration with them for me.

"You, Chels. You are the reason. I don't know *what* we're going to do, I just knew who I wanted with me."

Oh. I feel like a jerk for getting so worked up. I promised myself I wouldn't do that anymore, but it's a lifelong habit; it's a tough one to break. I attempt to reel in my "crazy" before responding. "Okay. Well, what do you want to do?"

Like a lightbulb, Liam's expression brightens. "I know." He puts on his turn signal, hangs a U-turn and seconds later, we're headed in the opposite direction. He pulls into a restaurant called *The Cabin* and opens the car door. "Do you want to come in to pick something to eat?"

I think for a second. "No, it's okay. I trust you."

Liam smiles. "I got you." Closing the car door, he strides confidently inside the restaurant.

I know. He always does.

He emerges fifteen minutes later with enough food for six people.

"What did you buy?" I gawk at the brown paper bag.

"A little of this. A little of that." He smirks, putting the car in reverse, turning to throw his arm around the back of my seat and pulls out of the parking spot.

I want to ask him where we're headed now but decide to place my trust in him fully, I have to hand over the reigns. He'll keep me safe, so I don't need to know where we're going. I'm confident he'll respect my limitations no matter what, and being able to place that level of reliance on another human is a massive step forward. I don't have to carry the heavy world on my back alone.

We pull into *Tudhope Park*, and Liam finds a secluded corner of the parking area to stop.

"We're going to have a picnic."

I look down at the outfits we're wearing and raise an eyebrow. "A picnic? I'm supposed to sit in the grass in a near-white, tight dress?"

Liam gives me a devastating grin. "Trust me, the last thing I want is for you to ruin that dress." He has a little flush in his cheeks that causes my face to heat. "I have blankets in the back." He hops out of the car, opening the trunk where he indeed has three blankets, then grabs the bag of food from the back seat.

I step out, nervous to walk around the grassy park in heels, but today is Liam's day, and it's the least I can do for him.

Thankfully, there are paved walking paths through the park, so traversing the area in impractical shoes isn't as difficult as I expected. For added assistance, I carry the blankets in my right arm, allowing Liam to loop his arm through mine and the gesture gives me confidence I'll be fine.

"Is this spot good?"

I scan the area. No errant soccer balls, no trees for predators to hide behind, no notable dangers; plus, it has a delightful view of the water. "This is perfect."

Liam lays out the largest of his three blankets, places the food in the middle of it, and holds my hand as I slip off my shoes to take a seat in the corner. He places a smaller blanket around my shoulders, and it amazes me he realized I was cold before it even registered to me.

Opening the bag, he removes so many choices. Mac and cheese, rice, roasted potatoes, a few different salads, and several drink options.

"Is today carb loading day?"

"I'll burn it off another day. Today is just a day to kick back and enjoy."

I smile, knowing he wanted to enjoy today, and he picked me to do that with. It might seem like an insignificant gesture because we've been friends for so many years, but after the turmoil the past few months have brought, feeling valued is immeasurable.

Liam is propped back on one elbow, laying along the right side of the blanket, sipping his ginger ale. I'm watching him stare out at the water, appreciating the sense of peace and security he gives me. I can't help but wonder what he's thinking. What goes on in the head of someone who doesn't have childhood trauma to contend with? What I wouldn't give to take a peek inside his mind for a minute.

"Are you staring at me?" Liam's amused voice breaks through the sounds of the waterfront park that had been lulling me.

"I guess I was. Sorry." I turn to face back to the water. "I was wondering what you were thinking."

The sun is setting slowly, and as it drops in the sky, so does the temperature.

"I was thinking it's getting cold." Liam pats the space in front of him. "Come here."

I am cold, and his body heat is a welcome reprieve from the chilly air. I shuffle over with the gracefulness of a walrus. My awkward squirm elicits a chuckle from Liam, causing me to stop in my tracks and glare at him. He opts to move closer to me instead of making me wiggle the rest of the way.

We lie on the blanket, side by side, with my head propped on his left shoulder. Now is the moment for me to give him his gift, but I'm nervous about how he'll react.

"Um. I got you something."

"Yeah? You didn't have to do that." His smile tells me he's excited to know what I've gotten him, making me more apprehensive.

"It's nothing, really. Just a silly gift." I try to set his expectations low, so he won't be disappointed. I reach into my purse, removing the rectangular object wrapped in white wrapping paper with graduation caps scattered everywhere, and hand it to him.

"I guess it's not a Lamborghini."

"I don't even have my own vehicle," I joke back, but if there were ever a failed attempt at a joke, that would be it. Reminding him I sold my car for drug money, then a trip to rehab doesn't set the right mood for the day. "Open it."

He tears into the paper and when he sees the item I decided on after countless hours of searching for the perfect graduation gift, he takes thirty painstaking seconds to reply. "Chels. Wow. This is... I don't know what to say. This is perfect."

"You really like it? You don't have to say that to spare my feelings."

"I love it." He holds up his newest possession, and the smile on his face reaching his eyes tells me he really likes it.

I look at the framed photo with a copy of the drawing Isla gave both of us when I was in the hospital, with song lyrics written on it from *Always* by *Panic! at the Disco* and only Liam would know what they mean to us both. I think back to the night he was willing to wait outside my house, putting himself in harm's way just to keep me safe, and I believe with my entire heart he'll never make me face hard things alone again. He's my light at the end of the road.

The further the sun sinks on the horizon, the deeper the blue sky becomes overhead. Stars dot the expanse above us, and I try to take in each one.

Staring up at the stars, I'm grateful to have this man I call my best friend by my side. Someone I can enjoy conversation with as much as these moments of silence. I don't know where I'd be without him.

"When you look up at the stars, do you ever feel so small and insignificant? Like you couldn't even count them, so trying would be pointless." I know he's more significant to me than anything under the sun or any star.

Liam rolls onto his side to look at me. The shadows created by the streetlamps lining the path enhance his handsome features. "It would also be pointless to count the number of freckles on your nose, but I know you have thirty-three, and that's important to me."

My breath catches in my throat. "How could you know that?"

"The night… um, the night Zach and I came for you. After they stitched you up in the hospital, you fell asleep. I was so relieved you were safe. I couldn't sleep, so I stayed and watched you."

If he were anyone else, that would indeed be creepy, but with Liam, I feel… what do I feel? Flattered? Valued? Loved? I feel loved. I roll to face Liam who has his head propped up on his bent arm while laying on his side. When I take in how he's looking at me, something about our relationship has changed. He's no longer just my best friend. He's my soulmate. He's my raison d'être.

I've never been so nervous in all my life, and that's saying something because I have been in some unfavourable situations. I have to do this though—I'm going to do something for myself without fear of consequences for the first time in my life. "Liam?"

He gives me a questioning glance. "Yeah, Chels?"

"I love you." My heart is pounding as I say those words. I'm conflicted about saying them because I know I mean it, but I don't want things with him to change. The potential for him pushing me away makes me want to swallow the words back down, but it's too late.

"I love you, too," he says so casually, I know he doesn't understand what I'm admitting.

I'm relieved for a second, as though I have a cowardly way out, and I can continue forward without our dynamic changing. But I know: no risk, no reward.

"No, Liam. I don't mean like a friend, though I do love you that way, too." Deep breath. "I love you like an albatross, or a gibbon."

He stares at me, unflinching. He's not saying a word; he looks confused. Why I am so bad at this? I have to stop reading animal books.

"I love you like if I didn't have you in my life, I'd never recover. Like you're the missing piece of my soul and I only feel complete with you around." I'm self-conscious of my admission and can't look in his direction. "It's okay if you don't feel the same way, just promise me we'll always be friends."

The split-second Liam takes to react has me expecting the sky to fall. I can't imagine a situation more catastrophic than Liam shutting me out of his life, which given my past, is a high standard.

He reaches his arm out to touch my cheek and force me to look in his eyes. "I can promise you that." He takes a deep breath and my stomach plummets. He's promising we'll stay friends, but that never works out when one person is in love with someone else who doesn't reciprocate their feelings. "I can promise that you'll always be my best friend. But Chels, I want to be so much more than your friend. I love you too, Chelsea Haynes. I've loved you for a long time, and I swear I'll love you until the day I die. There's nothing on Earth that makes me feel as alive as you do, and nothing that makes me happier."

Without thinking, I close the distance between us in the least romantic fashion imaginable on account of my dress clinging to the blanket, but I'm not concerned with my mode of transport right now. I'm only concerned with one thing: my lips on his. I wrap my hand around the back of his head, weaving my fingers into his curls, and pull him toward me. Our lips collide together with enough force we almost knock each other's teeth out, but everything in my life to this point has been intense—I expect nothing less.

I melt into his touch, trying to stay present in the moment, but my mind is freaking out. What if he's repulsed by me? What if, when I tell him the truth about my time with Sebastian, he won't love me anymore? What if, one day, he finds someone less complicated than me and realizes he doesn't love me as much as he thinks?

My focus is obviously not on Liam, so he pulls away with a concerned expression. "Are you not ready for this? Is this too much, too soon?"

I shake my head, not wanting him to make the wrong assumption. Jumping into a relationship a few months out of rehab is frowned upon, but Liam is… Liam. My reason for fighting all these years. Now that I've realized it and said it out loud, I can't imagine going back to how things were. I can't shove these feelings back down.

"No. This is what I want. I want you." That was misleading. I don't want him to think I'm ready to peel my clothes off in the park. A public indecency charge would not bode well for my recovery. "I mean, I want us."

He leans forward to kiss me again, and this time, we don't break apart until we can't breathe. Liam tilts his head toward me to bring our foreheads together again, and such a simple gesture evokes a visceral reaction in me.

"I love you so damn much, Chels. I promise I'll never let you feel anything less than cherished and incredible. Your strength inspires me, and you make me a better man." He pauses for a moment. "I've kept all of this in for so long and I was afraid you'd never see me the same way. I don't even know what to do with myself right now." He chuckles. "Pinch me."

A tear rolls from my eye and Liam kisses it. His touch is so tender and affectionate, I don't doubt a word he says—I trust him.

"The truth is, I think I've always loved you. My fear didn't let me see it until now." I say my revelation aloud, only realizing that as the words pour out. "I didn't... and I still don't think I deserve you, but if you'll have me, I want to try to be the woman you deserve."

"There was no time limit to how long I would have waited for you to say that. I knew I loved you for a long time, but I wasn't willing to lose you. As much as it hurt, seeing you with someone else who didn't love you like I do, I wanted to have you in my life, regardless."

Knowing I caused him hurt sends me back down a path of self-loathing. How can I ask someone to love me after I've hurt them?

"Chelsea."

I don't want to choke on my emotions, so I mutter, "Mm-hmm?"

Moving his hand on my cheek, reminding me it's still there, Liam continues, "I don't care about what happened, okay? I care about now, and I care about tomorrow. Whatever happened, I understand, and it never made me love you less." He kisses me again, bringing me back to the moment, and not allowing thoughts of my past, or anyone else, to come between us.

I shiver, and the sensation interrupts our intimate moment. "Sorry." I lean my forehead against his, imitating his gesture.

"There's nothing for you to be sorry for." He pulls the blanket tighter around me, rubbing along my arm. "I'm so happy right now, and I could stay like this forever, but what do you say we get out of here before you get pneumonia?"

As painful as it is to break up this love fest, I know we should get going. It's cold and late.

Liam stands first, reaching a hand down to help me up. Without shoes on, I feel tiny next to him. He bundles me up with the small blanket, pulling it tight and wrapping his arms around me. He whispers in my ear once more, "I love you."

"And I love you." I tilt my head to look up at him. "For the first time in as long as I can remember, I don't feel like I *need* to have everything figured out. I don't feel like I have a path to follow; no course to chart. But when I do figure out what's next, I hope you'll be part of it."

"Whatever comes next, we're in it together."

My smile threatens to break my face. I'll never comprehend how this man, when he was still a boy, saw any value in me. He's never wavered in his loyalty, support, or encouragement, and he loves me. This incredible man loves me. Problem-magnet Chelsea, with more issues than the *New York Times*. Me, who will deal with the effects of my past for the rest of my life. This girl, who will try to prove every day how much I appreciate Liam for teaching me that people can be trustworthy; for teaching me it's okay to let my guard down.

The End

If you enjoyed Chelsea's story, please consider leaving a review on Amazon and/or Goodreads. Your reviews help give me feedback so I can continue to learn, and also helps my books garner more attention from other readers. I would greatly appreciate your thoughts!

To easily access links to my books, visit linktr.ee/burdenofproofreading. You can also sign up for my newsletter and find my social media links there.

Thank you, my darling girl, age 11, for creating this perfect gift for Liam. I love you.

*Lyrics credit to *Panic! At the Disco**

Thank you to everyone who made it through Chelsea's journey. Did she drive you crazy at times? Did you want to shout at her and shake some sense into her? But did you also still love her at the end of it all? I hope so. I hope Chelsea's journey encourages you to live with compassion at the forefront of your mind because we can never truly understand someone else's motivations or struggles.

Now for some thank yous. Again, I have to thank my husband and children for coming along with me on the wild ride that is writing and publishing. All the nights I was sucked into my hole of editing or writing and my husband never hesitated to make dinner or somehow take other lingering tasks off of my plate; I can never truly express how much I love him for that. My daughter, Amaya, for being a little Cinderella, helping with housework and letting me talk her ear off about books. My youngest daughter, Linaya, for being an endless supply of encouragement and cheering me on.

I also have to thank my fellow indie authors who always keep me inspired to write, learn, and grow. I cherish each one of you. Celine Perron and Chelsea Eade in particular, for their assistance with this book. Also, Bruce Hanson, from the Barrie Writer's Group, for his kind words and critique, particularly on chapter two (which I couldn't seem to get right on my own); I'm endlessly grateful for your help.

To all of my readers, thank you all for allowing Chelsea to be a part of your life for a short while.

Much love,
Tiffany

With each of the novels in this series, I chose a musical artist to draw inspiration from to create the story. This book, obviously was Panic! At the Diso. Here's where I get vulnerable and real, sharing a story that isn't my proudest moment, but I pride myself on being transparent because life isn't always rainbows and cupcakes.

So, at one point, a few years ago, my husband was away on a work trip. He'd been gone for weeks, and it was the fifth time he'd been gone on an extended journey in as many months. Having recently lost my mom, I was drowning in the pits of depression. To say I was in a dark place is an understatement. I was barely existing.

My kids were away on a sleepover, so I was home alone with my dogs. I had every intention of not waking up the next morning. Without sharing any sordid details, I went to take my dogs out, and while I was waiting for them, I decided some music would be nice.

For no apparent reason, other than to save my life, when I opened my music app, a song by Panic! At the Disco came up called *Trade Mistakes*. One line in the song is "Let me save you; hold this rope." I'm not sure why it impacted me as much as it did, but I burst into tears. I let the dogs inside, and went down a rabbit hole, listening to Panic! At the Disco songs until the early hours of the morning. By that point, it wasn't long until I had to go pick up my kids.

And I did. Because of that song.

So, this entire book is essentially my long thank you to Panic! At the Disco for being vunerable and sharing their talents with the world. It's because of them I made it to pick up my kids that day.

Here's my ultimate playlist for We're All a Little Guarded. You can find it on Spotify at linktr.ee/burdenofproofreading.

(Please note, I do not make any claims to any of these songs. All rights belong to Panic! At the Disco or their record label. I'm merely sharing my inspiration.)

Northern Downpour
Stall Me*
When the Day Met the Night
House Of Memories
Ready To Go (Get Me Out Of My Mind)
The End Of All Things
Old Fashioned
Dying in LA
She Had the World
Behind the Sea
Time To Dance
Nine In the Afternoon
Do You Know What I'm Seeing?
Can't Fight Against the Youth*
Ready to Go (Get Me Out Of My Mind)*

Into the Unknown
Dancing's Not a Crime
C'Mon
King Of the Clouds
High Hopes
Mad As Rabbits
New Perspective
Folkin' Around
Don't Threaten Me With a Good Time
One Of the Drunks
The Green Gentleman (Things Have Changed)
All the Boys*
Lying Is the Most Fun a Girl Can Have Without Taking Her Clothes Off
(F*ck a) Silver Lining
Roaring 20s
Crazy = Genius
Casual Affair
Camisado
Vices & Virtues (Album Title)
Bittersweet*
Trade Mistakes
I Wanna Be Free*
Kaleidoscope Eyes*
Impossible Year
Too Weird To Live, Too Rare To Die! (Album Title)
Far Too Young To Die
The Good, the Bad, & the Dirty
Hurricane
This Is Gospel
Say Amen
They, Look Ma! I Made It
Golden Days
Always

Girl That You Love

A few special mentions:
Miss Jackson
Death Of a Bachelor
I Write Sins, Not Tragedies
LA Devotee
Mona Lisa Smile
Sarah Smiles
Overpass

*Indicates song is not available on Spotify Canada at the time of publishing

Also By This Author:

You Are Enough Series:
We're All a Little Broken: Book 1 (Zara's story)
We're All a Little Overwhelmed: Book 1.5 (Zara's extended epilogue)
We're All a Little Guarded: Book 2 (Chelsea's story)
We're All a Little Tired: Book 2.5
We're All a Little Scared: Book 3 (Isla's story)

This women's fiction series focuses on various aspects of mental health and overcoming trauma. It addresses anxiety, depression, panic disorders, miscarriage, adoption, grief and loss, racism, discrimination, and more, but in a light hearted way that will also make you laugh. The entire series is set in Muskoka/Bracebridge, Ontario.

Suburban Watchdogs: Long-time friends, Justin, Morrie, Brendon, and Josh, live in a small farming town north of the big city. When crime starts making its way onto their streets, the group of men brought together by circumstance, rather than choice, band together to keep their town safe. One movie night watching a good ol' gangster film is all they need to motivate them to take action, thereby forming the Suburban Watchdogs. If criminals think they can just waltz into the Suburban Watchdogs' territory without resistance, they are mistaken.

Justin takes matters one step further by adopting Karma. Karma is a... female dog, and she'll make sure you get what's coming to you.

Join the group of unlikely friends and their canine companion on their hilarious vigilante mission and laugh at the chaos and mayhem that ensues.

A New Leash on Life Series:
Coming Spring, 2022
This series will consist of sixteen interconnected standalone romantic comedies. Some characters from Suburban Watchdogs and

the You Are Enough series will have cameos or their own starring role!

Sign up for my newsletter or follow me on social media to learn more.

Linktr.ee/burdenofproofreading